WAS MURDER DONE?

Borgo Press Books by S. Fowler Wright

Arresting Delia: An Inspector Cleveland Classic Crime Novel
The Attic Murder: An Inspector Combridge & Mr. Jellipot Classic Crime Novel
The Bell Street Murders: An Inspector Combridge & Mr. Jellipot Classic Crime Novel (Prof. Blinkwell #1)
Beyond the Rim: A Lost Race Fantasy
Black Widow: A Classic Crime Novel
The Capone Caper: Mr. Jellipot vs. the King of Crime: A Classic Crime Novel
Crime & Co.: An Inspector Cleveland Classic Crime Novel
Dawn: A Novel of Global Warming
Dead by Saturday: An Inspector Cleveland Classic Crime Novel
Dream; or, The Simian Maid: A Fantasy of Prehistory (Marguerite Cranleigh #1)
Elfwin: An Historical Novel of Anglo-Saxon Times
The End of the Mildew Gang: An Inspector Cauldron Classic Crime Novel (Mildew Gang #3)
Four Callers in Razor Street: An Inspector Combridge & Mr. Jellipot Classic Crime Novel
The Hanging of Constance Hillier: An Inspector Cleveland Classic Crime Novel
The Hidden Tribe: A Lost Race Fantasy
The Jordans Murder: An Inspector Combridge & Mr. Jellipot Classic Crime Novel
The King Against Anne Bickerton: A Classic Crime Novel
The Mildew Gang: An Inspector Cauldron Classic Crime Novel (Mildew Gang #1)
Murder in Bethnal Square: An Inspector Combridge & Mr. Jellipot Classic Crime Novel
The Police and the Public: Some Thoughts on the British System of Justice
Post-Mortem Evidence: An Inspector Combridge & Mr. Jellipot Classic Crime Novel
The Return of the Mildew Gang: An Inspector Cauldron Classic Crime Novel (Mildew Gang #2)
The Rissole Mystery: An Inspector Combridge & Mr. Jellipot Classic Crime Novel
The Screaming Lake: A Lost Race Fantasy
The Secret of the Screen: An Inspector Combridge & Mr. Jellipot Classic Crime Novel (Prof. Blinkwell #2)
Spiders' War: A Novel of the Far Future (Marguerite Cranleigh #3)
Three Witnesses: A Classic Crime Novel
Too Much for Mr. Jellipot: An Inspector Combridge & Mr. Jellipot Classic Crime Novel
The Vengeance of Gwa: A Fantasy of Prehistory (Marguerite Cranleigh #2)
Was Murder Done? A Classic Crime Novel
Who Murdered Reynard? A Classic Crime Novel (Prof. Blinkwell #3)
The Wills of Jane Kanwhistle: An Inspector Combridge & Mr. Jellipot Classic Crime Novel
With Cause Enough?: An Inspector Combridge & Mr. Jellipot Classic Crime Novel

WAS MURDER DONE?

A CLASSIC CRIME NOVEL

by

S. FOWLER WRIGHT

WRITING AS "SYDNEY FOWLER"

THE BORGO PRESS

An Imprint of Wildside Press LLC

MMIX

CONTENTS

CHAPTER I.

MR. THOMAS BIRCHALL put down the test tube which he had been holding up to the light of his single electric bulb, in the hope of seeing that change of colour which would not come. He had heard the rattle of the letter-box flap of his outer door, and the fainter sound of a letter as it struck the uncarpeted boards of the tiny hall of his two-room Southwest London flat.

Failures of experiments were frequent enough, but his was an address to which letters would rarely come. Even tradesmen's bills imply credit, which he did not take; and the last quarter's rent had been lately paid.

He rose at once, though with no particular anticipation in his mind, and went to pick up the letter.

Interest quickened at the sight of a woman's writing, and one with which he had had an earlier familiarity. Why, he thought, should Dorothy be writing to me? But the Dorset postmark confirmed his recognition.

He did not return to the laboratory, but to the meagrely-furnished bed-sitting room in which he lived during the intervals of sleep and food which disturbed his work. Here a cold supper had been laid out by the woman who came in daily, and had left at an earlier hour. He might eat it within ten minutes of her departure, or she might find it untouched when she returned on the next day, and Mr. Birchall still working in the laboratory, oblivious of the course of time. Now he sat down and read:

Highview House, Osbury, Dorset
April 15th, 1935

Dear Tom,

We were talking about you and old times yesterday, and Alfred asked me to write. We thought that,

7

if you had nothing better to do, you might like to come here for a few days over Easter.

I don't know what it's like in London, but the weather's wonderful here—almost like midsummer.

We are about three miles from Osbury station, but Alfred will meet you if you will let us know by what train you are coming.

Always sincerely,

Dorothy

He read this twice over, as though a second perusal would reveal some explanation that was not there. It was, to his mind, an amazing letter. Not as regards Dorothy. He had never credited her own coldness toward himself, would always think that she would have married him in the end if his cousin had not appeared on the scene. But he had a fixed belief that Alfred Cuthbertson hated him, and a certain knowledge of his feelings toward the cousin who was in every way more successful than himself, and who had robbed him, as he thought, of the girl he loved.

Talked over old times, had they? And the result—the most bewildering result—had been an invitation to him to spend Easter at Highview House!

His own recollections went back on the same road, to the events of four—no, three—years ago, and the effect upon himself was of an opposite kind. Of course, he would not go! Bitter memories—bitter quarrels—what was the sense of reviving these?

That he could meet Alfred without quarrelling—was it a reasonable probability? That he should find satisfaction in seeing Dorothy happy in his cousin's possession—he knew himself better than to entertain so preposterous an idea!

But was she happy? The doubt, rising to sudden hope, shook his resolution. Had he thought that there was the faintest hope of success, he would have had no scruple in accepting the invitation, and seducing her in his cousin's house; nor was he sufficiently free from vanity to recognize the improbability of her preferring his uncouth, slovenly-clothed person to that of his handsome, light-witted cousin.

But reason told him that Alfred's consent to the invitation—in itself an unlikelihood only made credible by the fact that the letter was here before him—would be made more probable by the hypothesis that Dorothy and he were on quarrelsome terms.

8

By the most reasonable explanation, it was the patronizing gesture, half-kindly, half-contemptuous, of success to failure, of plenty to penury, of victory to defeat. Well, he would let them know at once that he was not to be patronized by them.

He searched for letter paper he could not find, discovering a dirty postcard with a note covering half of one side concerning the cause for the oblique rhombic prism which is the primary form of Glauber's Salts (NaO, SO$_3$); and scrawled across this, writing on the remaining space:

Sorry, but no money and no time.

T. B.

He put his hat on, and went out to post it at once at the pillar-box at the corner of Horseferry Road.

That would show Dorothy (and more particularly Alfred!) that he was not going to be patronized by them. No doubt, Alfred made thousands now, by work requiring neither knowledge nor brains. A fool doing that for which his brother fools, being able to understand, were willing to pay. And his own research work, of so different quality, had brought him, as yet, neither money nor the fame for which he would have had a higher regard. Well, it would be different when his grandfather died!—his grandfather, whose stinginess only allowed him now the four pounds weekly, which was the sole income he had, but from whom he expected to inherit, at his death, which could not be much longer delayed, a sum of not less than sixty thousand pounds. When he had that to spend, he might have a better chance of making Dorothy recognize her mistake.

So his thoughts went on through the night. In fact, the letter revived memories which their own bitterness had buried too deeply for thought to stir them during the last years, unless prompted by such a reminder as he had now. Speculation as to why the invitation should have been given stimulated his mind to dwell upon that which, for his own peace, had been better left. In the end he came to regret that he had been so prompt in posting the curtly-worded refusal.

CHAPTER II.

THE postcard was sorted out next morning from the little pile of correspondence which lay on the breakfast table at Highview House, at Dorothy Cuthbertson's left hand, and to which it was her habit to give attention when the coffee had been poured out, and she was satisfied that nothing of Alfred's immediate wants had been overlooked.

She was accustomed to give the morning correspondence a preliminary examination before passing across the table such letters as were addressed to her husband, and which her judgment decided were suitable for his immediate perusal.

It was a method of which he fully approved, holding that it is the first duty of a novelist to protect himself (and of his wife to protect him) from any mental disturbance which may obstruct the free exercise of his imagination in the morning's work on which it is (at least in theory) so constantly occupied. Wishing to judge all men fairly, and having soon to face a problem in which Alfred's character must be carefully weighed, it is fair for us to recognize that he could have had no correspondence which he was unwilling for his wife to see.

She turned over the pile of letters, observed the preponderance of bills without surprise or any other strong emotion, paused upon a letter which she opened with hesitation, and then said, with the inward relief of a trouble deferred: "Jorrocks can't get their royalty statement out till next week. They say you shall have it not later than Wednesday." (Alfred was always disappointed and angry of late when royalty statements came. However much they might resolve to anticipate disappointing results, the fact was always a bit worse.)

She glanced next at a card in a condition of dirt for which the post office had no responsibility, and hesitated again; but it was a matter which could not be concealed, and there would be no benefit from delay. She said: "Tom won't come. He says he's got no money and no time."

"He must come. The idea's too good to drop, and I don't know anyone else I can put it to as I could to him."

"I don't see how we can make him. The card reads a bit snorty to me. I don't suppose he's forgiven me for marrying you. I wonder what sort of life I should have had among all his smells. And living on the two pounds ten, or whatever it is, that your grandfather lets him have."

"Is that about what he gets?"

"I don't know exactly. I don't suppose it's much more. You know what your grandfather is. He probably thinks it's a fortune for an unmarried man. He'd call it being liberal with his favourite grandchild."

"If that's all he's getting, he ought to jump at the chance."

"Perhaps he would. I'm a bit doubtful myself. Anyhow, he can't jump at it before he knows what it is. It looks as though you'll have to go to him. It's not exactly a thing that you'd care to write."

"I'm not going to him." Alfred's voice was decided, and with a tone of displeasure at the suggestion. There was the dignity of a famous—or well, perhaps, distinguished—novelist to be maintained. To go to Tom with the proposal he had in mind would be far too like asking a favour. It would be the wrong atmosphere, the wrong environment. The idea would have to be too abruptly spoken. It was a matter to be propounded with discretion. Perhaps in a moment of conviviality. Perhaps first as a jest, until Tom's reaction had been observed. Go to him, and blurt it out in the first ten minutes while Tom would sit glowering at him, wanting to get back to his work, and wondering what the visit might mean? No, certainly not.

"I meant," Dorothy said in her equable manner, ignoring her husband's petulance, "you may have to fetch him here."

"You mean he mayn't have the fare?"

"He mayn't be willing to spend it, which comes to the same thing."

"You think I ought to run up to town in the car, and fetch him down?"

"You're really serious about this? The more I think about it, I like it the less."

"Of course I am. There's thousands in it—thousands. Take the car?"

"He makes two excuses—money and time. If they're genuine, it removes one. Of course, the truth is more likely to be that he just doesn't care to come."

Alfred considered this with the concentration which the importance of the issue required. He had taken a second helping of eggs and bacon—he was not one of those fanatics who consider that abstinence assists the clarity of the brain—before he spoke further.

"You'll come up with me?" he asked.

Dorothy looked doubtful. She understood clearly that she was to be bait for the trap, and that she must be prepared, if necessary, to persuade a reluctant man, which she had no will to do. But she was accustomed to let Alfred have his way in all but the fundamental issues of life, and thousands—if Alfred were right, as he mostly was when his own comfort or prosperity was concerned—would be very welcome indeed. She remembered opportunely that his credit was still good at the London stores.

"Yes," she said. "There are some things in town I should like to do. I'll send Tom a few lines in answer to this."

"All right. I'll trust you to pull it off."

Alfred went into the garden, and Dorothy moved over to the bureau to write:

April 17th, 1935

Dear Tom,

I've had your card, but you won't get out of it so easily as you think!

We're shopping in London tomorrow, and I'll call for you about two-thirty, and we'll run you down in the car.

Yours,

Dorothy

P.S. Don't be silly! It's certain to do you good.

Mr. Thomas Birchall received this next morning, hesitated, and decided that if she liked to call for him with no more encouragement, it would show that she was very much in earnest in her desire for his company during the coming Easter.

When she came, about fifteen minutes later than she had proposed, she found him with a suitcase already packed, and he made no difficulty about going down with her to encounter Alfred and the waiting car.

CHAPTER III.

THOMAS BIRCHALL, whatever awkwardness he may have felt in his first meeting with a cousin who was now his host, but with whom he had seldom before exchanged any but quarrelsome words, was unable to observe any sign either of unfriendliness or constraint on the part of Alfred Cuthbertson, or of the girl who had made her choice between them two or three years earlier.

They arrived at Highview House on Thursday evening in time for a rather late dinner, at which meal, and at breakfast on Good Friday morning, he was treated not only with the casual courtesy which is usually reserved for those whose friendship is too firmly based for the formalities that greater distance requires; but also, both then and at the subsequent walk which Dorothy took him along the top of the cliffs, with a measure of confidence as to the finances of his cousin's household, and other circumstances of his publishing experiences, which were the more surprising in that they were not of a wholly satisfactory character.

Somewhat bewildered by this sudden and almost intimate friendliness, he exercised a naturally morose and suspicious mind to discover its cause, and concluded that he was to be used as the medium of requesting their grandfather to render some monetary assistance, either by gift or loan, which, as the favourite grandchild, and one who was already receiving an income from him, it might seem natural to ask him to undertake.

It was an improbable hypothesis, such as the mind will only accept for lack of a more probable explanation; and it was one with which, he resolved in advance, he would have nothing to do. He knew the contempt his grandfather had for the writer's craft, and that news of Alfred's difficulties would only stir him to sarcasm, and the hope that they might incline him to do some useful work in the world.

But Dorothy's response to a few rather clumsy words which he spoke as they were returning along the cliffs, and which were intended to let her know in advance that he was not to be used in such a manner, was of a kind to convince him that he must look for a different interpretation of this sudden, inexplicable familiarity.

He decided that he must wait, in a guarded caution, until the explanation should appear; and, meanwhile, the food was good, the weather delightful. He enjoyed the comforts of a house which contrasted with his own manner of life, and which he had the leisure to appreciate in this enforced respite from work. He thought enviously that the financial privations at which both Alfred and Dorothy had hinted were very comfortably endured.

At dinner, conversation developed again on the same lines. Dorothy repeated the remark he had made about their grandfather during the morning, and he took the opportunity of emphasizing it in the direction he had intended previously.

He mentioned that he was himself requiring a sum of about two hundred pounds for some apparatus without which he could not carry out the experiments on which he was engaged to the conclusion at which he aimed, but he dared not ask the old man for the sum he needed, lest he should take offence, and withdraw the allowance already made, for he was of the temperament which will rather assist success than make the path of failure smooth.

He did not add, being too discreet for what might have been a dangerous confidence, that he had already drawn several smaller sums for similar uses, and each one with an increasing difficulty, and by means of lying as to the results and rewards which he had already obtained. He was now too deeply entangled in these mendacities to risk a further application, and preferred to accept his meagre allowance in silence, while waiting impatiently for the death which was slow to come.

Alfred met his half-measure of confidence with an unexpected sympathy. He said: "I can understand how you feel. I wouldn't ask the old skinflint for a penny myself, if I didn't know where I could get the next meal. But I don't like to think of you being held up for such a beggarly sum. I'd lend it you myself if the publishers weren't such ghastly frauds. But we must think out what we can do."

Thomas was more puzzled by this than he had been before. Was Alfred really disposed to contrive some way by which he could gain command of the sum he needed? Probably not. It was more likely that he had uttered no more than empty, courteous words. But if these people had suddenly gone mad with friendship for himself, there was no reason that he should not accept the benefits that the circumstances allowed. He saw that some increase of cordiality on

14

his side might be more profitable than his present attitude of watchful reserve.

And while he thought this, Dorothy did not let the conversation die.

"You see," she said, "Alfred made a lot of money with his first book, *The Blood-Stained Beads*, and then he made a contract for two more, with good deposits from the publishers, and it seemed as though he'd got nothing to do but to write two books a year and the money would roll in faster than we should know how to spend it; so that when we bought this house with the money we got from the first book, it seemed a very prudent thing to have done.

"And, of course, it's very pleasant to have no rent to pay, though the rates and the mortgage interest come to a big sum, and it's a good deal more expensive to keep up than we reckoned at first.

"But that wouldn't have mattered at all, if the publishers hadn't let Alfred down. They didn't advertise the next books half enough, and they hadn't sufficient enterprise to send them out on sale to the shops, and so when the contract was at an end it seemed prudent to make a change.

"So Alfred moved to Jorrocks, and, so far, they have proved to be worse than the firm he left."

Thomas murmured appropriate sounds of sympathy, in a voice ill-adapted by nature for such exercises, while he calculated: "Two books a year! Say 200,000 words, probably less. That's about 550 words a day—an hour's work if you reckon over six seconds for every word, which is absurd, especially for the pronouns. And he calls that work! I wonder whether he's going to ask me to collaborate with him to put some more guts into them. I suppose I could write half—300 words a day—without much interference with my real work, but it's not the kind of thing I should like Bevan to know that I'd taken on."

Edward Bevan, M.D., was Thomas's single friend—he who occupied a flat of more commodious extent under that in which Thomas lived. He was a consultant of some reputation, and an enthusiast in studying the course of various diseases by the inoculation of mice and other quadrupeds. Obviously, Thomas would not like him to know that he had been reduced to augmenting his income by the childish expedient of writing tales.

While these thoughts passed through his mind, Alfred continued the conversation. He gave many details respecting royalties, cheap editions, foreign translation and serial rights, and other fluctuant and too-precarious sources of a novelist's income, which it would be wearisome to record; but the point emerged clearly that, without

15

fault or failure on Alfred's side, the family income was falling short of the figure which Alfred's comfort and the upkeep of Highview required.

It seemed clear to the scientist that he was about to be asked to strengthen those wretched books, most probably by the addition of solid facts, such as people would naturally be eager to know. He thought now that he understood the reception which the confession of his own necessity had received. Doubtless, he was to be offered the £200 he required in return for the literary service so urgently needed. Well, if so, he might not decline. But there should be no hint of willingness on his part. Let them beg it of him, however awkward or humiliating it might be!

But, for the moment at least, he found that no such request, nor any other, was to be made. Dorothy was talking now, and she made her theme the difficulty of following public caprice, and the importance of seemingly-irrelevant notoriety on the part of the author in inducing the public to read his books.

"You mean," he asked, "that if Alfred were to climb the Nelson Monument during the night, and be seen on the top next morning wearing nothing but his school tie, there would be more people who would want to read his books during the week?"

It seemed an absurd theory to Thomas. Indeed, he would have reversed it in his mind, and thought that such an antic would supply convincing reason why sensible people would leave them alone; but Dorothy said, "Yes, that was the idea." And though Alfred had looked annoyed at the vision of his somewhat lanky figure being so indecorously displayed, he answered with equal definiteness.

Well, after all, people who read such books could not be expected to have their logical faculties in active and regular use! And if Alfred needed publicity, could it not be gained by the announcement that he had donated £200 of his surplus wealth to the endowment of scientific research?

But having reached this point, the conversation drifted inconclusively in other directions. It was not until evening came, and they were having coffee together in the drawing room after dinner, that the affability of which Thomas had been making unaccustomed demonstration had its reward, and Alfred put the proposition that was in his mind squarely before him.

CHAPTER IV.

"IT isn't the merit of a book on which sales depend," Alfred said. "Any publisher will admit that. If they could make even an approximate guess at how any book will go, they would amass fortunes without any risk at all.

"It's partly luck, and partly a number of other factors, some of which are very difficult to foresee, and, of course, largely a matter of the way a book's put on the market. There are few that a publisher can't kill by issuing them in such a way that he shows he doesn't think much of them himself; but there's one sure road to big sales, and that's to get the public talking about either the book itself, or the man who wrote it.

"Every actress comes to the time when her agent tells her she's got to have her necklace stolen, or her salary halved; and those who have any brains don't wait till they're pushed up to the fence; they have the stunts while they're young, and they're sure of getting onto the front page.

"Now what I've been saying to Dorothy is, why shouldn't an author do the same thing?"

Thomas Birchall, being a literal-minded man, as most scientists are, was puzzled by this opening. He was not aware that Alfred had a necklace of any value, and if he were wrong on that point, he was averse from being publicly known as the man who had stolen it, even though he should receive the solace of £200 for any legal inconveniences that might follow. He said doubtfully: "It's a good idea, I've no doubt of that. But I'm I afraid I shouldn't be able to help."

The reply was satisfactory to his cousin, who had not expected the idea that his assistance might be required to come so readily into Thomas's mind. It encouraged him to reach the point by a shorter route than he had intended to use.

He said: "Oh, but you could. You're about the only one I should care to ask. I mean the only one I could trust to play the game, and not to give me away.

"I shouldn't ask you to do anything difficult. Just to disappear somewhere for a few weeks, more or less, and to watch the papers, and come back at the right time. Of course, I'd make it worthwhile. Say £200 down and ten percent of the extra profit I make—compared with the book before—on *The Clue of the Twisted Spoon*, which comes out next month."

Thomas considered this proposition with some satisfaction, but more bewilderment. It sounded less repellent than stealing necklaces, but was the disappearance of a novelist's cousin sufficiently sensational to secure the desired result? Of course, he could stipulate for the £200 to be cash in advance, and he would be sure of that. But he had a sound instinct that there was more in the proposition than had yet been disclosed. He asked cautiously: "How would that help you, for me to clear out?"

Alfred felt that the opening of his proposition had been well received. It encouraged a rapid advance to the kernel of the idea, about which he had anticipated more awkwardness than he was experiencing.

"What I thought," he said, "was that we might be seen to quarrel, and then you would disappear, and enquiries would follow, and I should fall under suspicion of having made away with you; and just when the reporters were swarming round, and it would be getting very awkward for me, you would reappear, and say you'd been on a holiday somewhere out of the way, and hadn't seen any papers, and, anyhow, couldn't you go where you liked without the police making a fuss?"

"Alfred thought," Dorothy added, "that there might be some money in libel actions as well. Some of the Sunday newspapers would be almost certain to go too far."

Thomas heard this proposal without active dissent. Put in general terms, as it was, and by two people who were convinced of its practicability (at least, Alfred Cuthbertson was so convinced, and some weeks of talking with frequent reiteration of "Well, have you anything better you can suggest?" had brought Dorothy more or less to the same view), it sounded simple enough, and his part seemed to be mainly of a negative character. It was true that such a disappearance would interrupt his work, but that would soon be blocked for lack of the apparatus which he would thus be able to buy. If he had the cash in advance, he could order it before leaving, and it would be ready for delivery on his return. "Well," he said, "it's a queer idea, but I daresay you're right. You'd let me have the £200 at the start, so that I could have the things made while I'm away?"

The question brought a pause of silence. It was not entirely a matter of trusting Thomas. The money, at short notice, might not be easy to find. The original plan had been to offer half the amount, and it was only Thomas's statement that he was in urgent need of that sum that had caused Alfred to spring to what he felt would be an irresistible bribe. After next Wednesday, when Jorrocks's royalty cheque, overdue and now promised, would have arrived, it might be possible to manage it, but Dorothy had a conviction, based on past experiences of the same kind, that however moderately they estimated its amount, the reality would be something less.

Alfred was the first to speak, recollecting that the plan was not intended to be put into immediate operation. Its date must be that of the publication of *The Clue of the Twisted Spoon*, which was fixed for some weeks ahead. He said: "Well, I daresay we could manage that. I expect you'd want to go back to town first, and get things cleared up for leaving, but of course it wouldn't do to let anyone know that you expected to be away."

Thomas agreed that he would prefer to return to his flat. The question caused him to reflect that, if his disappearance were to be taken seriously, his rooms might be invaded by the police or other officious persons, against which he must be prepared, while avoiding anything which would have the appearance of having expected their coming. Evidently, this unusual proposition needed to be considered on many sides, as is common to any exceptional course of conduct which transgresses the normality of civilized life.

And with this thought came another doubt. If he should say nothing to anyone to stir alarm in advance, who was there who would be active enough to enquire, though he might be absent for half a year?

He understood the position sufficiently to infer that Alfred aimed at a prompt alarm. Two hundred pounds was an inviting bait, but he did not intend to go into this curious scheme without understanding every issue that might arise.

"I suppose you've thought," he asked, "that I'm not one of those who'd be missed in a few hours? You might find it simpler to do me in without any fuss following, than to get people stirred up because they didn't see me about."

"Oh, but Alfred's planned all that," Dorothy replied, with some natural pride in the genius of a husband sufficient to invent and solve the mystery of the blood-stained beads, which had been as improbable as most things are. "It will happen when some people are coming up the path, near enough to see you go over the edge, though too distant to interfere."

Thomas saw, with some inward annoyance, how completely the plan must have been developed before he had been taken into confidence. With what assurance, with what impudence, they had assumed that he could be summoned when they required his service! Anger stirred at the thought, but he controlled it with the determination that he would not allow resentment to obstruct his making of what had sounded like a very easy profit. Yet what was that which Dorothy had said, in her casual way? "When you go over the edge." It had a repellent sound. He gave his attention to Alfred, who, observing and partly understanding the effect of his wife's too-impetuous exclamation, was now giving a detailed explanation of the plan which he had evolved in a lively imagination for the resuscitation of his wilting fortunes.

"Of course," he said, adroitly meeting the feeling of annoyance which his cousin's expression showed, "we couldn't be rude enough to ask you down before we'd worked out a feasible plan. But there's nothing final in that. I daresay you'll think of a better one almost at once.

"But there's a place on the cliffs where the path goes close to the edge, or what looks like the edge to anyone coming up from this direction, but it isn't really the edge. There's a ledge a few feet lower that anyone could jump, or even fall, down to, without any danger at all, and by walking on for a dozen yards, till the ledge ends, which it does by the cliff top sloping down a little, and the ledge rising till they become one, he would get away—perhaps having to stoop a little; we should have to test that—without anyone coming up the path from this side seeing him at all.

"They'd just see us quarrel, and you go over the edge, and perhaps see me pass them afterwards in an agitated manner. And they'd be certain to talk, if they didn't phone up the police.

"If they should do that, I don't think the police here would believe much without enquiries. I know them fairly well. You'd have plenty of time to get away.

"But whether they bothered the police or not, they'd be certain to talk, and Dorothy, never suspecting that I could have committed a crime, would make an innocent fuss before the servants as to why you hadn't come back with me, and I should be agitated, and make some excuse that wouldn't sound true, and—well, we know Osbury! And we know the maids we've got here. Before night, it would be the talk of every house in the town.

"The police would be bound to make some enquiries, sooner or later. They mightn't accuse me of murder but they'd call politely to know what did happen, and I should give a reply which might have more truth in it than they would be quick to believe. And, in the end, they'd get me or Dorothy to give them the address of your flat, and ask the London police to ascertain that you had got home safely.

"If necessary, I could get something said in the right quarters to reach the local editor, and make sure of some guarded but provocative references appearing in the *Osbury Advertiser*. I know just how he'd rise to a bait like that.

"Or I might offer a reward myself for information by which you could be traced, saying that I was determined to clear my name. Some people would think it a proof of innocence, and some a bluff. I might get the whole country discussing whether I were a criminal, or suffering from an unjust suspicion.

"Oh, you can leave that side of it to me! I'll make sure that you don't disappear without a good deal of noise resulting."

Thomas listened to these lively forecasts with something more of respect for his cousin's brain than he had felt previously. He recognized that there are different varieties of efficiency, and that Alfred Cuthbertson might be able to manage his side of the conspiracy without assistance. But it seemed to him that it was one which might become very uncomfortable for its originator, particularly if he should delay his own return, on which point he saw that he was being trusted a good deal more than he might have been willing to trust Alfred, or anyone else, had the position been contrary to what it was.

"You'd be in a queer fix, wouldn't you," he enquired "if I lost my memory, say in an Irish village, and never came back at all?"

Dorothy answered that first. She said: "Not as much as you'd think, even then. Alfred says there's a law that a man cannot be prosecuted for murder unless the body can be produced, and of course it couldn't."

"I'm not worrying about that," Alfred added. "The more fuss there might be, the bigger sales we should have, and as we're to share the profits, the more you stayed away the more you'd come back, if I may put it in that way."

Thomas said that he had no doubt that he should. He made no further objections, and they went on to discuss the details of the conspiracy on a common assumption that it had been agreed in principle between them.

The next morning they took a walk along the cliff top, and inspected the site which had been selected for the pretended crime which was to make so rich a market for *The Clue of the Twisted Spoon.* Thomas did not think the ledge quite as safe or as broad as it had been represented to him, but he agreed that he might jump down to it, or even fall, without real danger of continuing his descent to the sea-beaten rocks below.

He was too destitute of imagination to be nervous beyond logical cause. He did consider, with a brief seriousness, that, if he were dead, his cousin might have some hope of inheriting their grandfather's fortune, which was otherwise out of his reach. But he reassured himself with the reflection that, were murder intended, it would hardly be staged in so particularly public a manner.

He thought that Alfred might need all his plausible mental agility to avoid consequences more unpleasant than he would care to encounter, even for the harvest which his imagination foresaw. But his own part appeared to be as simple as his own profit was sure.

He went back to London on the following Tuesday, promising to return in about three weeks, and having drawn a preliminary £10 from his cousin for the incidental expenses which he said the arrangements for his absence would involve. The remaining £190 was to be ready for his next arrival.

CHAPTER V.

THREE weeks later, Thomas Birchall returned to Highview House.

He had put the wild idea that Alfred might intend to murder him in earnest to gain their grandfather's inheritance out of his mind, and decided during the first week to go through with the project, though with an increasing reluctance.

Actually, his position as his grandfather's heir became less secure and his need of the £200 greater during the following fortnight, though he hoped and supposed that Alfred Cuthbertson was not aware of what had occurred.

The old gentleman, Eli Birchall, with perverse agility for one who had passed his ninetieth year, had mounted the four flights of stairs that led to his grandson's flat, and paid him a surprise visit, which may have been actuated by the curiosity of affection rather than any more malevolent impulse; but its result had been to expose the mendacity of certain statements which Thomas had made as to the condition in which he lived, and the successful activities in which his grandfather's liberality, which had now continued for nearly fifteen years, had enabled him to engage.

Mr. Birchall senior had been angry, scenting deceit. He had been sarcastic, suspecting failure. He had even hinted, in a most ominous manner, that a novelist who succeeds is preferable to a chemist who fails. Thomas had been tempted to retort that the novelist's success was not very securely based, but he saw that he might be drawn to indiscretion if he should commence to narrate the confidence that the Cuthbertsons had so recently given. With a wiser reticence, he talked of the work on which he was engaged, in which he was confident of success so soon as the new apparatus (costing £200), which he had already ordered, should be available.

The fact that he was able to spend such an amount, and that he did not ask for assistance to find it, did something to re-establish his shaken position in the old gentleman's mind, but Thomas saw clearly, when he had left, that it had become imperative that he should go on with an enterprise from which further reflection had made him more averse than he had been while under the influence of his cousin's optimistic plausibility, and Dorothy's quieter encouragement.

If he had a remaining reluctance, it arose from his dislike to doing that which, whatever profit it might bring to himself, must put ten times the amount into the pocket of a cousin whom he had never liked, and to whom his antipathy had now been stirred to greater intensity—first, by observing him in possession of the girl for whom his passion had been revived by a fresh proximity, during which she had shown a very friendly attitude to himself; and second, by the fear which his grandfather's words had roused, that he might be destined to lose the fortune which he had counted already his, and see his cousin possessing once again that to which he considered that he had staked out an earlier claim.

It was in this mood, with no goodwill in his heart, but with a determination to earn the £200, the possession of which had now become such an urgent need, that he went down to Osbury the second time.

There was, indeed, no real friendliness, and little trust beyond that which a common interest gives, between the conspirators on either side.

Alfred might be less than aware of his cousin's antipathy to himself, but his own judgment of Thomas was that he was both an uncouth boor, and a very evident fool. Dorothy, who had always felt a physical repugnance toward him which his vanity had failed to perceive, so that she would omit shaking hands if it could be avoided in a natural way, did not like him any the better because she had been constrained to adopt the measure of affability that his persuasion required. And it was in this atmosphere of latent hostilities that two incidents occurred, trivial in themselves, but necessary to chronicle, owing to their relation to the events that followed.

The occasions came owing to a fresh evidence of their own incompetence supplied by Messrs. Jorrocks Bros., Ltd., who wrote regretting that they would not be able to bring out *The Clue of the Twisted Spoon* on the date originally fixed. There would be an unavoidable delay of a week.

Alfred, who had planned that his cousin's disappearance should immediately follow, not precede, the publication of his new book, would not consent to alter his view of the advantage of having it already on sale, when the expected publicity should develop. He insisted that the event should be deferred for a week, to which, after a prolonged argument, Thomas rather sulkily agreed. He said that it would be an utterly wasted week, as he could do no work, and it would prolong the period which must elapse before he could be back in his own flat. He had a minor cause for grumbling in the fact that he had brought a very meagre supply of linen and other necessities, having foreseen that he could not take a packed suitcase when he set out on the cliff top stroll from which he would not return, and having no wish to leave behind more than the occasion required.

Beside that, he had now been at Highview House for nearly twenty-four hours, and there had been no mention of the payment of the £190 which was the condition precedent to the performance which he had undertaken. He might have been less concerned about this, had he not promised Wellers & Samuel, Ltd., the scientific apparatus manufacturers with whom his order was placed, that the amount of their *pro-forma* invoice, £169 3s. 10d, should be remitted to them not later than the following day. He had a conviction, which their name may have suggested, that it was only in a Pickwickian sense that they would put the order in hand until the cashier's department had recorded receipt of the required remittance.

Having this in his mind, he mentioned it with his natural bluntness.

"I hope that doesn't mean that you'll keep me out of the cash? I've promised Wellers that I'll send them a cheque tomorrow."

He caught Dorothy's eyes as he spoke, and thought that her reception of this remark implied something less than a belief that Alfred was prepared for immediate payment, though, beyond that, it was hard to read; but his cousin spoke before she attempted to do so.

"All right;" he said easily, "I'll go round to the bank in the morning, and see what can be done."

The casual tone, which treated the matter as a triviality or routine, reduced the effect of the ambiguity of the words, and Thomas felt he must wait to see what the morning brought. The conversation took place in the lounge, where afternoon tea was served, and at the conclusion of the meal he went out to sit on the terrace which overlooked the gardens on the south side of the house, beyond which was a view of undulating wooded country, falling away to the sea. On his right hand, the early April sunset had already reddened the sky. On his left was a glimpse of the blue, incurving bay. The evening was windless and warm, and most people, seated idly there, would have been conscious of the serene beauty of what they saw, to the exclusion of other thoughts.

But Thomas Birchall gave it no heed. His mind was on the plot which was not his, but in which he was now taking a willing part, and it was the sound of voices overhead which interrupted his thoughts.

The voices came from the open window of his cousin's bedroom, and though they would not normally have been audible to anyone sitting on the terrace below, anger or other kindred emotions raised the conversation at times to a pitch at which the words came clearly through the still evening air.

The fact was that the cheque which had been received from Jorrocks since Easter had not merely been disappointing, it had been of almost infinitesimal amount, the earnings of Alfred's last book having been insufficient, as yet, to cover the first advance which had been made upon it; and the receipts from the cheap editions of earlier books amounting to a very small sum, such publications doing more to increase the number of an author's readers than to augment his bank balance.

The position was therefore more critical than had been expected, and, in Dorothy's opinion, it was desperate, if so large a sum as had been agreed was to be handed over to Thomas tomorrow. Indeed, without the assistance of the bank, it could not be done. And to ask the bank was an unpleasant, and might even be an unprofitable, enterprise.

Mr. Duckfield, the manager of the local branch of the London & Northern Bank, had been of an effusive friendliness when Alfred had opened an account with him on purchasing Highview House, and first coming into that district to live. He was still affable when they met on the golf course, as they often would on Saturday afternoons, but Alfred's sensitive pride had noticed a subtle change, as his resources of idle cash had diminished during the last two years, and he had taken a gradually increasing advantage of the credit which the Osbury tradesmen had, at first, been so anxious to give.

We may sympathize with Alfred's feelings without blaming Mr. Duckfield for that. A bank manager's smile is an important part of his professional equipment, and must be graded with care. It is his business to know, and to foresee. He did not regard Alfred Cuthbertson as being in any immediate financial difficulty. His reputation, as yet, was high, his credit good. But he foresaw the probability of a time arriving at which Mr. Cuthbertson would ask for that little temporary accommodation which is so apt to assume a permanent character if it be too readily given. When that moment came, he might not refuse; but he would have serious, probing questions to ask, perhaps serious advice to give. But even that was no more than a likely guess. Alfred Cuthbertson's books were popular. The next one might be as great a success—or even greater—than *The Blood-*

Stained Beads, and the cheques which his agents sent might again be in four figures instead of three. Mr. Duckfield watched, and smiled meanwhile on his second grade, in a friendly, noncommittal way.

"I don't believe," Alfred said irritably, "the account can be as bad as you think. We can't have spent all that in the time. I expect you've made a mistake."

It was one of Dorothy's regular duties to keep a record of how the bank account stood, in the intervals of having the passbook written up, on the sound principle that a creative brain, such as that which Alfred possessed, should be relieved of the sordid or prosaic details of earthly life. It enabled Alfred to imply, with a mixture of incredulity and irritation, that it was primarily her own fault if the figures were of an unsatisfactory character.

"I haven't made any mistake," she replied, with a tone of annoyance which the unfounded accusation may have excused. "When they've paid Portby's cheque there'll be just under £160 left."

She knew that her accounts had been very carefully entered and checked, and she had previous experience that, if any mistake were made, it was always that there was less money in the account, not more than her figures showed.

"Then you should have told Portby's to wait."

"I simply couldn't do that. I'd put them off three times before, and they said they needed it particularly this week."

"Well, I'm not going to ask any favour of Thomas now. I'd rather ask Duckfield than him. And I shouldn't be surprised if he jibbed if I did, and the whole thing would be off. He's sulky enough now. You can see it just under the surface, though he tries to keep it from coming up. If he could get the money by murdering me in earnest, instead of me pretending to murder him, he'd be a happier man."

"Don't be absurd! You think any man hates you if he isn't always on his knees licking your boots. Suppose Duckfield jibs? That's quite as likely, if not a bit more."

"He won't do that. Not for such an amount. And if he did, we could ask Thomas afterwards. But I won't unless I'm obliged."

"I wasn't thinking only of him. What are we going to do for the next three months? There's the rates due now. That's nearly £30."

"You've got some cash in the house, haven't you?"

"I've got about £20. That won't go far. There's always wages to pay."

"What do you want me to do?"

"I want you to give Tom £90 now, and say he shall have the rest when he comes back. He ought to agree to that."

"No he won't. You'll find he'll kick like a mule, and I shall have to go to the bank at last, after I've made myself cheap to him."

The fact was that Alfred had brought himself to the point of one distasteful action, which he had mentally rehearsed, and which he felt he could probably carry through in a casual, offhand way. Indeed, in the rear of his mind, he had a half-admitted intention of doing nothing at all, but to present a cheque at the counter which he felt sure that the obsequious cashier would pay without the formality of referring to the balance of so valuable a client. If he *should* raise any question, then there would be time for the little talk with Duckfield, which should be more than sufficient to deal with the position.

Probably Duckfield would be most concerned to apologize for any hesitation the cashier might have displayed! After all, drawing £190 when your balance happens to be £160 is quite different from drawing £30 when you have no balance at all. It makes the £30 seem a comparative triviality—a mere discount upon the larger figures involved.

And after that—in a fortnight's time, when his new book would be out, and selling in quantities which could be only vaguely imagined, as the result of the publicity he would have obtained—he could either ask Duckfield for an overdraft of some really useful amount, or get his agents to draw an advance from Jorrocks, which, with the hope of a further contract to be fixed up, they would be almost eager to give!

And here was Dorothy, in her stupid, literal, unimaginative, feminine way, raising obstacles, asking him to humiliate himself further to a cousin he loathed with an intensity he had not realized until he had associated himself with him in this hateful enterprise— hateful, yes, that was the word. He realized that, as he got closer to it, he liked it much less than when it had been first, and vaguely, imagined. Now it was only pride, and the knowledge that, should it fail, his financial position would be really desperate during the next half-year, which prevented him from throwing it up, and telling Thomas to go back to the dirty room and the foul stenches from which he came! Couldn't Dorothy see that he had enough on his mind without worrying him in this senseless way?

On her side, Dorothy was even nearer to the point of throwing the whole thing up, of pleading with him to join with her in economizing, and making that £160 go as far as it would, instead of letting it pass into his cousin's pocket, leaving her bare to the world if the wild plot they had formed—and the nearer they got to it, the wilder she saw it to be—should miscarry. Suppose Tom should fluke it in some way? Should do something by which he would be discovered in a few hours, and the whole thing die out with no sensation at all? Would he return the money? She thought she knew Tom better than that!

It was only the hour she had spent that morning over the household bills, and the appalling total to which they came, which had silenced this intended proposal to call it off. She had compromised between her contending fears with the idea of giving Thomas half the amount. At the worst, there would be £60 left! There would still be the possibility of asking Mr. Duckfield's assistance at a later date! And should Tom refuse—well, she was not sure that her feeling would not be that of a great relief.

And now Alfred refused to listen, as he always would if he were crossed in his own plans. Was it fair, when he left all the contriving, all the unpleasant things, all the putting off of the tradesmen to her?

She may be excused—perhaps we should say that they may both be excused—if the argument went on to some heated exchanges, in the course of which things were said which would be regretted in cooler blood; until, in the end, Alfred gave way, as he usually would, if there should be a real contest of wills, and Dorothy found, as she would with the same frequency, that she had undertaken to do herself that which she had been urging upon him.

The bargain was that Thomas was to be asked to accept £100, and to wait for the balance until the plot had been carried through successfully, but it was Dorothy who must ask him to agree to this important modification of the bargain already made.

Thomas, listening below, and hearing high and angry voices gradually decline to more normal tones, did not understand this. Indeed, the disjointed phrases that reached his ears led him to radically misunderstand the nature of the dispute. But he understood that his cousins were liable to quarrel violently in their own room. Probably (he thought) they were at fundamental enmity, only concealed with difficulty in his presence and while they were drawn together by this plot, the success of which was essential to all. Was not he being outwardly polite to Alfred, his hatred for whom was only modified by an equally strong contempt? Might he not judge their manners in relation to their real feelings by his own? And, even now, they could not prevent their real bitterness breaking out when they were in the privacy of their own room!

Suppose that it might still be possible to reverse the fate by which it had seemed that all things fell into Alfred's hands, while his own remained empty? He looked ahead, and there was a new hope colouring the hatred that had possessed his mind for the last three years.

He had put aside the fear that Alfred would ever gain the fortune which he had long regarded as coming to himself at his grandfather's death. Apart from other plans which were in his mind, he relied upon the money which he was now to receive to enable him to demonstrate a success which would re-establish himself to Eli Birchall's favour. There was a pleasant comedy in the fact that Alfred would be unconsciously providing the means of checkmating any prospect of the inheritance which he might otherwise have had!

And now—looking ahead, if not at the moment—might he not find himself in possession of both the fortune that he had always regarded as his, and the girl of whom he had felt that he had been robbed three years ago? As he thought this, an unpleasant smile came to his face which there was no one to see. The evening became chilly, as well as dark. He went in.

CHAPTER VI.

THE second episode which it is necessary to chronicle arose out of the first, and may be more briefly told. Thomas went into the lounge, there still being more than an hour before dinner, and sat there looking at the afternoon paper, and considered rather disconcerting aspects of the adventure in which he was engaged, one or two of which had not occurred to him previously, especially in relation to the postponement of date to which he had so reluctantly consented.

As a result of these considerations, he decided that it would be necessary to send a telegram to London, and was considering how best it could be despatched, when Dorothy entered the room.

She had already dressed for dinner, and looked her most attractive as well as most capable self, as she greeted Thomas with smiling eyes and a word of apology for having left him so long alone.

He did not know the errand on which she came, nor that her smile was born of no love for him, but of a determination that her husband's bank account should be £60 in credit rather than £30 overdrawn. She had resolved that she would give him some soft words, and a sight of her seductive self smiling graciously in the low-cut, black-lace evening frock which, as she well knew, made the very best of what beauty she had, and the cost to him was to be either £90 or £100, according to how adroitly she could frame her request, and how complacent he might prove to be.

He only observed that she came from a quarrel with Alfred, the violence and spirit of which he overestimated (having no experience of how sharply married people may differ while maintaining a common front to the rest of the world), and that for him she had smiling lips and soft looks in the same hour.

He saw at the same moment how particularly desirable was the woman whom Alfred had meanly snatched from his arms, and (as he thought) how gladly she would now reverse the choice, if it should be possible for her to do.

31

But he had an immediate object he must not miss. He said: "This alteration of dates means that I may be longer away from London than I had planned. Is there a telegraph office near here?"

"There's one about ten minutes' walk on the Dorchester road. There'd be time, if it's urgent, to do that before dinner. But you can telegraph from the phone here."

Thomas did not appear to welcome the suggestion. He said: "Thanks, but I think I'll go out. I shan't mind the walk."

She had an apprehension that the telegram must be something he did not wish to disclose to her. If it contained any hint that he was not expecting to be back in London promptly, it might ruin everything! If there were risk of that, it became the more urgent that he should not be paid the whole sum in advance. She said: "There's no need for you to go out yourself. Annie can take it for you."

"No, I won't trouble her, thanks. I'd rather send it myself, if you don't mind."

He got up to go.

She had a moment's inclination to offer to go with him. There are advantages in a walk for such conversation as she designed, but it would mean changing twice before dinner. Apart from any question of time, it would seem an absurd suggestion to make. She fought down a cowardly impulse to postpone a distasteful task, and put the question of what the telegram might contain out of her mind, to concentrate on that which she had to do.

She saw that she must come to the point more abruptly than she had intended, if she were to detain him now Well, perhaps it would be the better way! "Wait a minute, Tom. I want to ask you something before you go."

He was aware of an undertone of excitement or nervousness in her voice, and misread its cause. He imagined, in a somewhat obtuse mind, that which he wished to believe. Having quarrelled with Alfred, she had come for counsel or consolation to him!

His thoughts leapt ahead to the time when Alfred Cuthbertson would be in the jail to which his crazy scheme would certainly lead—especially if his own return were delayed!

But how, if he were away, could he use the time as he (and doubtless Dorothy) would desire to do? For him to reappear would be the relief of whatever trouble Alfred might be experiencing. He must look farther ahead. And perhaps to a different end from that which Alfred designed.

He paused more willingly, and with a more amiable expression than she had expected to meet, giving her hope that the work of persuasion would be less difficult than she had feared. Alfred had been right, as he often was! She was the one to carry through her own plan to success, at which she must not fail through her cold dislike of the man to whom she would make appeal.

"I've been talking to Alfred," she began, "and I'm afraid there's rather more difficulty—but what I'm going to ask you isn't from him, but myself. It's my own idea, and when I've explained how Alfred—"

"You needn't trouble to do that," he answered, elated by her tone and manner as much by the half-finished sentences, the import of which he misread in his own way, and at the same time anxious to reach the point as promptly as possible, with the thought of the telegraph office in the back of his mind. He was not one to allow any woman, at whatever crisis of emotion, to interfere with his business life. "I heard," he went on, "the row you had in the bedroom. I was sitting on the terrace below."

The blunt admission confused her for a moment with the memory of the quarrel, and an effort to recall what had been said in those heated and confidential exchanges, and to realize what effect they might have on his mind. But he did not seem angered or even displeased. She felt that, however much or little might really have reached his ears, it must be boldly faced, and it would, at least, avert the necessity of explaining the purpose for which she came.

"Then," she began, "you'll understand how it is, and what I'm going to ask you now."

He misread her again, and with more excuse than before. It did not occur to him that she might blush with sudden confusion on learning that her quarrel with Alfred was overheard, for he supposed that it was the subject on which she was preparing to confide in him. He had simply helped her over a difficult stile. Helped her to come to the point, at which women are sometimes so slow to arrive. He supposed that he was helping her further now, as he said: "Of course, I do. We'll find a way to put that silly ass in his place, and...."

He might have finished the sentence without interruption, and before its implications would have been perceived by Dorothy's utterly unreceptive mind, if he had not accompanied it by what he felt to be an appropriate gesture, his arm coming round her shoulder, and his hand resting on her bare neck.

It was no more than that, but Dorothy was one of those people who are particularly averse from such physical contacts. With an exclamation of sharp astonishment, she pushed off his arm, and as she did so they were both aware that Alfred had entered the room.

There was a moment of angry, disconcerted, or bewildered silence, which Thomas was the first to break. He said: "I'd better be going, if I'm to be back for dinner," and pushed past his scowling but irresolute cousin out of the room. He went in a doubt of whether Dorothy's action had been one of spontaneous repulsion, or that she had been aware of Alfred's entrance a half-second before himself Finally, he decided that the latter was the true solution. How ready women were at difficult moments! Did it not suggest that she was more experienced in such situations than her cool aloofness would lead anyone but an observant scientist to suppose?

CHAPTER VII.

"WHAT the devil," Alfred asked, "was the meaning of that?"

He felt uncertain what had been the nature of the incident that his entrance had so abruptly terminated; doubtful, like Thomas, of whether Dorothy's sharp withdrawal from his cousin's embrace had been inspired by the revulsion her face expressed, or by the knowledge that he was a witness of what she did. He felt curiously unequal to the position, as he often would in the real crises of life, unless they could be turned aside with a light wit. It is so much easier to handle such situations in books, where everyone is under equal control, and the consequences can be decided without haste, at the author's will!

"I don't know," Dorothy answered angrily. "He said he'd do what we want, and then he put his hand on my neck, and I threw it off. I shouldn't have thought he'd dare! He heard the row we had in the bedroom, but I don't see what that could have done to make him think he could insult me like that. I suppose he thought that you didn't care."

The explanation gave a new direction to Alfred's mind. As Dorothy had done before, he began to wonder what could have been overheard, to endeavour to recollect what had been said. He asked: "What did he hear?"

"I don't know how much. He was on the seat under the window. We ought to have been more careful. He seemed to know what I was going to say before I could get it out, and I understood that he agreed."

"Well, I don't, if he does. I'm not going to have any favours that make him think he can be cheeky to you. I've a good mind to throw him out of the house."

Alfred felt very pleased with himself as he said this. He felt that he was handling the situation in the manly style it required, and at the same time getting his own way after all about paying the fellow off. He regretted this after reflection, when he realized that (as

35

Dorothy's misunderstanding led him to believe), he might have paid the smaller sum without further humiliation than the overhearing of the bedroom dispute had already caused. But these noble attitudes often do seem more satisfactory at the time than they will appear at a later hour.

Dorothy made no objection. She said: "I'm certainly not going to ask him anything further after the way he's behaved." She was conscious herself of a possible ambiguity in the incident as it had come to her husband's eyes, and her first intention at the moment was to let him see that it had been repugnant to her.

Seeing him to be convinced on this point, she was willing to persuade him that there was no occasion for it to be further noticed. In future, would Alfred be careful that she should not be left alone with his cousin, whose visit would so soon be over? She did not wish the plot to be upset because he had acted with a momentary boorish familiarity. It would be more dignified to pass it in silence, as a lapse of manners to be ignored in an uncultured guest.

Magnanimously, and with expressed reluctance, Alfred allowed himself to be talked over to this view.

It followed that Thomas did not become aware of the nature of the request that Dorothy had been about to make. He sat through dinner in a sulky silence, waiting for a storm which declined to burst. As the evening passed, he realized that, so far as Alfred was concerned, the incident was not to be a subject of further reference. He supposed that, while he had been at the post office, Dorothy had been clever enough to explain it away! He had read an old tale somewhere of a woman who had persuaded her husband to trust her against the evidence of his own eyes. Well, when she had come into his hands, she would have to watch her steps better than that.

He observed without resentment her subsequent coldness, which he supposed to be a garment of discretion which the occasion required; and the fact that he did not see her alone during the following day could be naturally ascribed to her husband's jealousy.

Alfred went to the bank in the morning, and though he talked to Dorothy, who walked down with him into Osbury, of what he would say to Mr. Duckfield, he found it much easier to stroll up to the counter and present his cheque for £190 for payment in his usual casual manner. He chatted pleasantly to a cashier who was simple enough to regard a live novelist with some reverence as he picked up the notes and stuffed them into his pocket-book.

He paid Thomas on his return, and they discussed once again some of the finer points of the plot, the success of which he was determined should not be hazarded by any oversight of detail on his part. Doing this, they regained something of their previous superficial affability; but the incident had increased the fundamental antipathies which could only be held in check as long, or so far, as a common interest remained.

CHAPTER VIII.

IT was shortly after breakfast on the morning of Tuesday, May 14th, that Dorothy rang the dining room bell, and instructed Bertha, the parlour maid, on her appearance, to inform the cook that Mr. Cuthbertson and Mr. Birchall would be out for lunch. From the conversation which took place in the girl's presence, it was made evident that the two gentlemen were proposing a long walk on the cliff tops in a westerly direction, when Alfred would show his guest something more of the beauties of the district before his return to town on the following day.

Dorothy said that she wished to provide the gentlemen with some sandwiches for their midday refreshment, which she would make up herself, on the necessary materials being brought to the breakfast table, together with an attaché case of suitable size in which to pack them.

These orders were, in themselves, sufficient to excite comment among the domestic staff, who knew that their master was disposed to prefer a lunch more adequate to the intellect of a great novelist, and more elaborately served; and that his opinion of those who self-eluded themselves that they prefer the discomforts of a picnic meal had been forcibly expressed in *The Mystery of the Blood-Stained Beads*.

It might seem surprising also that Dorothy, having a very capable cook, should wish to prepare the sandwiches herself, but there was a good reason for that.

Anyway, Dorothy was not one who allowed question or argument concerning any order she gave. The ham potted meat, fish paste, and minor requirements which she had ordered promptly appeared, and Bertha was able to observe her mistress cutting very regular slices of bread and butter as she commenced clearing the table, which she continued until Dorothy said: "You'd better leave the rest, Bertha. I'll ring when I've finished."

The cutting of sandwiches slackened as the parlour maid left the room. The fact was that those which had been made already had to be eaten immediately by the three conspirators, and though they had been frugal in breakfasting, in anticipation of this ordeal, it can be easily understood that they had not wished to be faced by such a quantity as the cook would have been sure to supply.

It is proverbial that nature abhors a vacuum, and in this case the space in the attaché case which was left vacant by the consumption of the sandwiches was promptly filled with a pair of black shoes, a soft hat, a tie of pronounced colour, spats, and horn-rimmed glasses, with which Thomas was to vary his appearance, after taking off the cap, the brown canvas shoes, and the neutral tie which he now wore.

These arrangements had been planned by Alfred, who said confidently that such minor alterations would be as efficient as a complete change of clothing in preventing identification through any casual observation which Thomas might encounter before reaching Dorchester, from which city it was agreed that he should proceed to Ireland by an indirect route.

At Dorchester, he was to purchase a light raincoat, of such material as might be worn without attracting observation on a fine spring day, and it had been calculated that he would be far from any probable following or identification before an alarm would be raised or systematic enquiry made. This was, at least, Alfred Cuthbertson's confident opinion, and it was received with the respect due to his reputation as an expert in mystery, and crimes of the more complicated descriptions.

The plan certainly worked smoothly enough at this stage. No one interrupted the consumption of those unwanted sandwiches, or observed Thomas filling the attaché case with less edible articles. The three conspirators left the house together, Dorothy saying that she had some shopping to do in the town, and that they could go in company till the roads divided. There was nothing singular in that, for Dorothy was a good walker, and frequently took her morning exercise in that way.

It was about noon when she returned, and about half an hour afterwards when Alfred also came back, with an appearance of some agitation, whether real or simulated.

He found Dorothy alone in the lounge, and she asked him, very naturally: "Gone all right?" expecting at least a few words of preliminary frankness, before the staging of the next scene in the drama which they had planned. But it seemed that Alfred had resolved that he must say nothing to reduce, even to his own mind, the realism of the part he played.

"I left Thomas," he said, "on the cliffs. He seemed to prefer his own company. I don't think we shall see him back."

Dorothy said: "Wait a moment," and put her finger to the bell. As Bertha entered the room, she spoke to Alfred again, and the maid must stand waiting for instructions while the conversation persisted.

"Tom not coming back!" her mistress was saying. "He can't really have meant that. Why, he's left his things!"

Bertha, who was an intelligent girl, and who found most of the interests of her own life in observing those of her master and mistress, did not overlook the combination of confusion and annoyance that were evident in Mr. Cuthbertson's reply: "Well, that's how it is. We had a few words, and he took the hump and walked off. I suppose we'd better send his things on." She had an impression that her master preferred not to be questioned while she was in the room.

As he said this, Dorothy turned to the maid, and gave the order for which she had been summoned: "Bertha, you'd better tell cook that Mr. Cuthbertson will be in for lunch after all."

"But not Mr. Birchall, madam?"

"Not so far as we know at present." Bertha spoke and acted as a well-trained parlour maid should, as though unable to hear anything not directly addressed to herself, but she was no less observant for that; and when she waited at lunch, she learned some further curious facts concerning the details of Mr. Birchall's going, which became the common gossip of the household staff, inside and out, in the next hour.

"I suppose," her mistress had said in the half-incredulous, half-sarcastic voice in which she addressed her husband in all allusions to the disappearance of their guest, "that Tom didn't eat up all the sandwiches while you were quarrelling? You'd better tell Bertha where you put the case down, so that she can give them to Cook. I expect she'll be able to make some use of them, before they get any staler."

Alfred looked confused at this, and was not quick to reply.

"You'll tell me next," Dorothy went on, "that Tom's gone off with the sandwiches."

"Well, he was carrying the case," her husband answered angrily. "I wish you wouldn't worry me about nothing." He shot her an angry glance, which Bertha supposed he had not meant her to see. He might be acting, which the maid was not likely to guess; but, if so, it was an exceptionally good performance.

Dorothy said stubbornly: "Well, it's all such a queer tale." The telephone rang in the lounge hall as she spoke, and she added: "Bertha, we'll excuse you a moment. You'd better see who it is, and tell them that we're at lunch."

Dorothy had made it a strict rule that Alfred's digestion was not to be jeopardized by his being called to the telephone during meal-time hours, and she expected Bertha to tell whoever might be put through, with such curtness or courtesy as their names required, that they must please ring up later; but she returned to the room to say: "If you please, sir, it's Sergeant Poole on the phone He says could you please spare him a minute? He said he must please speak to you now, sir. He couldn't ring up again."

CHAPTER IX.

POLICE SERGEANT POOLE, who had been in charge of the Baycliffe Road Police Station for several years to the satisfaction of his superiors, was a slow, silent, capable man, who was unlikely to allow himself to be stampeded into any rashness of act or speech; and the tale which Mary Gilkins brought to him, just as he was about to sit down to his midday meal, was not one which any experienced Police Sergeant would lightly credit. That is, not if he knew the parties concerned, as Sergeant Poole did, for he had been born in the same street as Mary Banning (which had been the woman's unmarried name), and was well aware that she had a somewhat hysterical imagination, which might be described in a worse way by unfriendly tongues.

He knew Mr. Cuthbertson also as a respected, law-abiding resident, and a literary man of some celebrity, who always had a joking word for himself, and was, from whatever angle his experienced observation considered him, particularly unlikely to throw strange men into the sea before he went home to lunch.

Still, the fact remained that Mrs. Gilkins had a circumstantial accusation to make, and that she was obviously disturbed and shaken by what she said that she (and two other people) had witnessed from the foot of the cliff road.

Mr. Cuthbertson (she said) had been quarrelling violently with another man, who was a stranger to her. High words had come on the wind, though they had been too distant to understand. Blows had been struck, and, from one of these, Mr. Cuthbertson's opponent had been seen to fall backward over the edge of the cliff.

Mr. Cuthbertson had leaned over for a few moments, so as though looking, with whatever emotion, upon the man who must have been dashed to death on the sea-beaten rocks below, and had then turned and come back down the cliff path, passing her without apparent recognition (though her Annie had been employed at High-view House for the last eight months, and it was not Mr. Cuthbertson's habit to pass her without a pleasant greeting), in a state of obvious agitation as he hurried back to his own home.

She said that it was not she alone who had seen the tragedy, but two other people—a young lady and gentleman who, walking more quickly than herself, had just caught her up and passed her—had also observed it, and had been equally horrified.

Indeed, the young man had made a motion as though to detain Mr. Cuthbertson as he passed, but the young lady had put a hand on his arm and said something which had caused him to desist, and they had then turned and hurried back, as though wishing to avoid association with the event.

Sergeant Poole listened to this surprising narrative with outward stolidity. He avoided several more or less obvious questions to ask: "Now, Mary, this young man and woman, I suppose you don't know who they were?"

"I can't rightly say that I do. They're not people belonging here. But I saw them turning up Crumbles Road. I should say they'll be staying at Mrs. Rickards more like than not."

"Yes," Sergeant Poole agreed, "I should say they might. You'd better sit there a minute, Mary, while I find out."

He went into the next room, where the telephone was, and rang up the Rickards Temperance Hotel, which was the only guest house as yet completed and occupied in the newly-developed Crumbles Road.

Mrs. Rickards answered the call. Yes, she said, she had guests in the house: a Mr. and Mrs. Wilber. Mr. Wilber had come last night, and his wife, as had been expected, had joined him this morning, having come from Bournemouth by the early train. She said, rather anxiously, that they seemed very pleasant young people. She hoped there was nothing wrong.

Sergeant Poole's well-known and comforting voice assured her that there was nothing against her new lodgers. He just wanted to know whether they had been out during the morning, and, if so, had they returned.

Mrs. Rickards said yes, they had. She became communicative. Like Mary Gilkins, she had known the Sergeant from childhood, and he was one of those men to whom others are inclined to confide the more because they are not likely to repeat what is said in a random way.

She said that, almost immediately that Mrs. Wilber arrived, they had asked her advice as to the best direction to take, and had gone out for a walk along the cliff tops, saying that they might not be back before tea-time; but they had returned within an hour in some apparent agitation.

When she had made a natural exclamation of surprise at this unexpected appearance, Mr. Wilber had appeared confused and was not quick to reply, but Mrs. Wilber, with more feminine readiness, had said that she had a headache, and they had thought it best to come in out of the sun. In fact, she had said, they hadn't got up to the cliffs. They hadn't been much beyond where the roads forked—where Mrs. Rickards had told them to be careful to turn to the left.

Since then there had been some exciting topic of conversation between them on which they had appeared to differ—not exactly quarrelling (the Sergeant would understand what she meant)—but they were careful to sink their voices if she should approach, so that she could say nothing of the subject on which they talked.

Sergeant Poole received this information without offering any similar confidence. He contented himself with repeating that Mrs. Rickards need have no doubt of the character of her guests. Should she tell them, she asked, that he had rung up? No, certainly not.

He went back to Mrs. Gilkins, and told her to go home, and not keep Albert waiting any longer for his dinner.

She had done rightly to come to him, but she had better say nothing, even to her husband, of what she had seen. She wouldn't like her Annie to lose her job owing to any mischief her mother made?

Left alone, Sergeant Poole would have settled down to his own bachelor meal while he considered the probabilities of the queer tale he had heard, and weighed the value of the support it received from the conduct of the two boarders at Rickards's Temperance Hotel. But before he had got the sausages out of the frying pan, Constable Ringwood came in.

"Mary Gilkins been in hindering me," the Sergeant said, in explanation of the fact that he was only preparing a meal to which he should have sat down half an hour before. "Seen Mr. Cuthbertson about anywhere this morning, Bill?"

Bill replied that he had. The novelist and his wife had passed him at about ten, or a bit later, with a gentleman who had been staying with them for the last few days. He had seen them separate, and Mrs. Cuthbertson take the Osbury road. Nothing singular in that, he remarked. Mrs. Cuthbertson often walked into Osbury in the mornings to give the trades people her orders. He supposed she liked to see what she bought. Showed more sense in that than most ladies did. And there weren't many these days who'd tackle the walk. Must have a better pair of legs than most ladies had.

Sergeant Poole listened patiently to this chatter until he saw that there was no more grain in the chaff. Constable Ringwood had a strain of flippancy in his narrative style which was not approved by his superior officer, though he rarely commented upon it.

Now he said: "You'd get further, Bill, if you said less. I didn't ask about Mrs. Cuthbertson's legs. Seen any of them go back?"

"The lady went back about the time you'd expect. I haven't seen the gentlemen since."

"All right, Bill. That's all I wanted to know."

Silently, he tipped the sizzling sausages on the heat-discoloured plate which was accustomed to receive the various delicacies which he fried for the three substantial meals of the day. When he had done this, he moved over to the telephone, and asked to be put through to Highview House.

CHAPTER X.

"MR. CUTHBERTSON in?" the Sergeant asked, without giving his own name.

Bertha's voice answered: "Yes, but he's at lunch. He can't speak to anyone now. Who shall I say rang up?"

"It's the Baycliffe Road Police Station. Will you ask Mr. Cuthbertson if he will kindly come to the telephone for a moment. I shan't keep him long."

It was with this message that Bertha returned to the dining room.

Dorothy looked at her husband, who did not rise, though he threw the napkin from his lap on to the table as though preparing to do so. She saw his hesitation, and the thought crossed her mind that he was better fitted by nature to plan than to act, that he was proving less equal to the emergency he had himself created than she had expected that he would be.

But she suppressed a disloyal thought, asking herself how much might be reality, how much acting now? If it were acting, she had to admit that it was very cleverly done.

She was conscious of a growing confusion in her own mind between what had really happened, and what everyone was to be induced to believe. But perhaps it was exactly that at which Alfred aimed? To increase the verisimilitude of the affair. And, as he hesitated, her normally dominant impulse to remove the minor worries of life from his shoulders to hers caused her to say: "I'd better see what it is. You'll let the rissole get cold if you go now. They ought to know better than to ring up when we're at lunch."

As she finished this sentence, she had already risen, and was leaving the room.

Sergeant Poole heard her voice, pleasant but firm. "Mr. Cuthbertson can't come now; he's at lunch. Is it anything I can do?"

There was more than his usual deliberation in his next words. He still considered that the tale he had heard was of a particularly improbable kind, and that, even though it had some basis of fact, which he was inclined to believe, it was almost certainly exaggerated beyond recognition of the original incident.

Beside that, he was aware that the Osbury Exchange was not free from the suspicion of listening in. The telephone was not a medium which he approved for any communication of a confidential kind.

"There's a gentleman been staying with you for the last few days, Mrs. Cuthbertson," he said. "Perhaps if I could have a few words with him?"

Dorothy, under a confusion of impulses, avoided direct reply. She said: "I could give Mr. Cuthbertson a message if that would do."

"The fact is, Mrs. Cuthbertson, we had a report that the gentleman who was staying with you had had an accident on the cliffs. There may be nothing in it at all. If you could ask him to speak to me for a moment?"

"I'm afraid I can't do that. He went back to London this morning."

"Thank you, Mrs. Cuthbertson." Dorothy became aware that she was cut off somewhat abruptly, without any indication of whether her statement had been believed. She went back to the dining room.

Bertha heard her report of the conversation. "Sergeant Poole wanted to speak to Tom. He said he'd heard that there'd been an accident, but he didn't know whether it were true. I told him Tom went back to London this morning."

Bertha thought of Mr. Birchall's bedroom, left with his things littered about, and of how the two gentlemen had started out equipped (she believed) with an attaché case full of sandwiches; and she thought, with reason, that there was some funny business somewhere.

Dorothy thought that Alfred had engineered the event in the way that he had meant it to go; but she wished he would be less realistic in his performance so far as she was concerned. He needn't keep up the pretence when there was no one to overhear.

In the meantime, Sergeant Poole had rung up Rickards's Temperance Hotel again. He asked to speak to Mr. Wilber.

"Sorry to trouble you, sir," he said, "but I believe you may have witnessed an accident on the cliffs when you were out this morning."

There was a moment's pause, and then Mr. Wilber replied: "No, there's a mistake somewhere. I didn't see any accident."

Sergeant Poole said: "Thank you, sir. Sorry to have troubled you," and rang off. He would have taken the reply differently had he not heard, faint but unmistakable, a woman's voice while the reply paused. It had said: "Don't say we saw anything, Jack, if it's about that. Say we saw nothing at all."

He decided that this was a business for which the telephone was not a suitable medium of communication.

He put his notebook into his pocket as he said: "I may be out for the next hour, Bill. Or perhaps more."

CHAPTER XI.

SERGEANT POOLE had determined to commence his enquiries by interviewing Mr. and Mrs. Wilber, and to decide upon his further actions when he had satisfied himself that they had given him a frank account of their own experiences, which he thought he should be able to obtain at a personal interview.

He was received by Mrs. Rickards, who said that her guests were upstairs. She confided to the Sergeant that she would have supposed them to be a honeymoon couple had they not arrived on different days, and from opposite directions. She hoped anxiously that there could be nothing wrong.

"Nothing," Sergeant Poole assured her, "if they'll answer a few questions sensibly, as I don't doubt that they will."

She led him, as they spoke, to the lounge which was provided for the general use of her guests, whose privacy was restricted to their own bedrooms, and went upstairs to announce his presence.

He had waited about five minutes, and was pondering the advisability of a more active pursuit of these reluctant witnesses, when a young man of pleasant exterior, but in a state of obvious nervousness and annoyance, entered the room.

The Sergeant rose as he entered: "Mr. Wilber, I think?"

"My name is Berry—John William Berry."

"Mrs. Rickards said Wilber. It was Mr. Wilber I wished to see."

"I expect it's the same thing. Will Berry—Wilber. You see it's an easy mistake to make."

He pronounced the first name quickly, and slurred the final syllable so that the difference was not great. Sergeant Poole, avoiding expression of opinion upon the point, went on: "I understand that you and Mrs. Berry were witnesses of something that occurred on the cliff road this morning."

"You mean Miss Mills and myself?"

"It was Mrs. Wilber, I understand."

"Officer, if I help you in this matter, will you help me? I arranged to meet Miss Mills here for a few hours, and, for reasons that matter to no one except ourselves, it seemed best to say that it was my wife who was coming. If there's any trouble that you want me to get mixed up in, I shouldn't wish that to come out."

"No, sir, I don't know whether we could avoid that. We shouldn't try to make any trouble for you or the lady, beyond what we couldn't help. So I am to understand that you did see something going on that looked like being against the law?"

"I haven't said that. I saw two men quarrelling up the road. They were higher than we, and too far away to hear what it was about. They got to blows, and the one disappeared from sight. After that, the other came back and passed me, coming this way."

"You mean the one man went over the cliff?"

"I shouldn't like to say that."

"Where else could he disappear to?"

"I don't know. I haven't been that far myself. I'm a stranger here."

"You could show me the place?"

"Yes, more or less. I suppose I could."

"You could identify the man who passed you?"

"Yes. I don't think I could make a mistake about him."

"Thank you, sir. I may say you're taking the right attitude. We'll do anything to help the lady as far as justice permits. You won't mind if I make a few notes on what you've said, just to get the facts clear? And after that I should like to see Miss Mills. You can tell her that I shan't keep her long."

Mr. Berry made no direct answer to these requests. He said: "I hope it's not a serious matter?"

"I can't say yet, sir. It may be nothing at all. I shouldn't mention it to anyone, if I were you. Not till we know more."

Sergeant Poole had come to the private conclusion that it was either nothing at all, or else a crime for which Mr. Cuthbertson was likely to spend the next fifteen years in a convict's clothes, or undergo a briefer but more painful ordeal at the hangman's hands. But he had also considered that justice would be no less sure if it moved with deliberation. If Mr. Cuthbertson's visitor had gone over the cliff, he had certainly been dead for some hours, and as to the criminal, he did not suppose that he would be foolish enough to confess his guilt by attempting immediate flight, or that he could escape if he did. He intended to interview him in the next hour, and, unless his explanation were satisfactory, it would be very difficult for him to escape subsequently. But he was not going to make himself a public fool by giving credence to an improbable charge before he had established it on a solid basis.

Of course, an inspection of the rocks at the cliff foot might give substance to the tale by providing the body of a murdered man, but he could not do everything first, and a consideration of the state of the tide caused him to decide that was, in any event, a matter which must be left to a later hour. He asked: "Can I see the young lady now?"

"I'm afraid not. Miss Mills has gone back to Bournemouth."

Sergeant Poole was a man of equable temperament, but he may be excused if he looked angry.

"She was here," he said, "when I came in. So Mrs. Rickards said."

"She was just about to leave then."

"She won't do herself any good by that. I shall have to have her address."

"She says she saw nothing at all."

"Is that true?"

"Who can say but herself?"

"I should say you can, sir, if you were both looking at the same thing. Mrs. Rickards told me that you were both staying for two or three days."

"It was a misunderstanding."

"You'd better let me have her Bournemouth address. It'll save trouble in the end—trouble for her."

Mr. Berry hesitated. "I must take your promise for that," he said at last. "It's 33 Fountain Road."

The Sergeant noted this, wondering whether it were true, and asked: "I suppose you're not going away today too?"

"I can't answer that. Probably not before tomorrow. It depends upon whether I get through the business I've come to do."

Sergeant Poole had not expected this reply. He had supposed that the business which brought him to Osbury was abruptly ended. But Mr. Berry, willing to be confidential on any matter which diverted attention from his feminine friend, went on to explain: "I am the representative of the Brownhills Equipment Co., Ltd. I came down here to interview a Mr. Birchall about an order which he had placed with us, concerning which a difficulty had arisen."

"Birchall?" the Sergeant repeated doubtfully. "I don't know anyone here of that name. Do you know his address, sir?"

"He wrote us from Highview House, near Osbury. We understood that he was staying here with friends."

"That's queer, sir. I mean it looks as though he might be the gentleman—I mean that, if I've got the tale right, the one that turned back and passed you was Mr. Cuthbertson, who is living at High-view House. I'm told that his visitor went back to London this morning."

"That's bad luck for me, if it's true."

"You mean if he had gone back to London?"

"Yes. It's a wasted journey, and I shall get blamed by the firm, more likely than not."

Sergeant Poole saw an alternative. He said: "They could hardly blame you if your customer met with an accident this morning."

Mr. Berry admitted in his own mind that that would sound the better report. The fact was that he had made the journey without encouragement from his superiors, who had thought that the questions which had arisen concerning some details of the apparatus that Mr. Birchall required could have been dealt with by correspondence, and were otherwise scarcely of sufficient importance to justify a special journey in search of the customer.

It was only after considerable argument that Mr. Berry had obtained permission to make the journey, on the purpose of which his own conscience was not clear, for he had seen in it, from the first, an opportunity for the advancement of his own private affairs, such as had rendered it difficult, even for himself, to tell how much of honest judgment there had been in the urgency of his opinion that Mr. Birchall's instructions required the elucidation of a personal interview.

But if now he must return to report that his journey had been abortive, owing to Mr. Birchall having already returned to London, and it should afterwards become public knowledge that he had used the occasion for a secret meeting with Clara Mills—well, a request for his resignation might be a more probable sequel than the advance in salary which he had been confidently anticipating at the close of the financial year.

"I was intending," he said, "to call on Mr. Birchall this afternoon. If I can't see him, I ought to get back to London tonight."

"You can do that," Sergeant Poole assured him, "if you catch the five-fifteen. It's the only good train after midday. If you see Mr. Cuthbertson when you call, you might notice whether he's the gentleman who passed you this morning. You might let me have your address, in case I want to get in touch with you again, but we'll hope there won't be any need."

Mr. Berry made no difficulty about that. He produced a business card, and crossed out his firm's address, pencilling his own above it, with a natural thought that he should prefer that such communications should come direct to himself.

Sergeant Poole departed without further reference to the written statement he had suggested. He had still a very doubtful mind as to whether it were an improbable murder with which he dealt, or no more than an empty scare. And there was still more than two hours before Mr. Berry would be due to leave on the five-fifteen.

CHAPTER XII.

IT was the custom after lunch at Highview House to adjourn to the lounge, where coffee was served, without which Alfred said that he found it difficult to keep sufficiently awake to do a good afternoon's work.

It was a time at which, after Bertha had brought in the tray and retired, trivial matters of household routine would be discussed, and gossip exchanged, before Alfred retired to his study on wet afternoons, or would go out for golf or tennis, if the weather were sufficiently favourable.

Dorothy, trying to maintain the usual atmosphere on this occasion, found her husband moody and monosyllabic in response. The feeling came over her again that, if this were his genuine mood, he was proving less equal than she had expected to meet the ordeal that he had himself contrived; or that, if it were acting, there was no need to continue it so persistently when there was none but her to observe. And from this doubt she was suddenly struck with a cold fear. *Suppose realism had gone too far?* Suppose that Alfred had thrust his cousin from the edge with too strong a push, and had seen him stagger over the brink of the lower edge, to fall to certain death to the rocks below? It was easy to think that the quarrel, simulated at first, might have become real, the latent antagonism between the two men being as strong as it was.

Suppose that Tom, out of perversity, or a last-minute dread of being forced over that which had the look of a sheer edge, should have refused to fulfil his part, leading to a real quarrel, and serious blows? It was easy to think of him being sent over at last with too sharp a push—

The thought having entered her mind, she felt that she must have assurance that it was not true. The suspense would be too much to endure.

"Alfred," she asked suddenly, "there wasn't any accident, was there? Tom didn't really go over the cliff?"

He stared at her with mingled irritation and anger. "Don't be silly," he said. "Over the cliff? Why should he? Didn't I tell you he'd gone back to London? You might get me into serious trouble if you go saying things like that."

"Sorry," she said. "I think my nerves must be a bit queer to-day."

"So I should think," he replied, receiving the apology with less grace than she had expected. "I never heard such an absurd suggestion from you before."

She wondered again how much was acting, how much sincere, and then realized that he might be of the same doubt of herself. Either of them, if not both, might be rehearsing for later hearers, keeping up the pretence. And again the doubt came to her mind: where did reality end, and pretence begin? Grant that her momentary fear had no foundation at all—assume that Tom was now on his way to the solitary retreat from which he would emerge at his own time—it remained that they had started something which they could not stop, or at least only at the cost of a confession which would make Alfred the laughingstock of the world.

Apart from that almost impossible relief—and even that might not be believed!—they had to go through with the comedy they had commenced (if it could be called by so light a name) until Thomas Birchall should decide that the time of intervention had come. And what reason had they for trusting Tom?

She sat silent with these thoughts, lighting a cigarette, and then another, as she rarely would in the afternoon, and Alfred sat opposite to her, equally silent, but making no motion to go to his own room, as his habit was if he did not go out. It was as though they waited nervously for some unescapable doom, as those may sit who are conscious of an unpaid rent which they have no means to discharge, knowing not the day nor the hour, but that the bailiffs will surely come.

They heard the doorbell ring, and then Bertha's voice at the door, and that of a man in reply.

"I wonder who that is," Dorothy said. "It's someone she's showing in."

Alfred made no reply, and next moment Bertha appeared at the door to say that Sergeant Poole had called, and would like a few words with Mr. Cuthbertson.

Alfred said: "Ask him to step in here."

"Shall I go?" Dorothy asked.

"No. Why should you?" he replied, with real or affected irritation. "Poole can't have any private business with me"; and then, as the police officer appeared, with more of his habitual manner asserting itself: "Well, Sergeant, what can we do for you this afternoon?"

Sergeant Poole took the offered seat, and made a suitable acknowledgment of Dorothy's friendly greeting, without anything in his manner indicating the business on which he came. He was too conscious of his official position, and of the duties which it involved, to be diffident of social distinctions, or easily moved by the reactions of those into whose conduct he found it necessary to enquire.

Circumspectly, perhaps somewhat slowly, but with a certainty which men who would have boasted of nimbler wits would have occasion to dread, he proceeded toward his goal.

"It's about Mr. Birchall. I felt I ought to look in," he said. "I've had reports from two or three people this morning that aren't easy to believe, but which I've got to clear up one way or other."

It was Alfred to whom Sergeant Poole spoke, but Dorothy was quick to reply.

She had regained coolness and self-control now that there was something to face, something to be done, and in this more natural, recovered mood, she had seen instantly that if they appeared to understand the nature of the accusation which would be made, it was like a plea of guilty on Alfred's part—a demeanour the significance of which she was sure that the police officer would not fail to see.

And though she knew that that would be no more than to develop the plot on the lines they had first contrived, she had an instinct of danger, a feeling that they had started something that would now go on far enough, or too far, without further impulse from them.

"I hope," she said, with a smile that made light of the possibility before it was spoken, "that Mr. Birchall hasn't been doing anything wrong. He's Mr. Cuthbertson's cousin."

She mentioned the relationship in such a tone as to suggest that it removed him from suspicion of all offences beyond those of the most venial kind, and Sergeant Poole, faintly influenced by the tone and manner of her reply, answered: "No, ma'am. It's not that the gentleman has done anything wrong. It's a question of an accident, if it's not all a mistake, as I hope it is."

"Then I've no doubt that it is. Mr. Birchall hasn't been out in a car all the time that he's been here, and if he'd been involved in an accident, I'm sure he'd have told us about it. It's only this morning he went back to London."

The Sergeant accepted the presumption that "an accident" implied a car, without remark, or indeed surprise, for it was a time in which most accidents did. He said: "No, ma'am. It sounds like a mistake. Could you tell me which way he took when he went back? I suppose he went from the Osbury station?"

Dorothy had sufficient discretion not to attempt reply to this question. She looked at Alfred, transferring the conversation to him.

"I really couldn't say," Alfred answered. "It was all rather sudden. You see I went for a walk with him along the cliffs, and was expecting to bring him back for another night, and he—well, he rather lost his temper over something I said, and perhaps I did too, and he said he was going back if I felt like that, and—well, we went different ways."

Sergeant Poole considered this statement with an open mind. He saw that, to a point, it was frank and true, being supported by the evidence he already had. He saw that the rest might be no more than Mary Gilkins's hysterical exaggeration, and was disposed to congratulate himself inwardly on the discretion with which his enquiries had been made. But he did not therefore deviate from his intention of clearing the matter up in a thorough way.

"Thank you, sir," he said. "That's very much what I had understood, and, of course, it's no business of mine. But when you parted, could you tell me which way he went?"

"Yes, I can tell you that I turned back, and came home, and he went on along the cliff path."

"That wouldn't be the way to Osbury station?"

"No. It would be walking away."

"Then it doesn't look as though he were on his way to London?"

"Well, he said he was going back home, and that's where he lives. There is a road, as a matter of fact, that might have brought him back to Osbury if he turned sharp off to the right by Griffin's Inn."

"Yes. Do you think he knew that?"

"I don't think he knew the district at all. And, at the moment, I don't think he cared which direction he went in, so long as it wasn't mine. But, of course, he'd soon begin to look round and enquire. You can't easily get anywhere in this country where a way to London isn't easy to find. But perhaps I could help you better if you'd tell me what the tale is that has come to you. Tom isn't very friendly to me, but I shouldn't like to think that he had got into any mess."

"The tale that was brought to me was that while you were quarrelling, he went over the cliff."

"Over the cliff? You mean he fell, and would have been killed? You surely didn't believe that! Is it likely I should be sitting here without having reported it, or made any effort to save him?—or I suppose it would be a matter of recovering the body. No one could fall from those cliffs and expect to live."

"That's true, sir. No, I don't say I believed anything; but when a report comes in, we're bound to make enquiries and clear it up."

"Yes, so you must, of course." Mr. Cuthbertson rose with the words as though the interview would naturally conclude at that point. He added: "I expect you'll like a drink, Sergeant, before you go?"

But Sergeant Poole did not rise. He answered: "Thank you, sir, but I don't think I will. I don't often take anything. Not at this time of day. I suppose you could let me have Mr. Birchall's address?"

"Yes. You're welcome to that. What is it, Dorothy? I never can remember numbers myself"

Dorothy answered readily: "It's 22 Thames Mansions. It's a little side street off Horseferry Road. I don't remember the name of the street, but I find that's enough for letters: off Horseferry Road. I think it's S.W."

"Thank you, ma'am. That's good enough."

Sergeant Poole entered the address in his pocket book, and got up to go.

"Sorry to have been so much trouble," he said. "I don't suppose you'll see me again."

It was an assurance which would have been more convincing had he not followed it by asking Alfred: "I suppose, sir, you could show me about where it was that he went off? That is, if it should be necessary to make any more enquiries, as I'm not saying it will."

"Yes. I suppose I could, more or less. I don't see what good that would be to you. He isn't likely to be there now."

Mr. Cuthbertson smiled as he said this, as at a good joke which he had made, to which others should give a smile in response.

Very faintly, Sergeant Poole responded, as he replied: "No, sir. I shouldn't say that he would."

Dorothy touched the bell, and Bertha promptly appeared to conduct the police officer to the door.

When he had gone, Dorothy called her into the room again. She said: "Bertha, Mr. Birchall went back to London rather suddenly. You'd better have his things packed, and send them after him. I'll let you have the address. If you hear any other silly tale about him, you'll know that it hasn't a word of truth, and contradict it at once. I can rely on you for that?"

Bertha said: "Yes, madam," with the demure and ready response which a well-trained parlour maid would give in her sleep if she were asked to drown herself in the bath.

When she had gone, Alfred said: "Quite right, Dorothy. I'm glad you said that."

The words were appreciative in tone, and brought back a little of the normal confidence that had existed before; but still neither was sure of the other, between what was acting and what was real, being too deeply entangled in the net that they had been active to weave, and uncertain what the next hour might bring.

CHAPTER XIII.

A FEW minutes after Sergeant Poole had departed, a second visitor was announced.

Mr. Berry had called to see Mr. Birchall on business, and, being informed by Bertha at the door that he had left for London that morning, he had hesitated, and then asked if Mr. Cuthbertson could see him.

Mr. Berry had an excuse for feeling that fate was treating him hardly in more ways than one. He did not exactly desire that the customer who had just placed a fairly important order with his firm should have been thrown over a cliff, but he had appreciated Sergeant Poole's suggestion that it might be a better tale with which to return than that he had abortively rushed to Osbury to interview a man who was on his way back to London before he had made an effort to see him.

But there was a contrary aspect of the matter, leading him to prefer greatly that an accident or crime should not have occurred.

He had wired Miss Mills to meet him in Osbury at short notice, under circumstances with which this narrative is not directly concerned, and with a moral obliquity which it is not necessary to judge, but which had brought retribution in advance of the intended error. For he was well aware, in the secret counsels of his own mind, that while he had asked her to meet him for a few hours only, for which he knew that her own holiday in Bournemouth provided a simple opportunity, he had hoped that he could have persuaded her to stay for a longer time; and whatever errors there had been regarding names and probable period of occupation, they had not arisen from any misunderstanding by Mrs. Rickards of what he had said to her.

Having no intention of returning to London that night, it had seemed to him that it would be expedient in itself to defer his proposed interview with Mr. Birchall until the later part of the day, while, from a different angle, it had been as necessary as it was desirable to devote his attention to Miss Mills during its earlier hours.

In the result, while he had gained nothing at all, he had involved a girl to whom he was very passionately attached in the danger of an unpleasant ordeal, and some exposure of indiscretion (even if there should be no worse suspicion attached), in view of the fact that she was under an engagement to another man which, for the time at least, family circumstances made it difficult for her to break; and he had involved himself in the danger of being censured by his firm for an abortive journey which had only been sanctioned at his own urgency, with the possibility of even graver consequences if the subsequent disclosures should lead them to the belief that he had been actuated by consideration of his own interests rather than theirs.

He now asked to see Mr. Cuthbertson with a feeling of irritation against the malice of circumstance which might be directed very easily to a more personal antagonism.

Alfred looked at the card which Bertha presented, and the name of Wellers & Samuel, Ltd., which he had heard from Thomas before, was an indication of the status, and to some extent of the business, on which Mr. Berry had called. Directly it was a business which was not his, and with which he might be wise to have nothing to do; though that question may not be easy to decide without being clearer than Dorothy was as to whether he were still seeking to augment or lessen the trouble and publicity to which he was heading, on a course which had already passed beyond his control.

"What sort of man is he?" Alfred asked, the question indicating the hesitation with which he handled the card.

"He's a pleasant young gentleman, sir, but he looks a bit flurried."

"Well, show him in."

Mr. Berry entered the room, and the eyes of the two men met in a mutual recognition and memory of that earlier hour when, but for a girl's restraining hand on his arm, the younger would have obstructed one whom he believed to be hurrying from the scene of a fatal crime.

Dorothy, having no knowledge of their previous meeting, watched with a fresh surprise the difficult effort with which her husband controlled himself to ask: "What can I do for you, Mr. Berry?"

The young man, to Dorothy's greater wonder, appeared to be in an equal confusion. He began sentences which he left unfinished: "It was Mr. Birchall. I mean I wanted to see him in reference to.... If you could tell me where he could best be found?" As he spoke, he had a vision of rocks and of a body flung and battered against them

61

by the waves of a beating sea. He believed that it was a murderer who had risen as he entered the room, for though Mr. Cuthbertson had now recovered his self-control, he had looked at him, he thought, in those first seconds of recognition, with the eyes of a guilty man.

"*If you could tell me where he could best be found.*" How would a man with such a secret upon his soul react to those sinister words? Mr. Cuthbertson, now master of himself, took them quite easily. He seemed most concerned that his visitor should not continue to stand. When he was seated, he said: "I'm sorry you've just missed Mr. Birchall. He returned to London this morning. It's bad luck if you came here specially to see

(Was there a sarcasm, Mr. Berry must wonder, even a threat, in that last simple-sounding expression of sympathy? A reminder that he had been seen that morning making no effort to meet with Mr. Birchall, and with a girl on his arm?)

Mr. Cuthbertson, now in control of the situation, continued: "I am Mr. Birchall's cousin. I suppose there's nothing I can do for you on his behalf?"

"No, I don't see that you could. I wanted to get clearer instructions about a certain part of some scientific apparatus he's ordered from us."

"Then I should be no good at all. I'm less interested in science than crime. I suppose you know his London address?"

Mr. Berry (such are the distressing limits of literary celebrity) was unfamiliar with Mr. Cuthbertson's name, and unaware of his occupation. The statement so casually made sounded to him like the almost incredible effrontery of a guilty and probably cornered man.

It caused him to blurt out in reply: "Yes, I know his London address. What I wasn't so sure about was whether he'd be there when I got back. If he was the gentleman I saw out with you this morning, I thought I saw him fall over the edge of the cliff."

He had scarcely uttered these words before he was half-frightened, half-ashamed, of what he had said. It seemed a monstrous accusation to make against a man in his own house, in the atmosphere of that civilized, cultured room. But Mr. Cuthbertson took it without visible offence.

"You would have alarmed me, Mr. Berry," he said, "if you had said that two hours ago. I should have feared lest my cousin had met with an accident after he left me. But a police officer was here just before you arrived, from whom I learned that there is a tale going about that I am myself responsible for throwing Mr. Birchall over the cliff.

"Sergeant Poole was too discreet an officer to mention the origin of so absurd a tale, and I am interested to learn that I owe it to you.

"I do not know whether you may have anything to lose, but, even if not, it may be worth your while to remember that the law of slander may sometimes be invoked in the criminal courts."

Mr. Berry found it difficult to outface the assurance of Mr. Cuthbertson's manner, the cool sarcasm of his voice, but he had an obstinate unwillingness to credit the innocence of the man to whom he attributed all the anxieties and disappointments of a day which he had commenced with very different hopes.

"The police," he said stubbornly, "were not told by me."

Mr. Cuthbertson did not answer that. "Now that I have warned you," he said, "I must ask you to leave my house."

Mr. Berry went, and Dorothy said: "I suppose he'll try to make more mischief when he finds that Tom hasn't got back."

Alfred said: "Why shouldn't Tom have got back? It seems to me that you spend half your time dreaming."

She admitted to herself that he played the game more thoroughly than she was able to do.

At the Railway Station Mr. Berry found Sergeant Poole waiting to see him. He gave an account of the interview from which he had come, mentioning the threat of criminal proceedings which had been made against him.

The police officer did not appear to think that that need be regarded seriously. Certainly not so if Mr. Berry had discretion to confine his confidences to the police, as he was recommended to do.

CHAPTER XIV.

THE incidents of the next three days were numerous, and, for the most part, of cumulative rather than separate importance, requiring that they shall be briefly chronicled.

The Cuthbertsons' household staff were not intentionally disloyal, nor did they believe the rumours that came to them, which stopped scarcely short, if at all, of accusing their master of the gravest crime (except treason) which is familiar to English law. But they were human and feminine. They discussed that which excited their own minds. They exchanged the gossip which came to them for that which circulated within the house. That which came from without had its main source in Mrs. Gilkins's cottage: her Annie was a natural channel, though only one among several, through which it flowed.

It may be said that these two sources of mingled fancy and fact bred together, producing progeny distinct from either, though having features of both. Within forty-eight hours, there were few indeed of the aborigines of Osbury and the surrounding district, and not many of the visitors on whom its prosperity depended, who were not acquainted with some of these whispered tales.

Both Alfred and Dorothy, when they went out, were conscious of a curiosity which stirred almost audibly round them, and of unmistakable hesitation or reserve in the greetings of those whom they had previously regarded as obsequious friends.

Yet during these first days—indeed, until the end of the week—there was an absence of any reference in the public press such as Alfred had expected to stir, and it is doubtful if the event had resulted in the sale of a dozen extra copies of *The Clue of the Twisted Spoon*.

It was not that the world of journalism was unaware of the excitement by which Osbury was so deeply stirred. Indeed, the representatives of two Sunday newspapers had appeared on the scene with the almost miraculous celerity with which vultures will swoop to a desert death. But it seemed that Alfred had defeated his own purpose by the very gravity of the issue that he had raised. The most audacious of editors will hesitate to give publicity to a tale of a prominent novelist throwing his cousin five hundred feet into the sea, in the absence of a dead body, or any overt action by the police by whom, it is understood, the alleged circumstances have been investigated.

And even the disappearance of Thomas Birchall could not be said to be of an emphatic kind. He was a man without family ties, living alone. He had no business obligations to observe. He had broken no appointments, had left no debts. His flat was closed, but so it had been during his visit to Osbury. Under what necessity was he of returning to it when he left his cousin, as it was said, earlier than he had intended to do? Why should he not have decided to complete his holiday elsewhere?

The tale, in all its varieties and implications, was discussed in several Fleet Street offices. It was admitted that it had some queer features, and that there might be developments at any moment such as would bring it on to the front page of the next edition. But at present it was too dangerous: tempting, but too dangerous, far.

Meanwhile, Mr. Berry had survived the first ordeal of reporting his non-success to the General Manager of Weller & Samuels, Ltd., with more credit than he had expected to gain.

He had put in a report in which truth, though somewhat adulterated, and used with economy at times, had been wisely predominant.

He represented that, being unable to find Mr. Birchall at home, he had followed him by the road that he was said to have taken with Mr. Cuthbertson. He told of the struggle which he had witnessed, and of his subsequent interviews with Sergeant Poole, and at Highview House.

The General Manager agreed that the matter was not one to be shouted abroad, but finding, on further enquiry, that Mr. Birchall had not returned to his flat, and a letter addressed to him there remaining unanswered, he decided to hold up the order until he should be more fully informed, and that Mr. Berry had done a service to the firm by the information his journey brought. On Thursday evening, Mr. Berry was courteously invited to Scotland Yard, and induced to sign a statement of his Osbury experiences, the matter having been brought to the notice and co-operation of the Metropolitan police owing to the request they had received to investigate the question of Mr. Birchall's return to London.

He was also persuaded to use his influence in correspondence with Clara Mills to induce her to commit herself in a similar way, on a bargain that it was not necessary that either statement should assert that they had been in each other's company, or more than casually at the same spot, at the time when they had observed the struggle upon the cliff, and that this irrelevant fact should not be needlessly brought out in their evidence in the event of a prosecution occurring.

Sergeant Poole, after sending Constable Ringwood searching along the shore at low tide for a body that was not there, had waited until he received a telephone report from London next morning informing him that Thomas Birchall had not returned to his flat; and then, having also received a tale which he did not like concerning the gossip which was filtering out of Highview House, cycled over to the head police station in Osbury High Street, and laid the matter before the Inspector there.

Inspector Reid took it so seriously that he resolved to report to the Chief Constable at Dorchester, who came down on the following day.

Sir Henry Tombs (with a dozen added initials) was a retired military officer of solid rather than brilliant qualities, and of a disposition to appreciate Sergeant Poole's cautious and thorough approach to what he recognized to be an unusual case, of the kind by which the reputations of police officers are sometimes made, and more often marred. He praised him both for what he had done and what he had left alone.

He instructed him to continue his enquiries with the same discretion he had already exercised, and arranged for a further conference to be held in Dorchester on the following afternoon, at which Mr. Frampton, a prominent solicitor of that town, who commonly acted for the police, would be asked to be present.

When the hour of that conference came, Sergeant Poole had acquired some additional information which threw a new and sinister light upon the enigma of the probable crime.

The question of motive, which had seemed to be entirely lacking (beyond the vague statement that Mr. Cuthbertson himself had made that he had been quarrelling with his cousin as they walked, but as to the subject of which difference he had since declined to inform the police, only saying that it was no more than a trifling matter), appeared to be supplied by a statement which the housemaid, Ethel Harding, had certainly made to Annie Gilkins, in a confidence which the latter young woman had found it hard to keep, though Ethel had denied it with protestations, tears, and self-contradictions at the police station during the evening.

Her tale had been that, as she had come up the garden path on the evening of Monday, May 13, the blind of the lounge not having been lowered, and the curtains only partly drawn, she had seen Mr. Birchall in the act of embracing her mistress, as Mr. Cuthbertson had entered the room.

Mr. Frampton, whose reputation had been built on the things which he had avoided saying, heard the facts of the case, both proved and doubtful, with this last ominous addition, and had more to say concerning the legal difficulties of the position than of any method by which they could be overcome. He did not overlook that on which Mr. Cuthbertson had most surely relied when the plot was formed—the illegality of instituting a prosecution for murder in the absence of the body of a murdered man.

But even this might not, he said, be an absolute impediment. There was a recent case in which legal ingenuity had overcome it, when the body of a murdered child had been incinerated beyond recognition or recovery. Finally, he advised that an opinion should be obtained from the office of the Attorney-General, who, in a matter of such difficulty and importance, would probably conduct the prosecution, if he should advise an arrest.

Mr Frampton, having given this advice, took instructions to prepare the necessary statement very cheerfully, and was engaged upon it during the following day, until he received a telephone message from Osbury which informed him that it would not be needed, developments having occurred which justified the police in taking immediate action.

The representative of the *Sunday Record*, who had waited in Osbury on Saturday afternoon for some hours after the rival journalists had left in despair of any development such as would induce their editors to make the case a feature of the next morning's edition, was destined to obtain a scoop which would be the envy of the competing press.

Alone among the Sunday newspapers, the *Sunday Record* appeared next morning with these headlines half covering its front page:

PROMINENT AUTHOR ARRESTED
ON MURDER CHARGE

A MYSTERY OF THE CLIFFS

The fact that legal proceedings had commenced constituted an annoying restriction upon much interesting matter which the Editor of the *Sunday Record* would otherwise have released for publication; but sufficient remained to indicate that the major section of the community, to whom a murder trial is of greater attraction than any matter of social order or foreign war, and may even have priority to the sporting news, could look forward to some pleasant reading during the following weeks.

The anticipatory diligence of their reporter had also enabled them to embellish the account with photographs of Alfred Cuthbertson, of Dorothy, and of Highview House. The utmost diligence of the Fleet Street staff had not been able to secure any pictorial representation of Thomas Birchall, but that omission would doubtless be remedied by the following Sunday; and meanwhile they were able to give a view of Thames Mansions, as the side of that substantial block of buildings appeared from the Horseferry Road, with a cross to mark the window of Mr. Birchall's bedroom, through which he had doubtless looked out on many occasions before the evil hour when he had left it for the last time to be hurried by the Southern Railway express to Osbury and a violent end.

CHAPTER XV.

ALFRED had come in on Saturday afternoon, rather late for tea, and with no cheerfulness in his looks.

He had had a round of golf on the links with Mr. Duckfield, after three other members of the club had excused themselves from accepting him as an opponent. Mr. Duckfield, an expert in gradations of cordiality, had been polite beyond criticism, and reserved beyond misunderstanding to anyone in Alfred's condition of nervous and now somewhat apprehensive irritability. The bank manager's attitude might be ascribed to the rumours of which he was sure to be well informed, or to the necessity which he had felt a few days before of writing a formal letter to Mr. Cuthbertson drawing his kind attention to the fact that his current account was put in credit as promptly as possible.

Neither explanation was likely to be satisfactory to Alfred, who was experiencing all the discomforts of a surrounding suspicion, and the absence of £200 which might have remained in his own account (even if there were no more serious reason for disquiet in his private thoughts), without compensation of the expected publicity on which he had relied for his financial recovery.

The afternoon had been dull, with gathering cloud, and a cold wind from the northwest, and Dorothy, aware that Alfred was more sensitive than herself to climatic changes, had ordered that a fire should be lit in the lounge, where tea would be served on his return. It would normally have been a pleasant meal, in contrast to the chilly dullness of the fickle spring weather without, but Alfred did not respond to one or two deliberately cheerful remarks, and after a few minutes of mutual silence, Dorothy said sharply: "Alfred, I wish you'd speak frankly for once. Isn't there any way we can stop it now? I feel I can't stand any more."

"We can't stop anything now," Alfred replied, with no cheerfulness, but more naturalness in his voice than she had recently heard. "I suppose it will come alive or die down. What do you want me to say?"

"I was wondering what Tom will do if there's no publicity. You will remember he was to watch for that, and not come back till it had become sufficient for the purpose."

"I expect there'll be plenty yet. It's only the fifth day." She noticed that he answered without animation, and that the energetic methods with which he had spoken of stimulating such publicity when they had discussed the project appeared to have gone out of his mind, but she said nothing of that. She turned the subject to say: "I was in at Fryer's this morning. They said that *The Twisted Spoon* was selling quite well. They'd got several copies just on the right as you go in. There are some press cuttings by the afternoon post. A very good one in the *Onlooker*. I've put them on your desk. Is your cup ready?"

"Yes," he said, passing it over the low table, and then rose as he added: "I think I'll have a look at them now. I'll bring them in here."

As he stood, he could see down the drive to the front gate, into which a car turned. He looked at it with a frown. "It's that damned policeman again," he said. "You can tell Bertha to say I'm sick of the whole subject. I won't see him again."

"Sergeant Poole? Oh, he isn't so bad. I rather like him. I can't tell Bertha to say that. I'll see him, if you'd rather not. I can easily say you're busy, or not feeling well."

"I wish you would. I've said all there is to say about ten times over already. There's two of them. I don't know whether they're both coming in."

He sat down again, the press cuttings being apparently forgotten. A minute later, Bertha appeared with the expected information that Sergeant Poole had called, and would like to see Mr. Cuthbertson.

Dorothy said: "Show him into the drawing-room."

Sergeant Poole had brought Constable Ringwood with him. He said: "You'd better wait here, Bill. You'll know what to do if—" His voice became indistinct, so that Bertha could not follow what was said or understood between them, but it rose again to end with: "But I don't suppose there'll be any trouble." He allowed himself to be led to the drawing room, where Dorothy promptly followed, giving Ringwood a friendly word as she crossed the hall.

CHAPTER XVI.

SERGEANT POOLE, through a varied experience of over thirty years, had never previously arrested a man for murder, and he was in some uncertainty as to how Mr. Cuthbertson would act on the realization that his last moment of freedom, his last chance of life, would be gone if he should submit himself to the authority with which he would be confronted. It was in that sombre light that, Sergeant Poole considered, the accused man could not fail to regard it, for the evidence which had come to his hands in the last hour, when added to that which Mary Gilkins, Mr. Berry, and Miss Mills had supplied, added up to a damning total, even without the addition that Ethel, under sufficient pressure, must consent to give.

He was conscious also that he was acting with no further warrant than the verbal authority of the Chief Constable given to him on the telephone no more than fifteen minutes before, when he had informed him of the latest development; but he wasn't worried about that, recognizing both that the responsibility for the decision was no longer his, and that the circumstances would have justified action on his own initiative.

"You'd better get him at once—get there before he hears. He'll most likely be off, if you don't. A man like he is sure to have his plans ready." So Sir Henry had said, and he had acted accordingly, telling Bill to come along with him, and driving to Highview House as though the police were a superior race, to whom the law of speed limit did not apply.

He would have much preferred that the man whom he must regard as a murderer, rather than his wife, had entered the room. He had no intention of informing her first of the business on which he came. Before she could make the excuses for Alfred which had already taken shape in her mind, he was quick to say: "It wasn't you, ma'am, it was Mr. Cuthbertson that I asked to see."

"I'm afraid you can't see him this afternoon. He's not very well, and he's got some work to get through before post-time. If it's anything I can do for you—"

"I'm afraid not, ma'am. I'm sorry, but I shall have to see him. It's not a matter that can be put off."

Dorothy recognized the determination in the officer's voice, and decided that it would be better to give way readily than to make too stubborn an opposition to that which would almost certainly be yielded at last. "Wait a moment," she said. "If it's so urgent, I'll see what I can do.

She returned to inform Alfred of his persistence, supposing that he would wait in the drawing room, but he had no intention of incurring a needless risk. After a moment of hesitation, he followed, and when she entered the lounge he was close behind her.

He pushed her gently aside, and, as Alfred rose to meet him in mingled irritation and surprise if not alarm, at this unceremonious intrusion, he said: "I'm sorry, Mr. Cuthbertson, but I have my duty to do. I must arrest you for the wilful murder of Thomas Birchall, and I have to warn you that—"

He was interrupted by Dorothy's indignant voice. "Why, Sergeant, what utter rot! Mr. Birchall's not been murdered at all. You'll make yourself the laughing stock of the whole county if you do that."

Sergeant Poole was polite, but unmoved. "Sorry, ma'am," he said, "but I have my instructions to carry out."

Alfred had become very pale. He found it difficult to maintain the cool demeanour which had been possible, under somewhat similar circumstances, to Carlton Boyes in *The Clue of the Twisted Spoon.* He controlled his voice, though his hand shook, as he replied: "You can make any use you like of anything that you hear from me. I say, like Mrs. Cuthbertson, that it's utter nonsense. I suppose I can see the warrant?"

"Sorry, sir. But I haven't got one. I'm acting on verbal instructions. Of course, as soon as you get to the station, you'll be properly charged, and brought up on Monday morning."

"No warrant? So I supposed! Look here, officer, you'll be sorry all your life if you don't go slow on this matter. Why, what evidence can you have? We know perfectly well that Thomas Birchall's alive. You can't arrest me because of some silly tales that are going about. Don't you know that you can't prosecute anyone for murder unless you can produce the body of the dead man?"

"I don't rightly know about that," Sergeant Poole answered unmoved, "but there's plenty of body in this case. We got it out of the water this afternoon."

"You don't mean to say—" Dorothy began, in a tone of incredulity, and was interrupted by her husband, who seemed to have regained something more of manhood, as he realized the extremity of peril in which he stood. "There's something we don't understand here, Dorothy, and we'd better find out what it is first, and talk afterwards. You might try to find Soome on the phone and ask him to come to me at the police station as soon as he can."

Mr. Soome was the local solicitor who had dealt with Mr. Cuthbertson's legal business since they had settled in Osbury.

"Yes, I'll do that," Dorothy said, but without moving. "I suppose I can come too, Sergeant? I can pack a suitcase for him to take?"

Sergeant Poole did not reply directly. He said: "You'd best keep out of this, ma'am, if you'll be guided by me."

"Keep out of it? I should think not! I shan't keep you waiting more than three minutes. I shall have to come to see Mr. Soome."

She touched the bell as she spoke, and said, as Bertha very promptly appeared: "We're all going down to the police station together. I want you to tell Cook to keep dinner back till we return. And get Mr. Soome on the telephone, if you can. You'd better try to get him at Seven Elms. If he isn't in, give them a message to say that I want to speak to him on important business, and to ask him to wait in till I ring again. If he's in now put him through to the bedroom phone."

She went out with the word, and Sergeant Poole made no further demur. So long as he fulfilled his main objective of getting his man quietly within the police station walls, he had no inclination to make difficulties on any questions of detail. It would be far better for Mrs. Cuthbertson to come along, if she wouldn't take good advice, rather than have any scene here. Mr. Soome would doubtless take her in hand when he should join them at their common destination, and in any case, it would be Inspector Reid's responsibility then.

Dorothy appeared again in little more than twice the time she had promised. "Mr. Soome," she said, "has gone away for the weekend, but I got his partner, and he'll be there before us, if we aren't quick. He says he'll go to the High Street station, unless he hears differently in the next three minutes."

They went out to the car together, with the Sergeant's hand unobtrusively but firmly on Alfred's arm, and Bill Ringwood vigilant in the rear.

Alfred said nothing further. He had a sense of physical sickness which he felt, if he spoke, he might find it hard to control. His studies and inventions in criminology had not included exact information as to the treatment of accused persons when in the hands of the police, but he had a vague belief, not wholly without foundation, that various indignities and discomforts would be gratuitously added to the unavoidable miseries that such detention involves.

Well, whatever might be before him, it was of his own planning that it had come. As a man makes his bed...but such reflections brought no comfort at all.

CHAPTER XVII.

IT is very difficult for a young and ambitious solicitor to feel low-spirited when he has just been retained in what is likely to be one of the most sensational murder trials of his generation, even though he may be required to spend the evening with the wife of the accused man; and it is creditable to Ernest Willerton's natural sympathy of disposition that he left Dorothy at a late hour on Saturday night somewhat consoled by the feeling that she had found a friend as well as a legal adviser on whose ability she could rely with such confidence as the position allowed.

He had returned with her from the police station to Highview House, after receiving Alfred Cuthbertson's emphatic assurance that he had not thrown his cousin over the cliff, nor seen him fall. He said further that he had left him descending the road which, as it proceeds westward, trends somewhat away from the cliff edge. He said with equal emphasis that he did not believe that Thomas Birchall had fallen into the sea, had been drowned at all, or was dead by whatever means. He said that he was convinced that he would be easily found and so dispose of an absurd accusation. He could not say what body or bodies might be cast up by the tide, over which he had no control, but he was certain that that of Thomas Birchall had not been one.

He said, beyond that, that he wished his wife to explain to Mr. Willerton the full circumstances which had led up to the present position, when he would understand how grotesque the accusation was, and he must use the knowledge which he would gain from her at his own discretion, or as the course of circumstances might require.

Mr. Willerton thought that it would be a good plan to talk the matter over with Mrs. Cuthbertson, and agreed to return with her to Highview House, only delaying to obtain what information he could from Sergeant Poole as to the strength of the case which he had to meet.

Comfortably seated in Alfred's place, and eating Alfred's excellent dinner (but Dorothy had arranged for an equal portion to be sent to him, having no confidence in her husband's digestion surviving the police station's cuisine), Mr. Willerton was content to listen, with no more than an occasional question, to Mrs. Cuthbertson's surprising narrative of the genesis of the cliff top incident which had now assumed so tragic an aspect.

"You will understand," she said in conclusion, "why it is almost impossible to believe that Mr. Birchall's body has been washed up by the sea."

"Yes," the solicitor replied, "I can see how it looks to you, and I'm not going to express an opinion as to the line of defence which we should take in so unusual a case until I am sure that I have got all the available facts, and have had more time to consider them than has yet been possible.

"But there are two points which I should like to make clear, so that we may exercise our minds in the right direction.

"First, I'm afraid that it's no use for you to say that you don't believe that it's Birchall's body that's been found. I'm sorry to tell you this, both for Mr. Cuthbertson's sake, and because he was someone you knew, but it's better to face the facts."

The gravity of Dorothy's face deepened as she heard this, for she saw how serious was the position with which Alfred was threatened if it could be proved that it was Thomas's body which had been cast up by the sea. She said: "I'm sorry for Tom's sake, of course, though I can't say that I was ever very friendly with him. Indeed, I didn't want him to come here at all, but Mr. Cuthbertson persuaded me that he was the right man for the plan that we were silly enough to try. But it's naturally Mr. Cuthbertson about whom I'm most concerned, and I still can't believe that Tom isn't alive and well. It seems such an incredible thing. I don't think I should believe anyone unless I should see…should see the body myself."

"Well, you could do that. You wouldn't expect it to be a pleasant sight, after being five days in the sea. But I ought to tell you that I learned from Inspector Poole that you mightn't find it easy to identify if you did. I understand that it's been a good deal disfigured, probably by the crabs, and especially the face and hands, which were the easiest to get at.

"But the clothes and the contents of the pockets make identification absolute, unless we are to suppose that someone changed clothes with him after he parted with Mr. Cuthbertson, and then fell into the sea on purpose to lead up to the present charge.

"You'll see with a moment's thought that that's too fantastic to be considered; you might put the improbability at many millions to one. If we should try to set up such a defence we should come a cropper, and I don't think we should deserve to do anything else.

"You've got to face the fact that your cousin was drowned at about the time when your husband says that they parted, after he had pretended to throw him over the cliff; and more or less from the same place. Of course, we'll enquire into all relevant questions of tides and currents, and get any possible help we can, or keep quiet if we find they work out in a way that's no use to us. But we've got to admit what it's no use to deny, and try to think out some plausible theory—the truth, if it's any way possible to get at it—to account for how he could have got drowned after they parted that morning.

"And that brings me to the second point I want you to have clearly in mind. If your husband really blundered in what he did, and threw his cousin into the sea, it may be far best for him to say so, and give a true account of what happened, with the explanation which you've just given to me.

"I don't mean that it would get him off. It's just possible we might persuade a jury even to that, but it's not a result of which we could have more than a faint hope. And I won't even say that it would reduce the charge from murder to manslaughter, because that might depend upon the question of whether they were engaged in an illegal act at the time, and that raises other questions of fact and law on which precedents might not be easy to find.

"But I do say that, at the very worst, if we told the truth of a tale like that, we should be sure of a reprieve and probably a release after a few years, with considerable prospects of wriggling out even better than that.

"But if your husband says that he saw Thomas Birchall walking away, and it isn't true, and the jury don't believe him (and I can tell you that if it isn't true, he won't be believed; and even if it is, it would be about the stiffest fence I ever met to try to get them to listen to such a tale), why then you'll see that he can't explain what did happen in such a way that he might get acquitted, or perhaps convicted on no more than a minor charge. The prosecution can place the worst possible construction upon what occurred, and we're shut out from reply.

"And that raises another question on which we ought to be ready, and on which you should be able to help: I mean the question of motive. It isn't necessary to prove motive in a murder charge under English law, but a case isn't considered very satisfactory by the prosecution if no motive appears, and naturally the jury, under such circumstances, will be more reluctant to believe that a deliberate murder occurred.

"The prosecution is certain to look for some explanation—to put forward some theory—as to why your husband may have wished to make an end of his cousin's life, and if they can do that we shall have a much harder task to convince a jury that Thomas Birchall's death occurred in an innocent way."

"Well, I can answer that question at once," Dorothy replied, with some relief in her voice, as of one who sees a feeble thinning of clouds far off in a blackened sky. "Alfred hadn't the remotest reason for killing him, or anyone else for that matter. It wasn't the kind of thing he would have thought of doing, not in a thousand years. The idea's simply absurd. It all seems like an impossible nightmare to me."

"Well, I'm glad that you can say that. It clears the ground quite a lot. But as to Mr. Cuthbertson never having such thoughts in his mind, I don't want to say anything to worry you, but everyone knows that he's written books in which murders were committed in most ingenious ways, and—"

"Yes, but that's quite different. Those books are only a kind of game."

"Yes, I daresay they are. You mustn't take that remark too seriously."

Mr. Willerton had regretted it the instant that it was made, seeing its futility, and aware that his hostess was maintaining a difficult self-control which would be unlikely to outlast his own departure. Whether she were the wife of a murderer, or a mere unfortunate fool, it was equally hard for her! But his own mind went on to a rapid reflection which, he feared, would occur as quickly to other minds. Suppose that Alfred Cuthbertson had designed this murder with the subtlety of one of the plots of his own books, relying first upon the presumption that the body would not be recovered (would there be probability of that?). The body, as it was, had been five days in the sea. He must certainly make himself familiar with the movements of tides and currents along the coast. And secondly, he considered the fact that, if Cuthbertson should prove to have miscalculated upon that point, he could rely upon this tale to protect him from the worst consequences of the crime. Looked at in that way, it had much of the far-sighted ingenuity of the devices of one of his own fictitious criminals. Mr. Willerton saw that it became more than usually important to probe the question of any possible motive which might have impelled him to such an act.

"I'm not questioning what you say," he went on, "about the absence of motive, but you can be sure that the prosecution will try to set up something of the sort; and what I want us to do is to guess what it will be, if we possibly can, so that we may be the better able to refute it at the right time.

"There are many reasons for which one man may hate another, even to the point of desiring his death, but most of them come under one or other of two headings—greed and jealousy.

"Now suppose we take that of greed first. Is there any question of inheritance by which your husband may benefit through his cousin's death?"

"No. I don't think so. Their grandfather is alive, and is supposed to be rather rich—very rich, if Thomas was right about what he has hidden away. In fact he—Thomas, I mean—had an allowance from him, which, as far as I know, was about all his income. But Mr. Birchall didn't like Alfred. I think he offended him when a boy. And he thought writing stories was waste of time. Alfred has said to me more than once that he didn't expect a penny from old Eli, as he called him. I think they both assumed that Mr. Birchall would leave everything to Tom when he died."

Mr. Willerton heard this complacent explanation of the absence of motive with an amazement which his face did not conceal.

"You think," he asked, "that there would be no motive in that?"

She looked at him with puzzled eyes. "No," she said, "I don't see how anyone could make much of that. It would be a wicked thing to suggest. And besides, Mr. Eli Birchall is still alive. He needn't leave his money to Alfred because Tom is dead. It's not like there being a settled will." Mr. Willerton admitted that there was some argumentative force in the distinction she drew. The motive was not so simple and strong as it would have been had Alfred become the certain heir to the old gentleman's fortune by his cousin's death. But it still seemed to him that there was abundance of motive here—especially as Thomas was admitted to be the favourite grandchild. Indeed, the two evil passions which he had mentioned as those which inspire the majority of such crimes might be said to have joined forces here. Jealousy and greed might have combined to urge the fatal push which had sent Thomas Birchall reeling over the edge.

He did not therefore decide that Alfred must be guilty of the alleged crime. He knew that there are few relationships in which it cannot be shown that the living do, or may, benefit by another's death. But he saw that the prosecution would not be embarrassed by lack of motive to be suggested—that is, if they should discover the facts, as they doubtless would.

That was bad enough, but he did not intend to leave the subject until the alternative possibilities had been explored.

"Well," he said, "we can't alter the facts, and I'm glad to know what they are. But before we leave the subject of motive, let me ask you one more question. You'll forgive me if I have to ask something that might be offensive under less serious circumstances. Is it possible, however remotely, either that you might yourself have been a subject of jealousy between Mr. Cuthbertson and your cousin, or else that there might be some other woman over whom they would have a disposition to quarrel?"

Dorothy took the question without offence, but dismissed it lightly.

"No," she said. "You can put that absolutely out of your mind. There's no woman except myself, outside the house or in, to whom Alfred gives a thought, I'm quite certain of that. We haven't been apart for more time than it takes him to get round the links since we were married two years ago.

"And I don't mind telling you this: Tom asked me to marry him more than once before I met Alfred at all, and I turned him down. I suppose that makes my own feelings as plain as anything could."

Mr. Willerton, listening to this emphatic statement, did not doubt that he had heard an honest reply, but the circumstances that it disclosed did not sound to him quite as conclusive as she appeared to consider them. Still, the fact that she had been wooed before marriage by the dead man was not one that she would be likely to go out of her way to disclose in the witness box—she could be warned against that—and it was not a fact which was otherwise very likely to come to the ears of the prosecution.

He tried one more question. "That, you say, was before marriage—that is, more than two years ago. Have you any reason to think that Thomas Birchall still had the same feelings towards yourself?"

"You mean would he have married me now, if he could? I daresay that's likely enough, though I should say he cared more for his laboratory, and fifty times more for himself, than for all the women in Dorsetshire. But he never had a word of encouragement from me in his life, either before marriage or since."

Mr. Willerton felt that she had answered him with sincerity, and with as much frankness as a woman could be expected to show. He said to himself that the position might have been worse, though it might also have been better without deserving to be called good.

It was at the end of the meal that the conversation came to this point, and, as Dorothy led the way to the lounge, Bertha stopped her in the hall to ask: "May I speak to you a moment, madam?"

Dorothy excused herself to her guest, and when she had shown him into the lounge she turned back to the dining room where the parlour maid was now busily clearing the table.

"Yes, Bertha, what is it?"

"We thought you ought to know, cook and me, madam, that Bill Ringwood'd got hold of Ethel."

Dorothy stared at the maid in a moment of startled bewilderment. Her mind occupied as it was, the words gave her no more than a vague impression that the young policeman had surprisingly abducted a quiet-mannered and otherwise respectable housemaid.

"Got hold of Ethel?" she asked. "You mean the girl's gone off with him?"

"No, madam, she's in now. But he's had her at the police station for two hours—it was her afternoon out—and she's been crying ever since she came back."

Dorothy saw her mistake now, though she was still bewildered as to what the girl could have said to make mischief in a matter which seemed to be so far removed from her own sphere. She asked: "What can she have been saying there?"

It was a simple question, but Bertha showed a reluctance to say what she plainly knew, which did not make the enigma less.

"I think, madam, she's the one to tell you that for herself. I expect it's more lies than not."

"I should think that's unlikely. I've always found Ethel a truthful girl. Tell her that I want to speak to her in the lounge. You needn't mention that Mr. Willerton's there."

Dorothy spoke without any thought that she herself could be involved in the girl's tale, but she judged, very soundly, that whatever had been taken down at Osbury police station should be equally known to her husband's solicitor.

Bertha, with fuller knowledge of the nature of what the girl had been saying, allowed an expression of doubt to appear. She had an impulse to warn her mistress, but she was reluctant to be the medium of communicating the tale, and she also saw that there was no use in attempting concealment now.

"Very well, madam," she said, "I'll see that she comes at once."

CHAPTER XVIII.

DOROTHY went back to the lounge. She said: "It seems that there's something else coming out now, though I've no idea what it is. They've had Ethel, the housemaid, at the police station all afternoon. I've told Bertha to send here in here. I thought you ought to know what she's been saying."

"No idea what it could be?"

"Not the least. But I'm prepared to believe almost anything after what's happened already today. Almost anything, I mean, except that Alfred would murder Tom, or anyone else for that matter. I'll never believe that. I know him too well."

Mr. Willerton was not much influenced by this protestation. He knew that numerous criminals, murderers included, have contrived to conceal the worst features of their characters from their households and closest friends. But he did not doubt its sincerity, nor that Mrs. Cuthbertson was as ignorant as himself of the disclosure the girl had made.

"I suppose," he asked, as the minutes passed and Ethel did not appear, "that there's no question of malice? The girl hasn't been found out in a fault? Or under notice to leave?"

"Oh, no. I think she's quite happy here. She's rather untidy in her work, and sometimes gets the rough side of cook's tongue, but I've rather liked her than not. She does her best in a slow way."

"Truthful?"

"I haven't found her anything else. I doubt whether she's got an imagination enough for a good lie."

As she spoke there was a sound, strange to the quiet dignity of Highview House, of scuffling and angry words in the farther hall.

Bertha's usually demure voice could be heard on a high note of expostulation or threats. The words "dirty little cat" came clearly along the passage, and through the barrier of the closed door, as further evidence of a lack of harmony among the approaching domestics.

But approach they did, by whatever means, until the altercation was on the other side of the door, and the words could be clearly heard.

There was a tearful, indignant protest: "I can't go in with it all torn. You can see that," to which Bertha's voice came grim in reply: "You should have thought of that before you began. You should come now if you were as bare as you'll be at the Last Day."

Dorothy rose, thinking that it was time for her to intervene in this undignified scuffle which was taking place at her door, and in the hearing of one who was still a guest, though he might be there primarily in his professional capacity. But Mr. Willerton said: "It might be wiser to let them fight it out in their own way," and she sat down again as the door opened, and Bertha appeared with a smaller, dishevelled figure firmly gripped by the upper arm. Bertha herself showed heightened colour, and some other indications of stormy passage since she had half dragged her prey through the kitchen door with the cook pushing behind. But her voice sank to its usual tone of respectful propriety as she said:

"I've brought Ethel to you, madam, as she wasn't willing to come alone."

Dorothy said: "Thank you, Bertha. Perhaps you'd better stay too, as you know what the trouble is."

She turned her eyes to the culprit, a sort, rather tubby girl, with a face naturally plain, and now swollen with many tears.

She was far from being in the state of nudity on which Bertha assumed that she would have to face her Creator on a later and even more important occasion, but the demands of propriety, as she understood it when in the presence of her mistress and a strange gentleman, required that she should use both hands to hold together a cotton blouse which, with a dingy garment beneath it, had been ripped from neck to waist as she had endeavoured to escape from Bertha's muscular grip.

"Bertha," Dorothy said, with her eyes on the tattered garments, "you might fetch a safety pin or perhaps two." And then to the wretched girl, as the parlour maid left the room: "You'd better sit down and tell me what mischief you've been at."

"Please, ma'am, I didn't mean any harm. I only told Annie, and she promising not to say it again."

"What did you tell Annie?"

"I only said what I saw. If I'd thought that it was the police wanting to know—"

"Will you tell me what it was that you saw?"

There was a brief interlude at this point, Bertha having returned with the required pins, and when the torn blouse had been fixed more or less in its former position, Dorothy repeated the question.

"Ethel, I want to know what it was that you say you saw. If you can tell the police, I suppose you can tell me. And if it's something that interests them, it's something I ought to know. Bertha, if she won't speak, you'd better tell me what you understand it to be."

"What it is, madam, is that she says she saw Mr. Birchall kissing you, and he only stopped when Mr. Cuthbertson came into the room. She says she wasn't spying, she just happened to be coming round the back drive, and the lounge was lit up and the curtains not drawn.

"Of course we know it's a lie, but she told Annie, and she must have told her mother, who says she saw the master throw Mr. Birchall over the cliffs the next day. And we suppose Mrs. Gilkins told the police, and they got Ethel into the station this afternoon, and wrote a paper out for her to sign, and now she says they put in a lot more than she meant, but she was too frightened to say anything when they told her she'd got to sign."

By the time this statement was finished, Dorothy had recovered her self-control from the emotions of sharp surprise, indignation, and fear for Alfred, through which she had passed as it proceeded. She did not suppose that her husband had shared Ethel's mistake, nor that the incident had led to a tragedy in which her reason still declined to believe; but she saw how greatly it might complicate the position that such an allegation should be in possession of the police. But what was done could not be altered now. It remained only for her to give the denial which was fortunately true, though it might not be believed.

"Thank you, Bertha," she said quietly. "Of course, it's an absolute lie. Mr. Birchall never kissed me in his life, nor I him. It is a thing, as Ethel should have known, that I shouldn't have allowed him to do."

"I said as you pushed him off," Ethel interposed between sobs which had broken out again as this conversation proceeded.

Dorothy took no notice of this interjection as she went on to say: "But I don't suppose you can do any more harm now, nor undo what you've done. You'd better stop crying and go to bed."

When the room was clear again, she gave the lawyer as accurate an account as she could of the incident which had obtained such unfortunate publicity. He did not doubt that she told the truth as far as her knowledge went, though it was evident that, like himself, she could do no more than guess what might have gone on in the mind of the man she had repulsed, or of the husband who had entered at so inopportune a moment.

Yet she spoke as confidently, and with the same evident sincerity, when she had assured him that Alfred had not taken the incident seriously, and that they had discussed it frankly.

"Well," he said, speaking as hopefully as he could, "it's just one more fence to be crossed on a rough course. I thought before that you were the best witness we've got, and I think so still. But I'd better be going now. I'll ring you up in the morning, and probably come round after I've seen Mr. Cuthbertson again. I expect they'll only ask for a formal remand on Monday, but we must be ready for anything. It's lucky we've got Sunday between. I shouldn't worry more than you can't help. Things often look better after a night's sleep."

He went away with the thought: "Well, the case might look worse, but it's difficult to see how"—and must console himself with the reflection that such cases may often be transformed to a better shape when a sufficient measure of legal and logical ingenuities have been expended upon them.

It was something to know the worst which he was likely to have to face, and that, he supposed, he had now done.

CHAPTER XIX.

MR. FRAMPTON prepared his brief. At an early hour of Sunday morning he had retained the services of Mr. Bigland-Buffitt, who resided in the outskirts of Dorchester, and was of an established reputation on the southern circuit, particularly as a prosecuting counsel in criminal cases.

It might be advisable to provide him with a leader at the assize trial, but, for the preliminary hearing at least, Mr. Frampton judged that he would be sufficient, in a case which he regarded as of almost prosaic simplicity, now that the body had been recovered and a motive provided.

Contrary to Mr. Willerton's natural anticipation, he had decided to have the case opened on the following morning, and then ask for an adjournment of not more than two or three days, leaving it to the defence to apply for further time, if they should elect to do so.

In this decision, he was guided by the facts that his case was logically complete, that he had some witnesses at call, that the others could be quickly brought, and particularly by the consideration that, if a committal could be promptly obtained, the case might be in time to be set down for the forthcoming Dorset Assizes, while a more dilatory procedure would involve keeping the prisoner awaiting trial for several months in the county jail. Such expedition had recently been urged by some of His Majesty's judges, who had dwelt upon the humanitarian considerations involved. It implies no criticism of their recommendations to observe the possibility that a murderer may have no overwhelming objection to some months of life, even under the conditions considered suitable for accused persons awaiting trial, when the alternative is no better than a shortened route to the scaffold.

However this may be, Mr. Frampton had no doubt that he earned the approval both of his fellow men and Superior Powers when he allowed his seat at St. Saviour's Church to remain unoccupied during the morning service, so that he might keep his promise to Bigland-Buffitt that the brief should be sent to him by hand not later than 6:00 P.M.

He now wrote in a neat, small, rapid hand, leaving wide spaces for counsel's subsequent annotations between the lines:

> Counsel will observe that there can be no reasonable doubt either as to the circumstances under which Thomas Birchall met with his death, nor as to the identity of the man by whose hand he died.
>
> It is true that none of the three witnesses who saw the struggle which terminated in his being thrown over the cliff was sufficiently near to be able to identify the victim, who was, besides, a stranger to them. But two at least (and probably Miss Mills also) will positively identify the accused, and other evidence will establish that the two men left Highview House with the expressed intention of walking along the cliffs, and were subsequently seen proceeding in that direction together.
>
> The defence will most probably recognize the expediency of admitting these facts, and may endeavour to set up (a) that the fall was accidental, or (b) that the accused acted in self-defence.
>
> Of these issues (b) appears to be the more plausible, in view of the evidence of those who witnessed the fatal struggle, and will probably be the only serious defence with which counsel will have to deal.
>
> In this connection, counsel's attention is directed to the fact that Thomas Birchall was some inches the shorter, and therefore presumably the weaker man.
>
> Whatever line of defence be taken (unless it be reserved), it appears to be unavoidable that Mrs. Cuthbertson be put into the box, and counsel will not overlook the importance of pressing her for an explanation as to the circumstances under which Thomas Birchall was invited to Highview House, on which point she may be less ready with her reply in regard to the incident witnessed by Ethel Harding, on which she will anticipate that an explanation will be required.

He wrote on for another half hour, covering with his far-divided lines several more of the large blue sheets on which, by established usage, such instructions must be set out, and was able to dispatch the brief by the hand of a waiting clerk nearly an hour before the time he had promised. After that, he attended the evening service with a conscience happy in the knowledge that he had done his part that day to maintain the social order by which he lived.

Mr. Willerton, meanwhile, had taken the instructions of a rather difficult client. Alfred Cuthbertson had insisted stubbornly that, be the appearances what they might, he had been in no way responsible, whether by malice or accident, either directly or indirectly, for his cousin's death. He protested that, before he turned to retrace his steps, he had actually seen Thomas Birchall regain the road, cross it, and set off rapidly toward a little hollow in the downs which had been previously chosen as that in which he should make the changes of clothes which had been arranged. He added, with equal stubbornness, that he did not believe that his cousin was really dead. He clung desperately to the point that the face had, admittedly, been disfigured beyond certain identification. As to the clothes, and the contents of the pockets, it was not beyond the resources of the human mind to imagine explanations. Might it not, for instance, be the device of an ingenious prosecution, which might honestly assume and believe that it had recovered the body of Thomas Birchall, and so endeavoured to provide the identification without which they could not hope to prove a crime of which they might honestly think him guilty?

He did not dispute Mr. Willerton's bluntly-expressed opinion that it was a wildly unlikely theory. But, he asked, was it more so than that the man whom he had seen walking away after he had pretended to throw him into the sea, should really have fallen in almost immediately afterwards? Even the most improbable solutions must be admitted to consideration when no probable one will resolve the enigma.

He urged that, in justice, he should be permitted to see the body on which the prosecution had fastened his cousin's name. Mr. Willerton was not disposed to think that such an application would be refused, but he pointed out that his inability to identify it would not be a factor of great value to the defence, as he could hardly be considered an impartial witness, unless he could support denial by pointing out some affirmative difference of a provable kind.

Beyond that, he said that he could not, as yet, see any prospect of successful defence on the lines of challenging the identity of the dead man.

He went away, at last, promising to scrutinize the evidence of identification with the utmost closeness, and to contest it in court, if he could find any ground, however remote, to which an intelligent magistrate could be expected to listen; and promising to see Mr. Cuthbertson again next afternoon, after the case would, as he supposed, have been formally remanded to a later date.

From that interview, he went to see Dorothy. During the short time in which his car covered the two miles or more which divided the Osbury police station from Highview House, his mind ran over the conversation he had had, and found little to encourage him to think that he would gain the credit of defending Alfred Cuthbertson successfully from the accusation which had been made against him; neither could he easily bring himself to the belief that he was advocating the cause of an innocent man.

Rather, he was disposed to think and resent that his client had contrived his cousin's murder by some such subtle plot as he would evolve in his own books, by which he had calculated to escape the penalty of his crime, and that he himself was to be no more than one of the puppets that the murderer had calculated to use. The ingenious device by which he had convinced his wife in advance that it was no more than a mock murder to which his victim was being lured, and which had also led Thomas Birchall to place himself in position to be thrown over the cliff, might be no more than the first act of the drama that Alfred Cuthbertson had devised for his own deliverance in the (perhaps improbable) contingency of the body being thrown up by the sea.

But he roused himself from these reflections, as his car turned into the gates of Highview House, to remember that he was Alfred Cuthbertson's solicitor, and that such thoughts should find no encouragement in his mind so long as he continued to hold that office; and that, be he guilty or innocent, there should be no lack of sympathy for the certainly-innocent woman whom he was now about to visit.

CHAPTER XX.

IT was midday when Mr. Willerton arrived at Highview House, and Dorothy received him with the relief of feeling that she could talk with a freedom impossible with the domestic staff, however loyal they might be, upon the subject which filled her mind.

"I hope," she said, "that you'll be able to stay to lunch. I've arranged to see Alfred this afternoon. Inspector Reid says that there'll be no difficulty about that at any reasonable time. But I kept away this morning, as I understood you would be there.

"I thought it might be an advantage to see Alfred after he'd talked it over with you, and heard what you advise us to do."

"It's not easy to answer that," the solicitor replied, "because I'm afraid your husband and I don't agree. He wishes to take the line of denying that anything happened beyond what you told me had been intended, which, of course, is what we ought to do if it's the truth; but I'm bound to say that it's very hard to believe, even for me.

"Following that line, he wants me to challenge the identification of the body, and, of course, I'm quite willing to do that if I can see the slightest hope of success; but if we do it beyond reason we shall only prejudice ourselves. In short, he urges me to take a line of defence in which I've no confidence, and it's only right you should know that, though it's what I'm sorry to have to say."

"I should be sorry," she answered, "if you don't approve of what Alfred wants, because you are so much more experienced in these matters; but Alfred isn't really a fool, though he may give you that impression at times, and with so much at stake—but suppose we talk that over at lunch?"

"I really ought not to stay, but if you're sure that you wish—"

"Of course I am. I ordered it early—twelve-thirty—on purpose. But there's one thing I ought to tell you. I've been questioning Ethel again, as it seemed the only thing I could do to help till you arrived; and I'm afraid they've got her to sign a statement which makes a great deal more of the incident than it really was."

She said this with gravity, and was surprised at the cheerfulness with which it was received.

"Why," the solicitor said, "that was what I was hoping to hear! She'll be their witness, and when we cross-examine her, she'll break down. That means a reaction in its effect, and if you afterwards tell the tale in the right way, as I can trust you to do, we may be able to make out that it was next to nothing at all. It's our best hope that the prosecution will try to play it for more than it's fairly worth. But of course, if we upset that, we're not much better off while the main issue remains."

As he spoke, the gong sounded in the hall, and Dorothy led the way to the dining room.

"You needn't mind Bertha," she said, as soon as they were seated. "She won't repeat anything, if I ask her not."

"I've no doubt you're right," he replied, with a memory of the parlour maid's vigorous advocacy of the previous evening, and a smile in her direction to which she gave the faint response that her training allowed.

"The real trouble is," Dorothy asked, "that you don't believe Alfred, and I suppose that you don't reckon to defend anyone unless you feel that they've told you the truth?"

The blunt question caused the solicitor to consider his position with care, and to answer in the same spirit.

"The question you put is often a very difficult one. As a rule we consider it our duty to accept the instructions we receive, unless we *know* they are false, which is much more than I can say in this case. My difficulty is really a double one. I am sceptical of my instructions—I think anyone would be—and I also think that they constitute a hopeless line of defence. If they be untrue, it is doubly my duty to urge my opinion that they will be irreparably disastrous.

"But I cannot refuse to accept an account which may possibly be correct, however faint that possibility may appear to be, so long as I continue in the office of Mr. Cuthbertson's solicitor; though a position might arise, or may already have arisen, in which it would be my duty to retire from the case.

"As a matter of fact, I do not suppose that the proceedings to-morrow will be of more than a formal character, and I had already resolved to talk the case over with Mr. Soome, my senior partner, when he returns to morrow afternoon, as to whether it might not be best for all concerned that Mr. Cuthbertson should take other advice."

"Then I most earnestly ask that you won't do anything of the kind. It would make me almost lose hope, which I've determined I'll never do. You say that you don't *know* that what Alfred tells you isn't the truth, and that while that position continues there is no breach of professional etiquette in advocating that line of defence. Well, beyond that, it seems to me that Alfred's got the most at stake, and it should be for him to decide. If you've told him you don't approve, and he still persists, he can't blame you for the result.

"But, of course, I don't want you to be advocating a defence that you don't approve, nor one that doesn't give us the best chance of proving that Alfred didn't murder anyone. I want to talk it out thoroughly with him this afternoon, and after that, if he still says the same, I want you to promise that you'll accept his own account of the matter, and stake everything on the defence which he prefers. Of course, it doesn't really depend upon whether it's Tom's body that's been recovered. He may have got into the sea some other way. But if my husband persists in doubting it, there's one thing that I think I ought to do, though I'd much rather not. I think I ought to see the body myself, if you can arrange it, and I could tell him what my opinion is."

"Yes, I could arrange that. And, whatever may be decided this afternoon, I shall be glad if you will. Of course, if you should see anything by which you would be able to swear that the body is not that of Thomas Birchall, it would alter the position immensely. We should have to start a search for him on the assumption that he is not dead, and his appearance should put an end to the case. I don't think myself that it is a possibility worth considering, but that is what the position would be.

"On the other hand, if you can identify the body, it will put that issue definitely aside, and I shall be relieved of the necessity of raising a question which is likely to do us more harm than good, if it be done without solid ground. And if you can't be sure, we shall be no worse off than we are now."

"Very well," she said, seeing that it was an ordeal which must be faced; "let me know when it can be arranged, and I'll come any time."

"There's one other point," he said, "which I ought to mention, on which your husband feels very strongly. He doesn't want any allusion made to the plot from which it seems that all this trouble has come, except as a last resort. He seems still to have a hope that Thomas Birchall will turn up alive, and that he will be released without the necessity of it being exposed.

"I don't see anything in it myself, because I think it's a matter that's bound to be brought in—it's at the root of any defence we have, whether bad or good, and if it's got to come out, I can't see that it matters when; but that's how he feels, and if that instruction continues after your visit this afternoon, I shall have to consider the expediency of reserving our defence until the trial. I don't see any great objection to that, though it isn't usual in murder cases, which are most often fought every inch of the way. But a committal's certain—there isn't a millionth chance of avoiding that—and the cross-examination of the prosecution's witnesses won't be affected one way or other."

"You mean that I, that anyone on our side won't be asked to give evidence until the trial itself? That we shall let everyone think just what they like till then?"

"That's the idea. But it isn't mine, it's what's being forced on me by the instructions I have received, if you can't get them changed. Though I don't say there aren't some advantages in reserving the defence. It's a matter of tactics, with arguments on both sides. I shouldn't let that question weigh with you too much."

"Well," she said, with a difficult effort of courage, which could not wholly control the fear that she was resolved that she would not show to others, or even admit to her own thoughts, "of course I'll do all I can, but it's Alfred's part to decide."

He went at that, promising to let her know when he had made the appointment for viewing the body, and she did not expect to hear from him again before visiting Alfred, for which she was due to start in less than an hour; but it was not more than twenty minutes before he rang up to say that the body of Thomas Birchall, if such it were, could be seen at the Osbury mortuary at four-thirty that afternoon, providing only that Sir Lionel Tipshift, the Home Office expert who had been called in, should have concluded his post-mortem by that time.

"I'm afraid," Mr. Willerton added, "you won't find it a pleasant sight. But you won't be expecting that."

She said that she would meet Mr. Willerton there, keeping her car waiting during the earlier appointment, and driving on to the mortuary.

Half an hour later she started to the police station, where the consideration of Inspector Reid permitted an interview with her husband which continued until it was time for her to start to the mortuary; but while she had no cause to complain of any individual rudeness, even of the warder who endeavoured not to listen to their conversation, she was disconcerted to find that the modern system of prison control—more barbarous in this respect, as in many others, than that of earlier periods—would not permit her to see him except in the presence of this official.

Obstructed as she thus was from any real intimacy of communication, she was yet able to obtain a clear perception of the mood in which he was meeting the peril to life and honour which his own folly, if not his crime had brought upon him.

He was in a condition of nervous irritability, hardly concealing the fear which he might have been equally reluctant to show even had they been in a position of greater privacy; but he professed the same incredulity as to the death of Thomas Birchall with which Mr. Willerton had been confronted previously; and he had a new theory which, he said, was at least as probable as that Thomas should have been drowned in earnest a few hours after he had acted the part of a murdered man.

This theory was that he might have been robbed by a tramp, who had afterwards fallen into the sea with his possessions in his pocket, and perhaps (if that were the case) wearing his actual clothes. Or, even more plausibly, that such a man might have picked up articles which he had thrown away when he disguised himself as it had been arranged that he should.

If this were so, it was a reasonable presumption that Thomas would make his existence known as soon as he should read of his cousin's arrest. Alfred expressed sufficient confidence in this development to relieve Dorothy's mind of any doubt she may have been fighting previously as to whether he were as absolutely innocent as she was resolved to believe, dismissing a traitorous doubt that what he said might be part of a deliberately adopted pose, or designed for the warder's ears.

He seemed to be genuinely glad, as well as grateful, when she told him that she was going on to the mortuary, though it was an ordeal which, he said, he would not have asked her to face; and he asked her to let him know as quickly as possible if she felt able to swear that the body was not that of his cousin.

She saw that, if she should be able to do this, it would at least be some embarrassment to the prosecution, even though it might be easy to throw doubt on the impartiality of her opinion, and, seeing it in this aspect, she was led to wonder how far a wife should go in her husband's cause, especially if he be in danger of a wrongful conviction; and from that thought it was no more than a natural progression to wonder whether Alfred was relying on her to deny that it was Tom's body which had been cast up by the sea.

CHAPTER XXI.

AS the attendant drew down the sheet, she forced herself to the resolution which would look steadfastly at the disfeatured face, the disfigured head, putting the horrors of corruption and mutilation aside, that she might detect any indication, however slight, of the Thomas Birchall whose remains they were said to be.

She had prepared herself for a repulsive sight, though she could only vaguely suppose what it would be, and her mood had been hardened a few minutes before when she had been in the waiting room with Mr. Willerton, and had heard, through the half-opened door, fragments of the conversation of a little group of men who had passed out through the passage to their waiting cars.

She had caught sight for a moment of a tall handsome man, very correctly dressed, to whom another, who was in fact the coroner's officer, had made some remark in a deferential voice, doubtless giving the information that, while the post-mortem was concluded, she had been waiting to view the body; for the reply came in a suave voice which seemed to assume the finality of its own decisions: "Mrs. Cuthbertson? Oh, yes, of course. The murderer's wife." To which Dr. Livermore, a local practitioner, who was Alfred's occasional opponent on the golf course, spoke a word of protest, and Sir Lionel Tipshift had replied with no alteration of his smiling suavity: "Oh, yes, of course. We assume nothing at all. 'Let all things be done decently and in order,' as the Apostle says."

Mr. Willerton had told her who he was as they looked through the waiting room window, and saw his liveried chauffeur respectfully open the door for him to enter his car. "That's Sir Lionel, the tame Home Office expert, who is always ready to give evidence for an official prosecution."

"You mean," she asked, hating the man for the cool assumption his words conveyed, "that he'll swear to anything?"

"No, scarcely that. But you can always get experts to contradict each other. You see they're allowed to swear to opinions, whereas other men have to swear to facts, and most of us find it hard enough to be right on them. A good many lawyers think that the expert witness should be entirely abolished, or else that one only should be allowed to give impartial advice to the Court. I instructed Dr. Livermore to be present in our interest, more as a matter of form than because it's likely to do any good, but he's a sound man, and he'll advise us if there's anything in Sir Lionel's opinion we ought to challenge. If there isn't—and I don't see what to expect in this case—we shall consent to burial without further delay, or otherwise we shall have to instruct some prominent surgeons to make a further examination, and contradict whatever Sir Lionel says. You'll find there'll be no difficulty about that."

He had talked more or less at random to occupy her attention during those minutes of further waiting, while the mortuary had been prepared for them to enter, and he so far succeeded that he took her mind off the coming ordeal to think of the expense which must be already incurred or inevitable in the coming days, and to suppose vaguely (and wrongly) that if Alfred's innocence were established, it would be his accusers who would have to bear it. And if he were convicted, what would that—what would anything matter? She supposed that, if she sold the house, it would realize all that could be required.

And after that Dr. Livermore had returned, and had greeted her with a cordiality pleasant to meet, being placed as she was, and had then turned to Mr. Willerton to say: "I don't see why we shouldn't consent to burial. If we do, I understand that the coroner will concur. Sir Lionel's opinion is that the body had been in the water about five days—more rather than less. But the cause of death wasn't drowning. He'll swear to that, so if you can make anything of it—well, there it is. But considering the height from which the man is supposed to have fallen, and the tide being barely up to the foot of the cliff at the time, it's really what you'd expect to find. Anyway, that's the fact. I can't say that he arrived at any conclusion with which I didn't agree. Oh, and you may like to know that they're bringing Birchall's grandfather down tomorrow morning to identify him, if he's able to do so."

After saying this, he had offered to come back into the mortuary with them if Mrs. Cuthbertson liked, which she had accepted with gratitude, and an unspoken thought that he probably supposed she might soon be needing his ministrations. And so she stood for a long minute gazing at the disfigured wreck of what had once been a human face, and asking herself, was it really Tom?

She withdrew her eyes at last, and turned to the two men who had stood slightly behind her to say: "It's no use. I can't honestly tell. I think it's Tom, and then I'm not sure. I can't say more than that the hair's very like, and I suppose there's not much in that."

Mr. Willerton saw that, on the instructions he had received, there was little help to be had here. He would have preferred a decided opinion, whichever it might have been. But it was the truth which, before everything, it was important for him to have.

"You wouldn't have questioned," he asked, "that it was Thomas Birchall, if the doubt hadn't been suggested to you?"

"I mightn't have doubted, but I think that I should still have said that I couldn't recognize him, the face being so...so eaten away."

"Could you swear: 'I was unable to recognize the body as that of Thomas Birchall, although he was well known to me'?"

"Yes. I could say that. Of course, I had not known him intimately. I knew him years ago, and he had been staying with us twice recently. I knew his face with familiarity."

"That is quite dear." Mr. Willerton made a note of the words of his first question, and read them out for her approval. At least, he knew where he was now, so far as the question of her identification was concerned. He asked: "Do you recognize these?"

On a slab at the side of the bare, cold, vault-like room, there lay, neatly folded, the tattered clothes which had been stripped from the dead man, and beside them, in a small glass case, not unlike those which may be seen on a jeweller's counter, were the contents of the pockets—an odd key, two pennies, a pocket knife, and a letter which had been sodden and dried, but of which much, if not all, of the blurred writing could still be read.

"I don't recognize the clothes," she said. "Not particularly, that is. I don't say that they weren't his."

"They have the tailors' name on," Dr. Livermore said. "I heard it mentioned that the police are enquiring when they were bought. They are from a firm near Horseferry Road. The knife has his name engraved upon it."

"Yes," she said, "I could identify that. I remember him bringing it out once at dinner when he stayed with us at Easter. I noticed because he pulled it out to peel an apple, as though he didn't know what a fruit knife was for. And the letter's one that I wrote to him myself. I wonder that he kept it in his pocket for such a time."

"Yes. It may have been just carelessness, but the prosecution will probably try to make profit out of it by suggesting that he had a sentimental interest in the writer. It's well that you should be prepared for that."

"I suppose," Dorothy asked bitterly, "they never try to be fair?"

"Oh, I don't know. They would say that they are scrupulously so, almost too much at times. But they go on the assumption that a murder has been committed, and that it's their duty to prove it. They have to rake up all the facts on one side, and we have to upset them as best we can."

She made no answer to that, being conscious that emotion rather than reason had ruled her words.

He went on: "There's one other thing that you ought to know. I rang up Frampton—he's the solicitor for the police—before I came out. I said I assumed that they wouldn't be ready to go further to-morrow than to give evidence of arrest and apply for a week's remand; but he said no, they meant to call some of their witnesses, and get on as far as they could. But he added that they couldn't possibly finish; so we shall be sure of an adjournment before we have to decide on our own course.

"I expect they want to get Sir Lionel's evidence in, without troubling him to come down again."

"Well," she answered, "I suppose it doesn't make any real difference." She was scarcely conscious of what she said, or what meaning it had. She felt exhausted in mind and body. Would that face haunt her for all her days? Why should all people and facts combine to convict Alfred of something which she told herself she was still sure he had never done?

Mr. Willerton's voice roused her. "You're sure that you feel fit to drive?" It was the second time he had asked.

"Oh, yes," she said. "I can do that. Ten-thirty tomorrow? A few minutes earlier? Very well. You can depend upon my being there."

She learned on reaching home that Constable Ringwood had called and served a subpœna upon Ethel Harding, requiring her attendance at the Magistrates' Court on the following day.

She went to bed immediately after dinner, anticipating a restless night, but when she waked the tea tray was at her side, and Bertha was drawing the curtains from windows that streamed with rain.

CHAPTER XXII.

MR. WILLERTON rose early on Monday morning, and a sky that was black with the prospect of heavy showers did not deter him from fulfilling the purpose which he had formed on the previous day, of taking an early walk along the cliff tops which he had known from childhood, but concerning which he wished to refresh his memory, in particular concerning the spot where, according to the tale which he was asked to believe, Thomas had allowed it to appear that he had been thrown over the edge.

He found it without difficulty, and recognized that its conformation gave some support to the story. He had no difficulty in believing that the fantastic idea, on which it seemed that the whole tragedy was based, had come to Alfred Cuthbertson's mind as he had gazed down upon it. But he saw that, to hostile minds, it might seem with equal plausibility to be no less than the cunning trap by which Thomas Birchall had been lured, so that he had walked willingly to the place which had been selected for his execution.

He saw also that a difference in position of not more than a dozen yards, which would be unappreciable to those looking up from the path as it approached the cliffs from the Osbury side, would be enough to make all the difference between life and death—fifteen yards of precarious safety, and, right and left, a sheer fall to the rocks below.

The sea was coming in now, and the waves threw up high clouds of spray as they beat the rocks with the urge of the southwest wind; but he knew that there would be little water or none at a lower tide; and it was easy to see that a man thrown down from so great a height on those granite rocks might be dead before he could be drowned by the rising waves.

Yet, he thought, if Alfred Cuthbertson had so thrown a man to his death when the tide was low, must he not have incurred an appalling risk that his victim would be seen before he would be covered or washed away? And would not that risk become immensely greater if he should select a time, as Alfred Cuthbertson had actually done, when there were witnesses to observe his crime? Did it not make the probability of sudden impulse, or even absolute accident, greater than he had previously considered either of them to be?

Perhaps for the first time, he admitted to his own mind that there was room for a genuine doubt. Why had not any of the three who were said to have witnessed the struggle investigated what had occurred at the time, instead of going back to Osbury? Could Alfred Cuthbertson have reasonably calculated on such a result? Had he subtly considered these questions, and relied upon them for his vindication, on the argument that it was incredible that he should so have designed Thomas Birchall's end?

Whatever the answer to these questions might be, he was resolved that the witnesses should not escape severe pressure as to why they had turned away with no effort to observe a dead, or succour an injured, man. On which reflection he went home to breakfast in time to get half an hour at his office before attending the court, which he reached at 10:20, to find it crowded to the doors, and to observe that Mrs. Cuthbertson was already there. Mr. Bigland-Buffitt had already arrived, and was in whispered consultation with Mr. Frampton and Inspector Reid, with Mr. Frampton's clerk, alertly respectful, leaning over from the bench behind. Their voices, low before, became lower still, as Mr. Frampton made room for his legal opponent to sit down beside him.

A few minutes later, the magistrates, and Mr. Lionel Waites, the magistrates' clerk, having been engaged in a preliminary discussion of the case in their private room, entered the court together.

The bench consisted of three on this occasion. There was Sir George Hawler, the chairman, a heavy man both in body and mind, but with a popular reputation for good humour and generosity when his prejudices were not concerned. He was also reputed to be able to tell a good after-dinner story, and to have a slow, dry wit in the latter part of the day, but brain and body moved with equal reluctance through the earlier hours.

Mr. Percival Bullows took the seat at his right hand. He had been a farmer during the War, and had had sufficient foresight to sell out while prices were high, after which he had speculated successfully in land values along the coast until he became known as a man of sufficient wealth to entitle him to the position which he now occupied.

The third magistrate was an eccentric, rather elderly lady, Miss Grigson Lait, who had reached this position of local dignity by conspicuous social services, and political subscriptions of a more private character. She was the frequent exasperation of Mr. Waites, owing to an obstinate preference for justice rather than law, and a habit of voicing opinions audibly which should, in his experienced judgment, be whispered only, until a final decision had been reached with some appearance of unanimity. At the moment, she was scarcely on speaking terms with Sir George, owing to a recent difference of opinion concerning the application of the licensing laws at their previous sitting, which she had carried against him with the somewhat unwilling support of the magistrates' clerk.

That gentleman, Mr. Lionel Waites, who sat on a lower level, supplied the law, most of the brains, and the majority of the decisions which these occasions required. In his private practice, he was Mr. Frampton's partner, in which capacity he had already familiarized himself with the case which the prosecution was about to submit to the consideration of the court.

It having been specially convened for this purpose, there was no precedent business, and when the magistrates had bowed to the crowded benches and taken their seats, the prisoner was introduced to the dock.

Guilty or innocent, it had to be allowed that Alfred Cuthbertson faced the moment well. He bowed slightly to the magistrates, to whom, in different degrees, he was personally known, and looked round for his wife, whom he greeted with a smile which won him sympathy from several of those who had come prepared to take his part rather than that of the law.

He heard Mr. Waites read the indictment charging him with the wilful murder of Thomas Birchall with some elaborations not necessary to record, and, on being challenged to plead, replied: "Not guilty, of course. I am absolutely innocent," in a voice that contrived to be faintly contemptuous of the charge, without disrespect to the court itself.

He showed no consciousness of the curiosity of the hundred eyes that were fixed upon him, or of the busy pencils of the reporters who constituted nearly half the occupants of the little court, and when the Chairman said: "You can sit down, Cuthbertson," in a tone that made the unceremonious form of address an insult rather than the familiarity of an equal, he took the narrow seat in the dock with a polite "Thank you, Sir George," that declined to observe the official rudeness with which the permission had been given.

Sir George Hawler thought: "The fellow's carrying it off very well." He was not surprised to see him in that position; was, indeed, subconsciously pleased at that which vindicated the soundness of his own judgment when he had objected to selling Highview House on the double ground that a man who made a living by writing books could not be a gentleman, and that he must be of an obvious financial instability, from which position he had only receded on Mr. Frampton's urging that he was not letting but selling, so that the second question did not arise, and that his own finances were not sufficiently healthy to admit of such an opportunity being rejected.

Mr. Bullows thought: "Poor fellow, I daresay he never really meant to give him the tip-over. But he's got to go through it now. Pity anyone saw."

And then Miss Grigson Lait, also with a measure of sympathy for a guilty man, thought: "It's the woman who ought to be there, more likely than not, rather than he. There's no doubt how she played them off."

And then they all turned their attention to Mr. Bigland-Buffitt, who had risen to set out the case against the prisoner.

CHAPTER XXIII.

MR. BIGLAND-BUFFITT was of an aspect less formidable than the name he bore. He had a pleasant voice, a plausible manner, and a gift of persuasive eloquence at times, which the average jury-man found it difficult to resist.

Now he set out his case with the lucid brevity which the occasion required, and with the voice and manner of one who dealt with matters beyond reasonable doubt, but which must yet be examined and proved in the patient way that the law required.

"It is possible," he concluded, "that a plea of unpremeditated violence which did not intend the full consequences which followed, perhaps under severe provocation, or even one of accident or of self-defence, may be put in.

"But when you have heard the evidence of those who witnessed the struggle, when you have considered the relative height and strength of the two men, and the fact that Alfred Cuthbertson made no effort for the rescue of the cousin he had thrown to this dreadful death, nor even to give information of what had happened, trusting evidently that the sea would retain the dead, or that it would be presumed that Thomas Birchall had come to an accidental end—when you consider these circumstances in the light of the fact that he had learned, a few hours before, and probably for the first time, that the man whom he now led to that fatal height was making love to his wife in his own house, I submit that you will have no difficulty in deciding to commit him on the more serious charge, remembering that jealousy can be no excuse for violence by English law."

He sat down for a moment after this effort of peroration, and then rose to call Sergeant Poole and the other witnesses, one by one to the box, to give formal evidence of arrest, of the finding of the body, and of the identification of the clothes and the contents of the pockets, which were now exhibited upon a small table in front of the magistrates' clerk.

This formal evidence being completed, with no reasonable doubt remaining as to the identity of the dead man, Sir Lionel Tipshift entered the box to give evidence as to the cause of death, and the injuries which, before that event or after, the body of Thomas Birchall had sustained.

The body, he said, was that of a well-nourished man of about thirty, five feet, four inches in height, probably not of the artisan class. Its condition rendered it impossible to state the cause of death with certainty. The back was broken, the skull fractured in two places, there was a compound fracture of the right tibia. Some, if not all, of these injuries might have occurred after death, and some certainly had. They were the natural result of the body being battered against the rocks by a high sea.

The one thing certain was that the man had not been drowned. He had been dead before he was engulfed by the water. The condition was in every way consistent with a fall from a great height, followed by being washed away by the sea. The body appeared to have been in the water four or five days. He mentioned that the appendix had been removed, probably within the last year.

Mr. Willerton, feeling that he was engaged in a somewhat perfunctory occupation, rose to cross-examine.

"The fact is that the body of this unfortunate man, whoever he may have been, was in such a condition that the cause of death cannot be ascertained?"

"Not absolutely. But there is no reasonable doubt."

"The only thing you can say definitely is that he was not drowned?"

"Much more than that. The great majority of causes of death could be ruled out."

"But many would still remain?"

"In theory, yes."

"It is difficult to say what injuries had been inflicted before death, and what after?"

"Some were certainly after death. Others were almost certainly before. It is true that the condition of the body renders it difficult to speak with absolute certainty on these points."

"Very well, now as to the time of death. Actually, it is as difficult to be precise as to the time, as the cause?"

"The body had been in the water for not less than four days. Death must have taken place before that."

"But it is impossible to say how long before?"

"With exactness, yes."

"Within a day?"

"It would be impossible to say with that degree of precision."

"Or two?"

"Possibly so."

Mr. Bullows whispered to the Chairman, who interposed: "Is it not a fact that Thomas Birchall is known to have been alive on Thursday morning?"

Mr. Bigland-Buffitt rose to say that that would be proved in due course.

Mr. Willerton said that that was not in dispute. He added, going further than he had intended upon the track which his instructions required: "He may be alive still."

Mr. Frampton remarked in a low whisper to Bigland-Buffitt that if that were the best card in Willerton's pack, they might consider his client already hanged.

Mr. Willerton sat down, and Sir Lionel Tipshift left the box, and the court.

Mr. Bigland-Buffitt rose to call his next witness, and was interrupted by Mr. Frampton, who had received a word from his clerk. It appeared that Mr. Eli Birchall had viewed the body, and was now available to give evidence. He wished to do so at once if possible, so that he might return to London by the afternoon train. The clerk had taken notes for counsel's guidance of the salient points of the evidence that Mr. Birchall would be prepared to give, and after a moment's consideration of these, Mr. Bigland-Buffitt decided to call him.

Eli Birchall appeared in the box, a man sparely built and still tall, though he stooped somewhat with the weight of his ninety years. In spite of that, he might have been taken to be twenty years younger, with good expectation of life to come. He was slightly deaf, and had a habit of raising his hand to his ear, but his faculties were otherwise unimpaired.

He said that he was the grandfather of Thomas Birchall, whose body he had seen in the last hour.

"You can identify him beyond doubt?"

"I suppose I should know my own grandson, shouldn't I? Didn't I give him the knife ten years ago?"

"I have no doubt that you did. And you swear that it is his body that you have seen?"

"Isn't that what I've just said?"

"Not precisely, though your meaning was plain enough."

Mr. Waites interposed to say that, if Mr. Willerton concurred, he proposed to treat that as an affirmative answer.

The examination continued.

"Mr. Alfred Cuthbertson is your grandson also?"

The old man turned his eyes in Alfred's direction. They showed no emotion. It seemed that age had deadened feeling, as sometimes, though not always, it will.

"Yes," he said, "he's another."

"Any other grandchildren?"

"Not that I've heard of."

"Any other near relatives?"

"Not that are living now."

"You are a gentleman, I believe, of considerable means?"

Mr. Birchall flushed with anger, showing that all emotions were not equally deadened. "You've no call to say that," he replied. "I daresay there's many meaner than me."

When it had been made clear that he had not been accused of being considerably mean, and the question was put again, he admitted, without enthusiasm, that he might have enough to last his time, or a bit more.

"In fact, for many years, you had been making an allowance to Thomas Birchall, on which he mainly subsisted?"

"On which he what? I helped a hard-working boy."

"And you made no similar allowance to Alfred Cuthbertson?"

"I suppose I can do what I like with my own cash? Alfred didn't ask, and he didn't need "

"So you may, of course," Mr. Bigland-Buffitt said soothingly. "And we may suppose that your testamentary dispositions would have continued to show your favour in the same direction?"

But this question proved to be another which Mr. Birchall was unable to hear properly, and it was an unfortunate circumstance that, when hearing or understanding failed, he was disposed to interpret remarks addressed to himself as being of an uncomplimentary character. To be accused of a testy disposition merely because he had made an allowance to his more deserving and more needy grandson, and had not considered it necessary to show similar generosity to one of whom he did not approve, appeared to him to be a violation both of politeness and reason, and his subsequent answers went far to justify an accusation which had not been made.

It was only after the exercise of much patience, and several oblique approaches to the question, that counsel was seeking to ask, that Mr. Birchall condescended to inform the court that he had, as yet, made no will, that being an occupation appropriate to severe illness, which he had not had, or old age, which he had not reached. Naturally, had he done so, he would have given Tom the preference, both as the better boy, and one who would not have wasted money in extravagant living.

Mr. Willerton cross-examined with caution. The answers which Mr. Birchall had given on the question of identification, as they stood, emphasized the recognition of the knife, which could not easily be disputed, rather than that of the body, which just possibly could, and which, in any case, he had been instructed to do.

To press the point further might lead to more definite assertions from the one relative who could speak with knowledge and presumable impartiality, and the position might become (if possible!) even worse than it now was.

But, apart from any question of tactical handling of a difficult witness, he was genuinely anxious, in his client's interest, to discover the truth. It was already certain, beyond more than a faint, almost fantastic doubt, that it was the body of Thomas Birchall which had been cast up by the sea. If that faint doubt, which would surely have occurred to no one had it not been suggested by the accused man, could be finally removed, he would insist on a different line of defence, while there might still be time to develop it to the best advantage, or withdraw from the case.

He therefore took the risk of pressing the witness further on this question, with the result that he obtained little more or less than the previous assertion. A man, Eli Birchall said, ought to know his own grandchild, if anyone did. Asked for any physical feature which he had been able to recognize, he could only mention the hair. It was Tom's hair. It was not a very convincing detail of recognition. Black hair, rather coarse in quality, and shortly cropped, is not an uncommon covering of the human head. But Mr. Willerton remembered that Mrs. Cuthbertson had spoken of the similarity of the hair also.

Mr. Birchall did not deny that the fact of the knife being in the dead man's pocket had materially assisted identification. Where else would Tom's knife be expected to be? In his mouth?

The grim jest moved the court to a stir of amusement, quickly suppressed. It might not be logical argument, but it seemed to many a fitting comment upon the line of defence which the questions indicated. Common sense said that it was Thomas Birchall's body; and Thomas Birchall's knife was where common sense would expect it to be.

The incident made Mr. Willerton additionally conscious of the futility of the contention that he had been instructed to raise; and as Eli Birchall withdrew from the witness box, and the prosecuting counsel rose to request the permission of the court that the witness should be released from further attendance on the usual conditions, he leaned over the dock, to ask his client whether he wished the question of identity to be further challenged.

Alfred Cuthbertson's reply showed irritation hardly suppressed. "Why," he said, "can't you see that he didn't recognize it at all?"

Mr. Willerton saw that his mind was unchanged, and that was clearly not the time or the place for further argument. For the moment, the question would not be likely to engage the further attention of the court. Mary Gilkins had entered the witness box.

Mrs. Gilkins was a very voluble witness. She had a tale to tell which she had already narrated, not only to the police, but many times to the admiration of breathless neighbours. Only her husband, a bricklayer of few words, and much readier blows, had refused to listen after the first hearing, saying that there would be less trouble in the world if she would learn to keep her trap shut, and that he would give her another clout if she went on while the oven burned.

Now, when her moment had come, with such an audience as she had never dreamed she would have until this event of supreme drama had come into her life, she did not require the help of the smooth skilled questions with which counsel will lead a witness gently forward upon the intended path. Rather, he must combine his efforts with those of the magistrates' clerk to hold her back sufficiently for the excited narrative to be taken down in the form which the depositions would ultimately require.

Mr. Willerton, as he listened, had a moment of better hope. He considered that, but for this woman's talk, there would have been no scandal at all. He understood that the other two witnesses of the alleged struggle, whatever they might be prepared to say now, had not been sufficiently disturbed by what they saw to take any action, or make any report upon it. But for the silent sombre evidence that the mortuary held, he might have thought that they dealt with no more than the chimera of an unstable brain. But, of course, there was the tale, equally fantastic in its own way, that the Cuthbertsons would have him believe.

He listened to a narrative blended of memory and imagination, and now petrified by many repetitions, and he saw that, if this witness could be discredited, he would have weakened the case for the prosecution at a vital point.

When his time came to cross-examine, he rose with some confidence.

"Now, Mrs. Gilkins," he began, "we have heard where you were on the path, and you have told us where the two gentlemen were when you saw them quarrelling. You were, in fact, about a quarter of a mile away?"

Mrs. Gilkins altered her manner, recognizing that the tone of the question was hostile. Was he going to call her a liar?

"I was where I said," she answered sullenly.

"Yes, I have no doubt that you were. You were about a quarter of a mile away." Inspector Reid passed a word along to Mr. Bigland-Buffitt, who rose to say that he understood that the distance was actually about 350 yards.

"Very well," Mr. Willerton went on, "I will accept that. You were about 350 yards away. You were, in fact, too distant to recognize Mr. Birchall, and if you knew Mr. Cuthbertson, it was because he came back and passed within a yard of where you were standing."

"I knew Mr. Cuthbertson."

"So I have said. There were two other people on the path at the time. Were they behind you, or in front?"

"They caught me up, and went past. They was walking quicker than me."

"Were they walking together or separately?"

"They was arm-in-arm. They was like lovers, as I should say."

"They were in front of you. They were arm-in-arm. How tall are you, Mrs. Gilkins?"

"I don't know what—"

"But I do. I must ask you to answer the question."

Mr. Waites looked at the witness. He thought himself a good judge of height. He said helpfully: "Shall we say about four-foot-six?"

Mr. Willerton said that would be near enough for him.

"The two people in front," he went on, "were probably taller than you?"

"I daresay as they was."

"And the path is narrow at that point?"

"I don't know what you're a-getting at," the witness broke out, in a tone of shrill excitability, "unless it's to make out as I didn't see what I saw, and with the poor man a-lying dead, as you may say, at the door!"

"I will tell you just what I am getting at. I am suggesting that you have exaggerated a very simple and trivial incident, and have used your imagination to fill up the gaps of what you only partially saw. I am suggesting that, but for this practically-invented tale, for which you are primarily responsible, no one would have connected Mr. Cuthbertson with the death of this unfortunate man whose body has been cast up by the sea, whoever he may be, or however he may have died. I am suggesting that, but for your too-lively imagination, none of us would be here today."

Sir George Hawler interposed: "We understand your contentions, Mr. Willerton, but would you please confine yourself for the present to questioning the witness? The time for speeches has not yet come."

"I beg your pardon, Sir George, but the witness asked what I was getting at, and I thought she was entitled to know."

Sir George's port-empurpled countenance took on a somewhat higher colour at this reply, which left him in doubt of whether he had listened to apology or rebuke. Being unable to determine this, he confined himself to enquiring: "Have you any further questions to ask Mr. Willerton?"

"If you please, Sir George. You have told us, Mrs. Gilkins, that you saw Mr. Cuthbertson throw some man whom you were unable to recognize over the cliff with yourself and two other people looking on. And after this surprising action you ask us to believe that Mr. Cuthbertson, seeing, if he had not noticed it before, that there were these spectators of what had happened, actually turned in your direction, and walked towards you, so that you are now able to identify him?"

"Well, that was what he did. I had to say what I saw. It was his way home."

"Of course it was. It was the natural way for him to take, after parting with Mr. Birchall, who went in the opposite direction, as he will tell the court in due course. But it would not have been so, if he had been engaged in a homicidal act. Do you realize, Mrs. Gilkins, that, from where you stood, he could have disappeared in a dozen yards, if he had desired to do so, by simply continuing on the path, as I am going to suggest that Mr. Birchall had actually done?"

Mrs. Gilkins did not answer this question directly. But she went to the root of the attack which was being made upon her veracity with an unexpected shrewdness in her reply: "When I said what I see'd, I didn't know as the body'd ever be washed ashore."

Mr. Willerton recognized that it must offset most of the effect which his cross-examination might have produced up to that point. That was the deadly fact that he had to face. The woman had said that she had seen Mr. Cuthbertson cast another man to his death. That man was certainly Thomas Birchall. And now a dead man, who his own grandfather had identified by that name, had been cast up by the sea. And if the Cuthbertsons' tale were to be brought out later, it would go far to support the accuracy of that which he challenged now.

110

But he gave no sign of these thoughts as he answered easily: "Well, unfortunately, dead men are often cast up on our English coast. It doesn't follow that anyone threw them in. And when you saw a man, as you say, fall over the cliff, it didn't occur to you to go to see if anything could be done to help him? You turned back to the town?"

"There was them there as had younger legs. You should ask them that."

"Well, perhaps I shall. I am asking you now."

"I thought I'd seen something as Sergeant Poole ought to know, and I went where he could be found."

Mr. Willerton sat down, not entirely satisfied that he had made the best of this cross-examination, but less inclined to blame himself than the difficult instructions he had received.

"Do you wish to re-examine?" Mr. Waites asked, looking to Mr. Bigland-Buffitt, who shook his head.

"There are two more witnesses to what occurred," he said, in a voice that might be addressed either to Mr. Frampton, or to a larger audience.

"Whom," Mr. Willerton commented boldly, "it will be very interesting to hear."

The magistrates meanwhile had been whispering among themselves, and the Chairman asked: "Do you wish to go further today, Mr. Bigland-Buffitt?"

"I have one witness that I should like to call."

"Then we will adjourn for forty minutes."

The magistrates left the bench, and the court became loud with the chatter of people whose hunger was not sharp enough to induce them to vacate places which they would not be likely to get again.

CHAPTER XXIV.

THE Osbury magistrates, not feeling it necessary to observe the precision of punctuality which they exacted from inferior mortals, were some minutes late in returning from lunch, and it was during the interval of waiting in the crowded court that Inspector Reid came in and reached over some intervening heads to pass a folded telegram to Mr. Frampton's clerk, who read it, and passed it to his principal, who read it also, and passed it to the learned counsel for the prosecution, who read it in turn, and then said to the prisoner's solicitor who was seated beside him: "Willerton, I think you ought to see this.

Mr. Willerton thanked him, and took the telegram. He read:

> Goldmans state that ready-made suit as described was bought at their store September Six, Nineteen-Thirty-Four, customer's name Birchall address not recorded.

Mr. Willerton read it, and smiled. "Ever given an old suit away, or do you prefer to bury them?" he enquired. "I should think most suits get outside the body of someone who didn't buy them before they come to their final end."

He thought that he had put the point rather neatly until Mr. Bigland-Buffitt said: "Body? That's just what seems unusual to me." After which he was not so sure.

He knew, in any case, that he had made no more than an academic debating point. The information the telegram gave made it about twice as unlikely as it had seemed previously that the dead man was any other than the Thomas Birchall who had walked out with Alfred Cuthbertson a week before, and whom three people would swear that they had seen hurled into the sea.

Against this cumulative evidence of identity; of what avail could it be to set up a defence fantastic in itself and which went to the very threshold of admitting the crime, and then to attempt to

112

avoid the logical deduction that the dead body supplied, by stubborn denial that it was that of the missing man? He saw, more certainly than before, that it was a defence doomed by its own weakness, however adroitly counsel might handle it when the trial came, and that it involved the almost fatal consequence of precluding any plea of accident, of provocation, or of self-defence, which a straightforward admission would have allowed. Was it likely that any able and experienced advocate, caring either for his own reputation or his client's welfare, would accept a brief so drawn? Certainly he must talk to Alfred Cuthbertson again—and to his wife, who seemed as sensible as she was loyal to a probably worthless man. But he remembered his resolution to consult his partner that afternoon, and, for the moment, he must turn his mind to other aspects of a difficult case, for the magistrates had returned, and a girl with a somewhat vacuous face was now entering the witness box.

Mr. Bigland-Buffitt had glanced at his brief before rising to examine the girl, and had read:

> Counsel will find that this witness is sullen and rather stupid. She has shown unwillingness to give evidence which may cause trouble to her mistress, and if this attitude can be brought out before the necessary admissions, as in her signed statement (copy herewith), have been obtained, the value of her evidence may be increased by the reluctance with which it is given.

She looked frightened and miserable as she stood facing the crowded court, but she took the oath in a very audible voice, and answered counsel's questions with nervous readiness.

Her name was Ethel Harding. She was eighteen last October. She had been housemaid at Highview House since her seventeenth birthday, the October before.

"Has it been a comfortable place?" Mr. Bigland-Buffitt asked, in his most casual and yet intimate voice The girl looked her surprise at a question so different from that which she had expected to hear, but answered readily: "Oh, yes, sir. Quite comfortable."

"You are not under notice to leave?"

"Oh, no, sir."

"Had you, on or before Monday, the sixth instant, any grievance against your mistress of any kind?"

The girl looked vacantly at him for a moment, her mind not following the introduction of a date into a question which was otherwise simple, and then said: "Against Mrs. Cuthbertson, sir? Oh, no, not at all."

"And on the evening of the sixth instant, had you been out, and did you return to Highview House at about seven o'clock?"

"Yes, sir. It was the Monday two weeks ago."

"And as you came in through the side gate, the dining room was lit up, and the curtain had not been drawn. Is that so?"

"Yes, sir; the mistress often has the lights on without drawing the curtains. Not till it's quite dark."

"And so you could see in?"

"Yes, sir. You can see in from the path."

"And will you tell the court just what you saw, in your own way?"

"I didn't look particular, sir. It was just what I saw as I walked in."

"And what was it you saw?"

"I didn't really see much, sir. Not to be sure."

Mr. Bigland-Buffitt maintained his suavity with a visible effort. He altered his approach to ask: "As to that, you have already made a statement to the police?"

"Yes, sir. They wrote it down. It wasn't what I saw. It was what they wanted to say."

"Indeed? We will come back to that. I suppose, since you signed the statement, you have discussed the matter with Mrs. Cuthbertson?"

"Yes, sir. Bertha told her the things that Inspector Reid had got me to say."

"And she spoke to you about them?"

"Yes, sir. She spoke to me this morning."

"And asked you to say that they weren't true?"

"She told me they wasn't true, if you mean that."

"But you must have known whether they were true. You knew what you had seen?"

"Not if she said I was wrong, sir."

"Not if she said you were wrong! We will come back to that. What else did Mrs. Cuthbertson say?"

"She told me to say that she's only told me to tell the truth."

There were some smiles at this somewhat ambiguous statement, and a quick laugh from the back of the court, that ceased abruptly as Sir George Hawler looked angrily in its direction.

The prosecuting counsel repeated the words with a slow emphasis which gave full value to the implication which they conveyed.

"And now," he asked, "after having had that admonition from your mistress, perhaps you will tell the court what you saw as you came up the path?"

"I thought I saw her kissing him, and the master came into the room."

"Kissing who?"

"Mr. Birchall."

"And after that?"

"I didn't see any more."

"Did Mr. Cuthbertson look angry?"

"Not as I saw."

"But you saw Mr. Birchall kissing your mistress as Mr. Cuthbertson entered?"

The girl had a fresh burst of tears as she replied: "I didn't ought to say that. It was what I said, but it wasn't true."

"It was what you 'thought' you saw?"

"Yes, but I know I was wrong now."

"The path goes very near to the lighted window?"

"It isn't far."

"About five yards?"

"It isn't far."

"You have nothing wrong with your eyes?"

"Not as I know of."

The learned counsel sat down, well content with the reluctant testimony he had obtained, and thinking it best not to return to the question of the statement which had been signed in Osbury Police Station, unless Mr. Willerton should oblige him to do so.

Mr. Willerton rose.

"Mrs. Cuthbertson talked this matter over with you this morning, after she heard that you had signed a statement at the police station?"

"Yes, sir."

"And she told you that you had been mistaken in what you thought you had seen?"

"Yes, sir."

"And you believed her?"

"Oh, yes, sir."

"But she told you that you must tell the truth, or whatever you thought to be the truth, when you came here?"

"Yes, sir. That was what I said, sir."

"Not exactly. But I have no doubt it was what you meant. You have Monday afternoons out, I believe?"

"Yes, sir, except the first in the month when—"

"Never mind that. When are you expected to get in?"

"I have to be back at seven."

"You don't like to be late?"

"No, sir. Cook's that cross if we are—"

"No doubt she is. Last Monday you were about ten minutes late?"

"It wasn't my fault, sir. It was because—"

"Never mind why. You were late, and in a great hurry to get in. Did you stop on the path to see what was going on in the lounge?"

"No, sir. I shouldn't ever do that."

"Of course you wouldn't. And the window would be visible for about half a dozen steps along the path?"

"Perhaps a bit more than that, sir."

"Well, say a dozen. All you could have seen even if you had been looking at the window the first second it came into view, was what went on while you took a few quick steps along the path?"

The girl, who had doubtless paused to see what she could of what, to her, must have appeared a surprising incident, hesitated in her reply. But she had already said that she was hurrying back, which was true, and repudiated the suggestion that she would spy on her mistress, which had been a natural denial to make. She could only answer: "Yes, sir. That was it."

Mr. Willerton picked up a copy of the statement which she had signed, which the courtesy of the prosecution had already placed in his hands. He read from it: "I saw Mr. Birchall and Mrs. Cuthbertson standing by the fireplace. I saw them embrace and kiss. As they did so, Mr. Cuthbertson was standing observing them at the door, on perceiving which Mrs. Cuthbertson pushed Mr. Birchall away."

He laid it down, and allowed a moment's pause, before saying: "Now, Miss Harding. I want you to think carefully before you answer. As your mistress told you, we want nothing but the truth. Nothing either more or less. I am going to suggest to you not only that that statement is untrue, but that it could not be true for a very obvious reason. It says that you saw your mistress and Mr. Birchall standing by the fireplace. The door is on the opposite side of the room. I suggest to you that it is impossible to see the door, or anyone standing near it, as you come up the path, that you could not, by any possibility, see both door and fireplace at the same time."

The girl looked so confused by this suggestion that it was evidently a new idea to her mind; and it was one to which a truthful answer was not easy to give. Could she say: "No, but if you walk over the grass, as I do when I see the room is lit up, you can see a good deal more"? She could find no better answer than: "I couldn't say about that, sir."

"No, I don't suppose you had thought of that. It shows how careful you should be before you let imagination get to work. Now we will come back to this statement. Do you often use such words as 'embrace,' 'observing,' 'perceiving'?"

"No, sir. I don't know as I do."

"In fact, whatever you may have said at the police station, whether it were accurate or not, it was something quite different from what was written down for you to sign?"

"Oh, yes, sir," the girl replied, with more sincerity in her voice than had been apparent in some of her previous answers, "it was quite different. I didn't make out very well what it all meant the way they twisted it round." Mr. Willerton felt that this reply, which was actually unfair to Inspector Reid, who had done no more than translate a colloquial statement into what he considered to be language more appropriate to the dignity of criminal proceedings, could not easily be improved, and moved instantly on to other ground.

"And now, Miss Harding, will you explain how you came to go to the police station at all? Did you tell them that you had evidence that you wished to give?"

"No, sir. I didn't want to say anything. It was Annie Gilkins did that."

"Annie who? Any relation to the Mrs. Gilkins who is sitting over there on the left?"

"Yes, sir. She's Mrs. Gilkins's Annie."

"So I supposed. The Gilkins family seem to have a good deal to do with the making up of these improbable tales. I believe Annie Gilkins is employed with you at Highview House?"

"Yes, sir. She's been kitchen maid since Dolly Bibbs left."

"And you said something to Annie Gilkins, and the next thing you knew, a tale had been taken to the police?"

"Yes, sir. She promised she wouldn't say a word to a living soul."

"I've no doubt she did. But some people aren't built that way. They find it easier to repeat all they hear, and perhaps a bit more. And I suppose when you tell a tale that you think no one will repeat, you are not quite as careful as you would be if you knew you'd be expected to come here and confirm it on oath?"

"No, sir, I expect not."

"You made as much of it as you could, and Annie Gilkins made it a lot more?"

"I daresay as she did." Mr. Willerton sat down at that, feeling grateful for the hint he had had from Dorothy during the luncheon interval as to the limited view of the lounge which could be obtained from the side drive, and feeling that if he went further he might fare worse. But Mr. Bigland-Buffitt was not equally content, and decided that the position could be improved by a few further questions.

"Just a moment, Miss Harding. I am sure that you are trying to tell the truth in a rather difficult situation, and I must remind you that you are under oath, and must not allow any sympathy for your mistress, nor any thought of possible consequences, to influence you in what you say. When you talked to Annie Gilkins, you have told us that you had no grievance against your mistress, and I suppose you didn't mean to do anyone any harm? You were just gossiping about what you had seen?"

"Yes, sir, it was just talk."

"Something you had just seen, at which you were surprised and excited, so that it wasn't easy to keep to yourself? But when the police asked you about it, you saw that it might make trouble, and wished you'd never mentioned it?"

"Yes, sir. Of course I shouldn't if I'd have known how Annie'd tell."

"So that you wished to say as little to the police as you could?"

"Yes, sir, I didn't want to say anything."

"And in spite of not wanting to say anything, you did tell them that you had seen your mistress in Mr. Birchall's arms when Mr. Cuthbertson entered the room?"

The girl looked at him miserably, and, as the reply paused, Mr. Bigland-Buffitt added: "Perhaps silence is a sufficient answer."

He felt that he had had the best of the legal duel, as Ethel Harding was at last permitted to leave the box.

CHAPTER XXV.

AS Ethel Harding left the box, Mr. Bigland-Buffitt rose to say that that was as far as he was able to take the case, his further witnesses not being available.

He would be ready to go on, at the convenience of the magistrates, on Thursday or any subsequent day.

Sir George Hawler engaged in a consultation with his colleagues, after which he said that it was evidently desirable that the case should be completed as promptly as possible, and they would arrange to sit again on Thursday, as Mr. Bigland-Buffitt desired.

Mr. Willerton rose to suggest that a week's adjournment at this stage might be more generally convenient, and would allow him more time to prepare his defence. He mentioned that he had only been instructed late on Saturday night.

Sir George appeared to be about to assent, when Mr. Waites rose from his place, and said something to him, of which "the date of the Assizes" was clearly audible at the reporters' table.

"I think we must continue on Thursday, Mr. Willerton," Sir George then said. "It is difficult to see how you can be prejudiced by the case for the prosecution being completed as promptly as possible. Of course, if you should desire an adjournment subsequently—if you should desire to resist a committal—but in a case such as this, where the—"

The conclusion became inaudible as Mr. Waites moved restlessly, with a rustling of papers in the seat under the high desk from which the magistrates looked down on the crowded court. Sir George Hawler knew it for a warning from the experienced lawyer below him that he was on the verge of a probable indiscretion, and he knew that the consequences had been unpleasant when he had disregarded it on previous occasions. (Yet why not point out the obvious fact that the homicidal bounder was certain to be committed for trial, which must be plain from the evidence of the witnesses already heard?)

His words fell to an inarticulate mumble, and Mr. Willerton, having no valid argument to urge in reply, and seeing that Mr. Waites was not disposed to assist his plea for a longer adjournment, had the sense to give way without further words. He said only: "Thank you, Sir George," as the Chairman went on: "The court stands adjourned until 10:30 A.M. on Thursday next, the—yes, thank you, Mr. Waites, the 23rd instant." He rose as he spoke, and withdrew with his two colleagues, while the little crowded court woke into a hum of voices, and a rustle of people jostling in the narrow gangway, or lingering to watch the faces or catch the words of the principals in a play, the first act of which had been so satisfactory in its suggestions of greater drama to come.

Mr. Willerton leaned over the dock to say with a cheerfulness more professional than spontaneous, that they hadn't done so badly for the first round, and that he would arrange to see his client again tomorrow. With an impulse of more genuine friendliness, he spoke to Mrs. Cuthbertson in the same hopeful tone, and gave her also the expectation that he would be ready for a further consultation on the following day; after which he hurried back to the offices of the firm, where he found that his senior partner had returned from his week-end absence.

Mr. Soome was one of those men whom the years do not decay but rather dry up, like some species of fruit, into a state of permanent preservation. His age might be anything between sixty and eighty years. His acquaintances—it was not observable that he had any friends—did not think of him either as old or young. Those of sufficient years to remember his youth were not conscious of any radical change. He had always been small, active, and lean. Now his eyes were as alert, his step as quick as his wits, and no one had yet suggested that his mind was a failing power.

At no time of life had he been embarrassed by the softer emotions. His virtues were probity and truth. His vices, avarice and a callous disregard for the consequences of that which might be done in a legal way. He was scrupulous of methods rather than of results. He was a good criminal lawyer, having a combative spirit, and an intellect that was cool and clear.

He had a well-founded confidence in the abilities of his junior partner, and now listened to the account of the case which the week-end had brought into the office with few interruptions, and those of an elucidatory rather than a critical character.

In the end, he complimented him upon the energy and skill with which he had handled a difficult defence up to that point, and declined to take it out of the hands of the younger man, though it was customary for him to handle the criminal business of the firm.

He declined also to express an opinion as to whether the accused novelist were wise or foolish in pressing for the defence to concentrate on challenging the identity of the body.

"I don't see how you can say that yet," he remarked. "He's the one man who knows for certain what happened on the cliff, and you can't trust what he says. You can't judge the line of defence that it's best to take till you hear what the other two witnesses have to say. It's a wild idea, but it may be the only chance that he's got. Of course, it's rubbish, but a clever criminal lawyer—say Romford or Willis-Jones—might bamboozle a jury with it successfully, if they had a weak judge. Birchall changed his clothes, and a tramp picked them up! Rotten nonsense, but it's just the sort of idea that might get half a million people signing a petition for a reprieve. By the way, what about costs?"

"I haven't mentioned them yet. It's evident that there's not much money about at the moment, from the conspiracy in which they say they were engaged. As a matter of fact, I know one or two tradesmen have been getting rather restless lately. Portsby consulted me for one, and, the Cuthbertsons being clients of ours, I told him to see what another call would do, but we should have been issuing a writ if Mrs. Cuthbertson hadn't sent him a cheque on the next day."

"Well, that's likely enough. But you can talk it over with Cuthbertson tomorrow. He'll have to pay to get out of this mess, if he ever does. But you'll find he'll dig it up somewhere. They always do, when it's a question of life or death. It's the kind of case that ought to bring £1,000 into the office before it's done, and there'll be counsel's fees to provide, which will make it a lot more, if he wants us to get one of the best men.

"Well, I'll see what I can do. There must be some value in Highview House. Cuthbertson put up nearly £2,000 when it was bought, and it wasn't a bad price."

"Well, there's something in that. But I don't propose to be paid with a second charge. He should use that with the bank. He's sure to be a good deal overdrawn, and they might let him have a bit, if they thought that they could get covered that way for what they've already found.

"And there's another thing. Whether he's got himself in this mess to sell his books, or because Birchall made love to his wife, or with the two motives a bit mixed, it doesn't alter the fact that it ought to bring him some good sales. You'll find the trouble there is that the publishers don't reckon to pay till about six months after they've made their own scoop. Still, you could take an assignment for what it's worth.

"But it's the press you must tell him to look to, if his other resources fail. The tale you've told me ought to be worth four figures if they sell it exclusively to one of the Sunday papers before Mrs. Cuthbertson gets into the box. Tell her not to give any interviews till she's consulted with you. She'd better refer any reporters here. Save her trouble, and we should fix up better terms than she'd be likely to do.

"And you would get almost any amount for a complete story from Cuthbertson's own pen, if he undertakes that it shall be written without reserve. 'Novelist caught in his own net!' You know the kind of headlines that it would make. But he wouldn't be expected to write that before the conviction. And there might be a stipulation that it shouldn't be published till after the date fixed for the execution, if it might prejudice a reprieve."

"You think a conviction's certain?"

"Nothing's certain in law. I think he's guilty, if you mean that. It's common sense. But of course that's only between ourselves. He's Frampton's murderer, and our innocent client; and it's our business to make Frampton feel as sick as we can. As to that, I should say you've done well enough for the first day."

CHAPTER XXVI.

BEFORE interviewing his client on Tuesday morning, Mr. Willerton had a further talk with Mr. Soome, who had now had the benefit of the very full reports of the first day's proceedings which had appeared in the evening and morning papers, and having had time to consider the unusual features that the case presented, he said frankly that he had altered his opinion during the night.

"I said that that talk about the body being someone else who was obliging enough to get himself drowned in Birchall's clothes, after Cuthbertson had either been seen to throw him over the cliff, or pretend to do so, if that's the version that you prefer, was all bunkum, and so it is. But there's one possibility that we oughtn't to overlook, in which case it would be next door to the truth.

"Take this publicity plot to have been genuine enough, and allow that Cuthbertson took his wife and Birchall into his confidence as far as he was obliged, it doesn't follow that he hadn't another card to play that he didn't turn up for them—or at least for both of them—to see.

"Suppose the corpse to have been part of the plot, which was to round it off into the sensation that it is now becoming? Cuthbertson doesn't tell his wife of this, seeing that it will be simpler for her if she only knows it as far as he had to explain to get her help. He'd presumably have to let Birchall know a bit more to get the suit and the things that the pockets held, unless, of course, he pilfered them out of his cousin's flat.

"If that were the case, he naturally wants you to take that line of defence, which will justify itself—and, of course, him, when Birchall decides that the right moment had come to stroll into the court."

Mr. Willerton heard this theory with the attention due to his partner's reputation, but with a very sceptical mind.

"I don't say it's impossible," he replied, "but in the first place, how would he get hold of such a very suitable corpse? And the letter in the pocket—is it what he would have selected for purposes of identification? The knife was a more evident choice."

"Of course," Mr. Soome replied, "it's not a probable theory, and getting hold of a corpse of the right kind, and then planting it on the spot, are about as difficult as anything could possibly be. But for all that, I shouldn't lose sight of the possibility. You've got to keep in mind that we're not dealing with an ordinary man. He's one who makes a living by thinking out improbable complications of crime. And, on his own account, this thing begins in just such an ingenious plot; and he takes you into his confidence half the way, and insists, beyond that, and against reason as it appears, that it isn't Birchall's body that's been fished out of the sea. It's so improbable that it's an absolutely silly defence, unless he knows that it's true.

"And, as to the letter, wouldn't it be natural to put more than one thing in the pockets that would be absolutely certain means of identification? As a matter of fact, it was that point which set me thinking on these lines. Two things only—a letter and an engraved knife. There might have been a dozen things, and yet nothing that could be connected so certainly with the missing man. And wouldn't Birchall, if he had really been pitched into the sea, have had his pockets fuller than that?"

"Most likely he would. But there's no argument in that, one way or other, because it was only the trouser pockets, and the left-hand jacket pocket, that were recovered. The right-hand pocket, and breast-pocket, and, in fact, the whole of the right-hand side of the jacket, had been torn away."

"Well," Mr. Soome replied, "there's a point there. And, of course, some of the things may have fallen out of the trousers pockets. I'm not wedded to any theory. But you shall insist on Cuthbertson telling you all the facts, as far as he knows them. If he wriggles at that, you can bet your last fiver that you're defending a guilty man. But whatever else you do, don't forget that it isn't a case we can defend unless he's ready to grease the wheels."

Mr. Willerton said that he would keep that point prominently in mind, and was about to leave for the purpose of interviewing Mr. Cuthbertson when he was stayed by the announcement that there was a trunk call coming through for him from London; and next moment he learned that he had put himself to needless trouble the night before when he had rung up Mrs. Cuthbertson to ask her to refer the press to himself, for the representative of the *Sunday Record* had required no prompting to enable him to see the advantages that might follow from an understanding with the solicitors of the arrested man.

"Mr. Willerton," came the politely urgent voice of the reporter whose stubborn persistence had secured the scoop of the previous Sunday, "I hope you won't mind me ringing you up, but I can't get to Osbury before seven tonight. I hoped you'd ask Mrs. Cuthbertson not to talk to anyone else till you've heard the offer we are prepared to make. I can see you about that tonight, if it won't be too late when I arrive, or else first thing in the morning."

"Well," Mr. Willerton said reasonably, "if you've got an offer to make, I can hear it now, before I see Mrs. Cuthbertson."

"I'm sorry, Mr. Willerton, but I ought to speak to the editor first. It's no more than formality in this instance, I can assure you of that. I'll bring you down an offer tonight that even the *Sunday Pail* wouldn't be likely to make. But it's not a matter that can be discussed on the telephone. All I ask now is that you won't fix anything up, or give anything away till I arrive."

"I don't mind promising that. You're first in coming to us, and we'll wait till 10:30 tomorrow morning before closing in any other direction."

Mr. Willerton felt that he had ended the conversation when he said that, and would have rung off, but the objection which the *Sunday Record*'s reporter felt to discussing such matters by telephone did not prevent him asking a further question.

"And, oh, I say, Mr. Willerton, could you tell me just one thing more? Are you serious in suggesting that the body may not be that of Thomas Birchall? Do you say that he's alive still?"

"Don't you think we'd better leave such questions till you're able to put your proposition before us?"

"Yes, of course, I see what you mean. But if you could just tell me that, I might be able to make a better offer than I otherwise shall. I only want it to tell the editor at the conference this afternoon."

"Well, you heard what I said in court yesterday. It isn't a suggestion we should be likely to put forward if we weren't serious!"

"Thank you, sir. That's quite enough. You'll see me tomorrow morning, probably by 10:25."

The cheerful voice ceased, and Mr. Willerton rang up Mrs. Cuthbertson, nominally to say that he was about to visit her husband, but really to impress upon her again that all reporters should be turned over to him

She replied, in a voice which showed the nervous tension under which she was enduring the slow hours of the day: "Oh, you needn't fear that I shan't do that. I'm only too glad. Bertha's sent four of them away already this morning. Three-thirty this afternoon? Yes, of course I'll come. Any time will be convenient to me."

CHAPTER XXVII.

MR. WILLERTON'S interview with the accused author was inconclusive, mutually irritating, and unsatisfactory.

Alfred Cuthbertson, who seemed to be in a state of maddened exasperation at the position in which he had been placed by his own deliberate folly, if not his crime, would neither recede from the position he had taken up on the previous day, nor would he take his solicitor into the fuller confidence which was urged upon him.

He persisted that, after a pretended struggle, which had followed the lines previously agreed and rehearsed, he had seen his cousin walk safely and swiftly away by a path which bent obliquely from the cliff edge, to which he had no cause to return. Was it likely, he asked, that the man who had played at being cast into the sea should return to drown himself in earnest at a later hour? Mr. Willerton agreed that the improbability was extreme, though his own deduction from the fact of that improbability was not one that his client would admit to have occurred.

Mr. Willerton reflected that all murderers were probably the same in that they would decline to acknowledge their guilt to their own advisers, thinking that denial should not begin farther away than themselves.

But when Alfred Cuthbertson reiterated that it could not therefore be Birchall's body, Mr. Willerton was cold in his response, recognizing that, while he doubted premises that he could not discuss, it was a waste of words to debate deductions that were based upon them.

He turned the subject to the question of costs, and faced a client whose temper was obviously on the verge of an uncontrollable explosion.

"Good God!" he exclaimed, "can't you leave such questions till you've done something worth making out a bill for? Why it's scarcely three days since the ghastly business began!

"Can't you wait till the job's done? I suppose I shall be able to pay my debts, as I always have. Or are you meaning to hint that I really did throw Tom Birchall over the cliff? Do you think that I shall end up in the condemned cell? And am I to pay in advance because you can't do better for me than that?

"Counsel's fees? That's looking a bit ahead, isn't it? I tell you, Tom may turn up any day now, and the whole thing will explode at once.

"You can't have any expenses yet that a ten-pound note wouldn't more than square. And what can I do about funds while I'm trapped here? Even a Jew could see that! I beg your pardon, Willerton. I didn't mean to be rude. And I don't suppose it's you. It's that skinflint Soome! But if you must have some cash, you'll have to ask Mrs. Cuthbertson, and she'll have to see the bank.

"I shouldn't think Duckfield will refuse what's required, when he knows what an infernal jam I'm in now. Anyway, you must please talk it over with her."

It was not a task that Mr. Willerton was willing to undertake. He had a confusion of feelings, half-resenting Alfred Cuthbertson's tone and manner, and half-sympathizing with him, and wishing that Soome had done this part of the business himself. But it is likely that he would have refused to continue to act in the case unless his client adopted a different attitude, had he not reminded himself of the probability that there would be funds to come from the *Sunday Record*, the destination of which could now be discussed with Mrs. Cuthbertson on her husband's authority, even if she were not entitled to allocate them on her own, that being a point he could not resolve till the nature of the offer should be disclosed.

CHAPTER XXVIII.

IN the afternoon, Dorothy drove to Soome & Co.'s office, it not being the etiquette of the profession (which has changed with the years) to visit even their lady clients during office hours, except when they are placed in the unfortunate position which her husband was now experiencing.

She was careful not to look either right or left as she drove through streets where she had been accustomed to the exchange of frequent greetings of friendly or formal kinds, keeping her eyes on the steering wheel and the road ahead, where they should normally be. For the fact was that a bad night had been followed by a worse morning, and she was in a mood to rebuff the advances even of genuine friendship, had the opportunity arisen, of which she had not yet had any recognizable experience.

It was not surprising that she had slept badly, nor that Alfred's idea—real or professed—that it was not Tom's body that had been cast up by the sea, could be seen in its naked improbability in the hopeless hours of the dark.

She told herself twenty times that they were facing that which they had deliberately planned, and which could not fail to bring the rich harvest of sales which Alfred had so clearly foreseen. Beyond that, it was no more than a nightmare of broken nerves which would disappear when Tom should return with the tale they had arranged at the first—that he had seen the papers, and hurried back. Or he might wire when he learned the sinister, unbelievable development which had occurred. There might be a telegram in the morning. So she told herself, but without belief. In her heart she knew she imagined that which would never come. For the nightmare in which she lay was one that would not dissolve with the waking hours, and there would still be that ghastly horror that the mortuary held.

It was an incredible, impossible thing, in which the wild folly that they had planned was so blended with its unthought-of sequel that it was hard to realize where fact ended and nightmare horror began.

It was as though they had raised a spirit which had proved to be beyond their control in sinister, unforeseeable ways, as though they had planted a simple seed which had risen in normal growth, and then broken into a poisonous, impossible flower. She told herself, as she lay through the wakeful hours, that she was caught in a hateful dream, from which she must surely wake to the sane security of the life she knew. But the plot with Tom was no dream. Where did reality and illusion meet? It was no dream, as she knew. The faint light of dawn showed in the sky through the open window. She heard the voices of early birds. She slept at last, as those will do who have lain awake through the darker hours.

She rose late. There was no note of discord until breakfast had been served, and as she ate with the appetite of youth and health, which does not easily fail, the telephone rang. Bertha answered it, in the usual routine, and came into the room to say, in her toneless, respectful voice: "It's the fishmongers, madam. They want to know if they can have a cheque if they send up." That was to be the first of a series of more or less similar episodes. The butcher, Portsby, was sorry that he would not be able to make further deliveries until his account had been settled to date. The rate-collector called, and talked of the necessity of issuing a summons unless he had a cheque by first post tomorrow. (But she had been expecting trouble about the rates.)

She met these minor annoyances in her usual resolute spirit. She told Bertha to tell the fishmongers that there was no need to send up. They would have a cheque during the week. (How, in any case, could a cheque have been signed when Alfred was not at home?) She went to the telephone herself to deal with Portsby, and reminded him, with some sharpness, of the £25 which he had had from her ten days before. He said: "Sorry madam, but there's a good bit still on the books," and she answered: "Well, there won't ever be any more."

After that, she rang up Morton, the rival butcher, who had been trying to get the account ever since they settled in Osbury, and gave an order which he did not refuse to take.

She saw the rate-collector, spoke to him frankly of that which he must already know, found him to be respectfully sympathetic, and received a helpful suggestion that if he could have a cheque dated a fortnight ahead, the threatened proceedings could be delayed for that period.

But she had had worse things than these to endure from acquaintances actuated by malice, curiosity, or mere stupidity, who
rang up on half a dozen pretexts, but all with the common object of
discussing the sudden shadow which had fallen across her life. And
this, she thought bitterly, was the publicity at which they had deliberately aimed, and of which Alfred had so lightly talked!

There had been Mrs. Ransom, who had kindly offered her a few
days' hospitality, "to give her time to look round," because she
could understand "how terrible it must be to have to stay in that
man's house."

That had been followed by a ring from Miss Jenkinson, who
had tried to cheer her by pointing out what a blessing it was that it
had been a childless marriage, and that there would be no future
generation to bear a dishonoured name.

Then there had been Mrs. Willoughby from the Cedars on the
other side of the hill, who had called with some pretext of reason,
though at an unusual hour, and had seemed comparatively tactful in
her sympathy, till she had made a remark showing that she shared
what was no doubt a general assumption, that Dorothy's lover had
died at the hands of a jealous husband, to whom she had been un-
faithful before, and whom she must now regard with a doubled hatred.

CHAPTER XXIX.

MR. WILLERTON received her with his usual courtesy. He said with truth that he was glad to see her. She had given him the impression of having both sense and character, and he thought that a further talk with her might be more fruitful than that which he had had earlier in the day with the accused man.

He had resolved what he would say before she arrived, but he found that it would be his part to listen to a woman who was evidently nearer the edge of hysteria than he had expected to see her.

"Mr. Willerton," she began, "I don't know what Alfred may have said to you this morning, but I want to ask you two things.

"The first is that you will push this case on as fast as you possibly can. I want you to get me into the witness box the first moment you can—on Thursday if possible, or else the next day. I want people to hear something that's really true for a change, and of course Alfred must do the same. I suppose he really ought to give evidence first, but you'll know best about that. If we don't do anything more, we can clear up this nonsense about me being fond of Tom."

"Well," Mr. Willerton admitted, "there'd be something gained if you could do that. One suggestion of motive would disappear. Of course, it would weigh with most people that you still stand by your husband and don't appear to regret Birchall's death. And when you've both told how the whole thing began— But I can't say that Mr. Cuthbertson is in any hurry for it to come out. Perhaps you can understand it, from his point of view, if he's really got any hope, however faint, that his cousin will turn up alive.

"As to that, we must judge according to whether we believe what he says, that everything went as you'd first planned that it would.

"But as to this idea of you having been in love with Birchall, are you sure that he didn't attempt that very slight familiarity that occurred with your husband's consent? Are you sure that it wasn't part of the plot, which may not have been told to you, that there should have been an apparent motive of jealousy for what Mr. Cuthbertson was to appear to do? Accepting everything that you say, it still seems hard to decide where the fake ends, and the reality starts."

"Yes," she said, in a quieter voice than she had spoken before, "I see what you mean. I get the same doubt myself. I lay awake all night trying to sort it out so that it would make sense, till I thought I was going mad. But I don't see how they could have planned that, unless they knew we should be seen from the path."

"You don't think your husband arranged for Ethel Harding to be outside, or to say what she did?"

"No, I don't. I don't think that part of it was meant at all. But, anyway, I want to get where I can tell the truth to everybody at once, and if they don't believe what I say—"

"Yes. I can understand how you feel. It's not a line of defence that any lawyer would like, but if it's got to be that, it's no use wobbling; and to a certain point—indeed, as far as your evidence goes—I think you will convince most people that you are a truthful witness. What's the other thing that you were wanting to ask?"

"I want you to tell me the best way to get some money, if possible without asking the bank."

"It is a subject I was going to bring up myself, though I was sorry to worry you about it. But I suppose you know that a case of this kind involves a good deal of expenditure. In fact, Mr. Cuthbertson asked me to discuss it with you this afternoon."

"It was good of Alfred to think of that. I hadn't thought about costs, but I expect he guessed that I should be running short for the home. I want about £200 to clear up all the pressing things—it seems that everyone's going to be pressing now."

Mr. Willerton avoided the question of Alfred's kindness. He said: "There'll be a much larger sum needed than that, but I don't see why we shouldn't arrange them both at the same time. You haven't seen any reporters yet? Not to give them an interview, I mean?"

"No, I promised you that I wouldn't, and I should have refused, whether or not. I told Bertha to cut them off if they ring up, without troubling to tell me; and to say I am not at home, and refer them to you, when they come to the door. There've been about six this morning, and one man—I think he was from the *Lantern*—got through the hedge after Bertha sent him away, and took a snapshot of me in the lounge. They've been photographing the house all the time."

"Well, you can't help that, but I don't want you to say anything to anyone till I've seen the representative of the *Sunday Record* tomorrow morning. He says they'll make a better offer than we're likely to get elsewhere."

"Offer of what?"

"Of money, of course. If you don't go into the witness box on Thursday, you might give them a good deal to print on Sunday which would be absolutely new to the public, and worth a large sum. Of course, it's risky, but they think it's worthwhile, even if they get fined now and then for contempt, and they're very skilful in going close to the edge without falling in. They won't comment on the case, but they'll publish an interview with yourself. At least that's what I suppose they'll offer to do."

"Well," she said bitterly, "I don't see why I should refuse. It's what Alfred aimed at, I suppose. Indeed, I shall be rather glad, if they won't print things that I don't say."

"You can rely upon us to protect you from that."

"Then I'll leave it with you to arrange. I'm going to the police station again now. They're very good about letting me see Alfred, but it's not much satisfaction with a space between us, and someone else always about. If only I could have a talk to him really alone!"

"I'm afraid they won't let you do that."

"It's a barbarous custom."

"I suppose it is. It's possible to defend it on certain grounds. They are about as logical as putting a man in jail to prevent him stealing, and even that may be defended under some circumstances. It's one of our modern improvements of procedure. But there's another matter about which I want to ask you while you're here. I want to know whether there's corroboration of any kind to this story of a plot to fake an appearance of murdering Birchall—I mean is there any independent evidence beside that of Mr. Cuthbertson and yourself? You see, it's a dangerous line of defence to take at the best, because it goes so near to admitting the whole thing; but if we set it up and are not believed, we should go, so to speak, straight down the drain."

"I'm afraid I can't think of any. You see, from the very nature of the scheme, it was essential to keep it as secret as we possibly could."

"Do you think Birchall may have told anyone? He must have had the idea in his head for about a month, and he had to make arrangements for being away."

"I can't say, of course. But I think it unlikely. He promised not to, most definitely. I don't say that that would have been certain to hold him back, if he'd had any reason for breaking faith, but why should he? And who would he have told? I never knew a man who had so few friends. It was just the same when he was—what you'd call running after me two or three years ago, and I was trying to make him see that I disliked him so much that it wasn't easy to be polite. Not that I succeeded in doing that. He was clever enough in some ways, but in others he had the densest head, as well as the thickest skin, that I ever met. But I'm getting wide of the point. I know he hadn't made many friends since, because he told us that no one would notice if he disappeared, unless we advertised it ourselves."

"He said that, did he?" Mr. Willerton became thoughtful. "I shouldn't mention that, if I were you. It might be taken in the wrong way. But if you can't think of anything or anyone who might corroborate your own tale—well, we must do without it as best we can; but I do ask you to try, because it might make all the difference in the end. The single straw turns the scale."

Dorothy was silent for a few moments, and the solicitor, seeing her hesitate on the verge of speech, waited without interruption, until she said: "There was one thing I meant to mention, and you've brought it back to my mind. I don't suppose it will give you what you want in the least, but I can't say it won't, and I thought it might be of use in another way."

"You'd better tell me, whatever it is. It can't do any harm for me to know."

"As a matter of fact, I did tell you. But it was only incidentally, and I don't suppose you gave it two thoughts, which might have been more than it's worth. But you'll remember that after that evening incident that they're trying to make so much of, which occurred at a few minutes after seven, Tom went out to the post office to send a telegram.

"It was because he wanted to get out to do that before dinner that I tried to ask him the favour I'd promised Alfred rather abruptly, and I've thought since that he may have misunderstood me in a— well, in a very thick-headed way. At least, I didn't quite mean to say that. I don't want to say unkind things about him now he's—at least, if he's dead. But I thought the fact that he did go out to send it—that he went at once, so that he was back, as Bertha knows, for dinner at half-past seven—rather shows that there wasn't anything serious in the incident in the way they've tried to get Ethel to make out."

Mr. Willerton listened patiently to this somewhat rambling statement, content that, the more freely she talked, the more certain she would be not to omit anything that it might be important for him to know. He said, as her narrative paused: "You mean that his mind was less occupied with yourself than in getting his telegram off that night, and that whatever happened between you and him, and which Mr. Cuthbertson oversaw, wasn't important enough, either in itself or its consequences, to divert him from doing that? Well, there may be a point there. But the telegram shows there was someone he was keeping in touch with somewhere, unless it were something to do with his business deal. I suppose you've no idea who it was to?"

"Not the least. I can only tell you that he wasn't willing to send it by telephone, or even for one of the maids to take it, so I thought it was something of a private character—something he didn't want us to know."

"You know nothing of it beyond that?"

"Nothing at all. But I got an idea somehow that it was because we had put off the date for a week because the publication of the *Twisted Spoon* was delayed, that he wanted to get it off in a hurry that night. I suppose there's no way of finding out what the telegram

"Yes, that's possible, but not without the prosecution knowing. It's a matter that the police should deal with. If we apply to the Postmaster-General for the telegram to be produced in the interests of justice, he won't refuse, if the application be made in the right way. But we've got to risk whatever it may disclose.

"I mean, we can't look at it and then put it back without anyone knowing, if we don't like what it says. Are you prepared to risk that?"

"Yes. I think so. Unless you advise differently. I don't suppose it will help us, but there's no saying, and I don't see how it can possibly be anything which could do us harm."

Mr. Willerton felt somewhat less certain of that, but he felt also that the position in which they stood was so bad that it justified more hazard than he would have taken had he been established on stronger ground.

"If you're willing to take the risk," he said, "I shall prefer to do it in such a way as to show that we want all the truth, being confident that we have nothing to fear. I shall ask the prosecution to have it produced. And now, if you'll excuse me, there's a coast guard officer been waiting for half an hour, from whom I want to get some information about the tides and currents along the coast. I don't want you to hope anything from that. It's just a matter of checking up wherever we can. And after I've seen him I shall try to get in touch with Frampton about this telegram before he leaves for the night."

CHAPTER XXX.

MR. FRAMPTON was actually putting on his coat to leave when a call came through from Soome & Co.'s office, asking if he could see Mr. Willerton conveniently, if he should be over in five minutes, on which he took it off, and said that he should be pleased to meet him.

He found time during that short interval to stroll into his partner's office.

"Willerton's on the way here," he said. "I expect he wants to put it to us that they'll admit that Cuthbertson did him in, if we'll agree to reduce the charge."

"Yes," Mr. Waites agreed, "I should call that a good guess. He's talked it over with Soome, and the old man's too wily to let him run on the rocks. Soome's just as quick to see that there's no way through as to spot any there is."

"Well, the question is, what ought we to say?"

Mr. Frampton was disposed to defer to his partner's opinion, recognizing that he had approached the case from a different angle, and with more impartiality than he had been able to do.

They both regarded it as a matter to be decided in their own office, rather than by the bench of magistrates whose comparative incompetence was too obvious to have ever needed explicit mention between them.

"I should say," the magistrates' clerk answered, "that it depends upon whether he's telling the truth now, and what defence he intends to set up.

"If he'd gone on the line of denying everything, and persisting that a strange body had got into Birchall's clothes, he'd have been convicted on the capital charge, and possibly had a reprieve on the theory of provocation, and other grounds, and ended with being a public charge for the next fifteen years.

"But if he's got the sense to face the court with a plausible tale that has enough truth in it to go down, you'll find murder's more than you'll get any jury to stand for. It'll be manslaughter in the end, and anything between five years and ten.

"Willerton's straight enough, and if he tells us that they're dropping the nonsense about dead men getting into each other's clothes, or whatever it is, and admit that there was a quarrel about the wife that came to blows in the end, in the course of which Birchall went over the edge, I think you might go so far as to say that, whatever the committal may be, we shan't press for a conviction on the capital charge.

"You see there's one point that's bound to weigh with a jury, if they have it put to them on the right lines. A man doesn't usually commit a premeditated murder with a little crowd looking on. Not if he's a sane man, as Cuthbertson almost certainly is."

"He might even get an acquittal from some juries on that ground," Mr. Frampton considered.

"I don't think he would. Not if you brief Jackson-Hicks, or perhaps Moole would be even better than him. There's the fact that Cuthbertson doesn't appear to have been in any hurry to quarrel, though it's clear that he knew what was going on. He didn't throw Birchall out of the house, as most men would have done—and some of us with the woman following him down the steps. He asks him to go out for the day—just the two men—and comes back alone with a tale that his cousin has left for London. It doesn't sound overwell when it's put like that."

"No. Perhaps not," Mr. Frampton said doubtfully. He rather wished that Willerton would have gone on with that silly denial that Birchall was drowned at all. It would have been a walkover for the prosecution then. But the significance of his coming over for a conference was too plain to be misunderstood. He added: "I believe that's him now."

He went back to his own room, into which Mr. Willerton was shown a moment later.

"Sit down, Willerton," he said genially; "I'm glad you caught me before I left. I suppose it's a safe guess that it's the Cuthbertson case that brought you over?"

"Yes, there's a little matter in which I thought you might be able to help. It may lead to nothing, but we want to get hold of all the facts about Birchall we can."

"Well," Mr. Frampton replied, supposing that Mr. Willerton was feeling his way towards the proposition he had in mind, "we want no more than the truth, and there can't be too much of that. If you've been able to make the crime specialist see that he isn't writ-

ing one of his own books, it may be simpler for you, and a lot better
for him."

Mr. Willerton, who saw the direction in which Mr. Frampton's
mind was working, and had no intention of disclosing the defence
before the necessary moment came, avoided the issue with some
adroitness.

"We have decided," he said—the plural pronoun being in recognition of the fact that he was only a junior partner in the firm
which had undertaken Alfred Cuthbertson's advocacy—"that it's
not a case in which we ought to simply plead not guilty and reserve
our defence. We intend to put both Cuthbertson and his wife into the
box and explain at once how the position arose. And it's something
I've just learned from Mrs. Cuthbertson that's brought me here now.

"She says that after the episode in the lounge concerning which
Ethel Harding gave evidence yesterday— I am not discussing what
it was, much or little or nothing at all—Birchall went out to the post
office, saying that he had to get a telegram off that night. We don't
know anything about what was in it, or to whom it was addressed,
but Mrs. Cuthbertson thought it might prove to be of some value,
and I thought the best course would be to mention it to you, as you
will be able to get the post office to produce it without difficulty.

"It must have been dispatched between seven-fifteen and seven-
twenty-five on the evening of the 6th instant."

"We shan't refuse," Mr. Frampton said readily, "to follow up
anything which may bear on the case. But it's a little difficult to understand how such a telegram can be helpful to you—and I'm not
foolish enough to suppose that you're trying to strengthen the case
against your own client—especially if you don't know anything
about what the substance of the telegram was."

"Well, we don't. And we don't know that it will assist us at all,
or you either, for that matter. But it is a risk that we are willing to
take."

Mr. Frampton said again that it should be procured, and that he
would arrange for Mr. Willerton to inspect it before the court
opened on Thursday morning, if not earlier. He was rather surprised
when the defending solicitor rose up to go, as though there were
nothing more to be said, but he considered that the request showed
that a reasonable line of defence would now be taken, and if it were
to be done without any attempt to bargain with him, he was not
likely to make complaint about that. He concluded that the telegram
must have some bearing upon the relations which had existed between Mrs. Cuthbertson and the dead man. Probably the woman
knew well enough what its nature was. Suppose Birchall had been

booking rooms to which he was persuading her to flee from her husband's roof? Or enquiring concerning an ocean cruise?

It looked as though Mrs. Cuthbertson had repented of a levity which had led to such tragic ends. She had decided that a living husband was better than a dead lover, and was now doing all in her power to reduce the ruin which she had caused.

He considered that it was a rather cheeky thing to have asked him to use the power of the law to procure a telegram which was likely to be of use to the defence rather than to him, but he did not seriously object. He did not wish the man to be convicted for more than he had done, nor punished beyond the equity of the case, especially not if he should have decided on frank confession of his offence. But he did not approve of the extension of mercy to those who deny their guilt.

CHAPTER XXXI.

IT is a Fleet Street custom that the staffs of the Sunday newspapers, who may be kept at work until an early hour of that day, do not return until Tuesday, when there will be a conference during the afternoon in the editorial rooms, attended by all the more important members of the staff, at which the leading features of the next issue will be discussed and decided.

Mr. James Beecher (more generally known as Jimmie), the reporter of the *Sunday Record* whose reluctance to quit his ground on the previous Saturday had enabled that periodical to publish the exclusive news of Alfred Cuthbertson's arrest, to the exasperation of half a dozen lively competitors, had attended such a conference on the day following the novelist's first appearance before the Osbury magistrates, and received the congratulations of his more or less envious colleagues.

The confidence which comes with success had given him courage to urge upon the editor not only that he should be empowered to purchase an interview with Mrs. Cuthbertson almost without restriction of price, but that he should be authorized to make a further proposal, to which (after using his telephone to consult the proprietors of the paper) Mr. Garbett had also consented.

He was at Soome & Co.'s office well before the appointed hour, and punctually at 10:30 he was shown into Mr. Willerton's room.

The solicitor greeted him with the cordiality usually shown toward those who are connected with the mysterious and sometimes sinister powers of the press, and which is seldom unmerited. He said: "I've kept off the other gentlemen till now, as I promised I would. There are four of them who have been told they can ring up any time after the next hour, and about a dozen small fry, and representatives of the—well, say the lower press, who've been choked off. So if you'll tell me what your offer is, we shall soon know where we are."

Jimmie said thank you for that, as he had reason to do. He came to the point at once with: "We want an exclusive interview with Mrs. Cuthbertson for next Sunday's paper. You can O.K. the proofs, and we'll pay you £500 on her behalf."

"You'd better double that and call it guineas, and we might talk."

Jimmie went on without appearing to notice this somewhat disconcerting interposition: "If we give £500," he said, "we shall naturally expect the first call on Cuthbertson's own account of the matter after—after the trial's over."

"There's no question of a trial at present—there's no committal."

Jimmie's eyes lightened as may those of a sportsman who looks where the thicket moves. "Do you mean you're going to resist that?"

"I don't mean anything except that assumptions are dangerous in these matters, when they go beyond present fact. But are we coming to terms, or must I see what the *Sunday News* is prepared to do?"

Jimmie, whose varied experiences had given him an adroitness in such negotiations that might have raised a diplomatist's envy, again avoided direct reply.

"I asked you yesterday," he said, "if you were serious in questioning whether it were Thomas Birchall's body which had been thrown up by the sea, and you rather snapped me up before you were kind enough to reply. But I wasn't asking out of curiosity, or to get a quick item of news. We're willing to offer £1,000 reward for the discovery of Thomas Birchall, if he's alive. And this cash will be in the office for him to pick up himself, if he should walk into the office before anyone else gives him away."

Mr. Willerton considered this surprising offer, which had the effect, as Jimmie Beecher had intended, of taking his mind off the question of the fee to be paid for the proposed interview. He said: "Well, I couldn't stop you doing that, if I would. It's good publicity for yourselves, and will cost you nothing if the man's dead, as I daresay you feel sure that he is."

"We can't be sure of that, if you're not. You ought to know a bit more than we do yet, though I hope you're going to let us in on the ground floor. We might do a good bit for you later on."

Mr. Willerton thought: "You mean when we want an agitation for a reprieve," but he only said: "I've no doubt you might, but it's present help that I value now. I don't say the offer isn't interesting, but I should like to hear Thursday's evidence, and perhaps complete some enquiries I've got on hand now, before I give a reply. But it's a thousand guineas for the interview, neither more nor less. You'll have to wait till Friday morning for that, and I'll tell you at the same time whether we want a reward offered for a missing man. If you agree, I'll have the terms set out by midday for us both to sign."

"You're asking a big sum."

"You can phone your editor, if you like, in the meantime, but if it's not definite, I must be free also to make the offer elsewhere. But I'll tell you this. The interview will be a surprise in more ways than one."

"If you say that, it's a deal," was the quick response. Jimmie knew there was no need to telephone, the figure being within the authority he had received, though it was the very maximum to which he could go. There might be some grumbling, when he made his report, that he had not managed a better deal, but he would stand or fall in the end by the substance of the interview which he would obtain; and he had an instinct for dramatic news which assured him that there was something here for which the *Sunday Record* would he willing to pay. So he said: "Call it a deal. I'll drop in again at twelve, if you want something in black and white, but you can trust us without that."

"I don't doubt," Mr. Willerton replied, "that we could. But it's always better not to trust to memories, when you can get a thing written down."

So Jimmie went out, and strolled round Osbury for the next hour, picking up the gossip of shopkeepers and waitresses on the topic which was in everyone's mouth, and returned at midday to put his signature to a document which certainly left nothing either to memory or to chance. The agreement recited that the *Sunday Record* would submit a proof of the proposed interview, and accept any deletions there from, while on its side accepting full legal responsibility for whatever it should decide to publish, and agreeing that the reward of £1,000 for the discovery of Thomas Birchall in living form should be offered if, and only if, it should be requested to do so on or before the following Friday, by Soome & Co., on their client's behalf.

"Well," he said, "it's a big sum. I've got to trust you that you won't let me down."

"You needn't worry about that," Mr. Willerton replied easily. "When you've got the interview, I shouldn't wonder if you feel you ought to double the cheque."

Mr. Beecher said that of course the editor might, though he was unable to recall such a circumstance occurring previously. He went back to London feeling some confidence that what he had done would be justified in its results, and did not return to Osbury until

Thursday morning, when the hearing was resumed in the Magistrates' Court.

CHAPTER XXXII.

WEDNESDAY was a busy day for Mr. Willerton, who demonstrated that though Soome & Co. might not be a firm which would exert itself without a reward in sight, it did not neglect its clients' interests when that essential preliminary had been observed.

The agreement with the *Sunday Record* had to be communicated to the accused man, who, somewhat to Mr. Willerton's surprise, showed no unwillingness that his wife should use that medium to disclose the plot which had brought him to the position in which he stood.

The solicitor, using his client's own assumption, though it was one in which he had no belief, said: "If it be true that Thomas Birchall be still alive, he should have appeared before the end of the week. On your bargain with him, he should have been watching the newspapers for whatever development may have followed his disappearance, and, on seeing the trouble that has arisen, he could have no excuse for not hurrying back, if he were intending to keep faith, as we must suppose that he would."

"He might," Alfred argued, "think that the publicity will be so valuable to me that I might not thank him for returning till the most dramatic moment has come."

"Well, so he might. But on our side, you may agree that it has already gone far enough. Even for your wife's sake you could not wish the anxiety to continue longer. And beside, if we aim to establish a doubt, however faint, of the identity of the body, we must show that we are in earnest ourselves in that belief. The offer of the reward, linked with the interview that Mrs. Cuthbertson will give, will at least show that the case is not of the simple nature which the first day's hearing appeared to indicate. And, by next Sunday, we shall be close to the time at which we must show this defence, if we are to do so at all.

"Mr. Soome's opinion, with which I agree, is that it is the kind of defence which cannot be reserved. If it is to win any credence at all, it must be stated frankly, at the first opportunity that the law allows. And it may be a relatively subordinate matter, but you can understand that Mrs. Cuthbertson is anxious to deny, as early as possible, the aspersions which have been made upon her own character."

"Yes," the novelist replied, but with an impatience which might arise either from the nature of the accusations themselves, or from the fact that Dorothy could trouble herself to resent them at such a crisis, "but they are absurd! They were no part of our plan. I had no idea that her name would come into it at all. They are too silly to be taken seriously."

"But they are being so taken. And perhaps the more so they are, the better it is for us, as there will be the stronger reaction if we can establish the fact that they are untrue, or force the prosecution to drop that part of their case. Two motives have been suggested, of which this is by far the stronger and more definite. If we can rebut it, we are not home by a long way, but we are a little distance upon the road."

"Well," Alfred Cuthbertson answered, with an unusual humility, showing the nervous tension which he endured, "you know better than I do how these things should be handled. I must leave them to you."

Mr. Willerton, hearing the note of despair in his voice, had the less belief that there was anything more than a desperate bluff in his professed anticipation that a living cousin might still appear to confound his accusers. He said: "I'm not absolutely sure, even now, that we're not going on the wrong lines. That was why I put the *Sunday Record* off till we've heard what the two other witnesses who were on the road at the time are going to say.

"If there is any indefiniteness on their part, or if we can get them to say that they didn't see what Mary Gilkins had sworn, it might still be the best course for you to say no more than that Birchall left you, and you saw him walk off.

"After all, because you quarrelled with him in the morning, there's nothing to prevent him drowning himself later in the day, and we would deal with Mrs. Gilkins's tale as the excited imagination of an unstable woman. An extraordinary coincidence, of course, in view of what occurred later, but still not beyond the bounds of possibility.

"But if two other people say that they saw you throw Birchall over the edge, as they probably will, I don't see how we can do better than give your own account of the matter, which Mrs. Cuthbertson will confirm."

He left his client on this understanding being reached, and went on to see Mr. Duckfield, with whom he had a sufficiently satisfactory interview.

The bank manager anticipated, when he was announced, that he had come to ask for substantial funds for the defence of a guilty man, which he was in no mood to provide.

He was relieved to hear that money was being otherwise obtained, and surprised when Mr. Willerton, in whose judgment he had a proved reliance, spoke vaguely, but not without some show of confidence, of an undisclosed defence, which would place a very different and unanticipated construction on the event.

He stated that Alfred Cuthbertson's account was (with charges) about £40 overdrawn, and when the solicitor pointed out that the sale of the novelist's books had not ceased, but was likely to be greatly increased by the present publicity, and added an assurance that, as far as he could ascertain, there was no doubt of his substantial solvency, Mr. Duckfield almost readily agreed to increase the overdraft to a maximum of £250, to provide for the current necessities of the household, against a second charge on Highview House, which was to be immediately executed.

When Dorothy called upon Mr. Willerton during the afternoon, he was able to relieve her mind with an assurance that he had put her into a position to discharge any household accounts of a pressing urgency; and he was also able to report to his senior partner that the whole of the money which would come from the *Sunday Record* would be available for the costs of the defence.

He spent two hours with Mrs. Cuthbertson, drafting matter for the proposed interview, to which he had given a title:

MRS. CUTHBERTSON DENIES AND EXPLAINS

which he felt would be preferable to leaving the wording of placards and headlines to the editor of the enterprising periodical in which it was to appear.

Having done these things, he went home with some justification for feeling that, if Soome & Co. were to be liberally paid, they were not failing to give such service as the occasion required; and even then his activities did not cease.

For he considered, during the course of his evening meal, that the two remaining witnesses, who were to be called by the prosecution, might not be long in the box, and it would fall upon himself either to apply for an adjournment at that point, or to keep the proceedings alive for a reasonable period subsequently. He did not wish to put Alfred Cuthbertson in the box until he had had time to consider the effect of the evidence which would be given by Mr. Berry and his lady friend, and—even more important—he wished to secure publication of Dorothy's account of the matter before that of her husband should be offered in evidence.

The result of these reflections was that he telephoned Mrs. Cuthbertson, asking if she thought that the parlour maid, who would have been in the best position to observe, would be a reliable witness as to the propriety of her conduct and that of Thomas Birchall during the time that he had been a guest under her roof.

Dorothy replied that Bertha would be not only a reliable, but a willing witness, and, on that assurance, he asked if she could be spared to come round to his house that night, so that her evidence could be discussed, and he would be ready to call her on the next day.

He regarded this as little more than a manœuvre for marking time, or as a dishing up of *hors d'œuvres* before the more substantial courses, rather than a matter of any vital importance, being unable to foresee that Bertha's presence in court on the following day would exercise a decisive influence upon the subsequent development of the case.

CHAPTER XXXIII.

IT was while Mr. Willerton was in his office, shortly before leaving for the court on Thursday morning, that Mr. Frampton telephoned him to say that the telegram had been obtained from the post office.

"It is," he said, "apparently of no great importance, though, as far as it goes, I should say that it will be of use to us rather than you.

"Anyway, I propose to put it in and prove it this morning, so if it's any good to you—well, there it is."

Mr. Willerton did not wish to show eagerness to learn its contents till he knew more. He said, in a casual manner: "Thanks. I didn't really suppose it could have much bearing upon the case. I'll have a look at it when I see you in court."

He was in his place before the magistrates entered, and Mr. Frampton, taking a seat at his side, showed him the original, in Thomas Birchall's rather scrawly hand.

It was addressed to Dr. Bevan, 20, Thames Mansions, London, S.W., and said no more than: "Staying till thirteenth." It was unsigned, but the sender had scrawled his name, and Highview House as his address, on the back of the form.

It was evident that he had relied upon Dr. Bevan knowing whom it was from, and that he had not regarded secrecy as of any importance—not at least sufficiently so to have adopted the simple expedient of using an imaginary name and address.

Mr. Willerton handed it back with a smile: "I'm afraid we can't either of us make much of that."

"Not a lot," Mr. Frampton agreed, and there was a measure of sincerity on both sides. It might easily have been a more revealing or surprising document. But they both placed interpretations upon it which they regarded as of some importance, and which differed according to their knowledge or theories of the circumstances under which it was sent.

Mr. Willerton rightly saw in it an important confirmation of the tale of the conspiracy which was to be set up as the foundation of the tragic position which had now developed, and which was, at the least, preferable to the motives of greed and jealousy which the prosecution alleged. The week's delay in the execution of the project, following the news of a similar delay in the date of the publication of *The Clue of the Twisted Spoon,* which last could be easily proved, was confirmed by the telegram; and though the reason for informing Dr. Bevan might not be of importance or relevancy, he felt that the result had justified him in following it up. He made an easy guess that the prosecution would place another construction upon it, as relating to the date of a possible flight with Mrs. Cuthbertson, to which Mr. Birchall's neighbour and presumable friend was an assisting party, and he saw that his possession of another and more convincing explanation would be proportionately discreditable to the theory which they would use their own to support.

Mrs. Cuthbertson entered the court as he handed the telegram back, and he told her the brief words of which it consisted.

"Something for us," he said, "if not much. But I suppose you don't know who Dr. Bevan is, or why he needed to let him know?"

"No, I don't think I heard him mention anyone of that name. He didn't talk much about his own affairs. I think I told you he said he hadn't any friends, and wouldn't be missed if he should disappear.

"But I think it's very easy to see why it was sent. He wanted someone to be expecting him back about the 13th, a neighbour evidently, who might have undertaken some duties for him—taking in letters, or what-not—while he was away.

"It looks as though he may have been doing more to help the plot than we gave him credit for at the time. Suppose that he had impressed on this Dr. Bevan that he would be back about the 6th, and that had resulted in his making a fuss a few days later, when he didn't arrive, and he would then have found that Tom was still staying with us? It would have been rather a damp squib, and I suppose Tom wanted to make sure that it wouldn't happen that way."

"Yes," the solicitor agreed, "that's quite a feasible explanation. It shows that two heads are always better than one." And as he said this the magistrates took their seats, and the second scene of the legal drama commenced with the routine preliminaries which an adjournment entails, after which John William Berry was called to the witness box.

Mr. Berry had had a bad time. Mrs. Gilkins's tongue, living up to its reputation, had made gratuitous trouble both for him and for

Clara Mills when she had embroidered her evidence with the unnecessary, even if accurate, statement that her two fellow witnesses had been arm-in-arm in what she considered to be a lover-like attitude, as they had watched the struggle upon the cliff.

This statement, distributed by the newspapers of the following morning to something between ten and twenty millions of eager readers, did not escape the eyes of the managing authorities of Wellers & Samuel, Ltd., and they were naturally curious for an explanation of why, and with whom, their representative had been strolling toward the cliffs, at a time when he had assured them that he had been active in pursuit of the customer whom he had travelled so far to meet.

He met this awkward question, which he had anticipated for an uncomfortable half hour, after reading an account of the previous day's proceedings in a morning newspaper, with a combination of truth and falsehood, hardy denial, and ingenious prevarication. His meeting with Clara Mills had been, he said, of an absolutely casual kind, unforeseen on either side, which had occurred as he was pursuing his customer, after calling at Highview House, and learning that he had gone for a walk on the cliffs. It was untrue that he had walked with her in any attitude of familiarity. That was an error of memory, or a picturesque invention, on the part of Mrs. Gilkins, whose evidence, it would be observed, had been assailed by the defending solicitor as being largely of that description.

Could he refuse to speak to a lady whom he caught up on the road, walking the same way as himself, whom he had met on a holiday occasion two years before? But as to any closer familiarity, or any attraction which had drawn him to Osbury on the excuse of business to be done at his firm's expense—why he happened to know that she was engaged to another man!

When the departmental manager to whom these explanations were offered reminded him of some material inconsistencies between them and the account he had given on his return, he could do no better than to challenge the accuracy of Mr. Macklin's memory. Was it likely that he could have said so, when it had not been the case?

Mr. Macklin appeared to be half-doubtful, half-convinced; but there was a coldness in his tone when he concluded the interview with: "Very well, that will do, Mr. Berry," which became an ominous memory when confronting the difficult realization that the evidence which he must now give upon oath would certainly be read by Mr. Macklin, as would that of Miss Mills, and if these accounts should appear to be inconsistent with the statement he had made a

150

few hours before, it was a poor hope that a second suggestion of defective memory on the part of his principal would be sufficient to bear him through.

It is not surprising that he entered the witness box with gloomy anticipations, intensified by the sight of Mrs. Rickards at the back of the court, and by the memory it brought of the names in which he had engaged her rooms, with some accompanying mendacities.

It was true that Mr. Frampton had given him assurance a few minutes before that neither Miss Mills nor himself would be interrogated by the prosecuting counsel except upon the direct issue of what they had seen; but there was little consolation in that, for it was immediately followed by a warning that there might be no similar restraint in the questions of the defending solicitor, who must be expected to challenge the quality of their evidence by every means in his power; and that any lack of frankness or appearance of evasion on his part might defeat itself by inducing questions of a more probing and personal character than he should otherwise have to meet.

Placed in this difficult position, he might have considered himself sufficiently chastised for the degree of moral obliquity to which the impulse of passion had so abortively led him, but he was suffering from the additional misery of a quarrel with Clara Mills, who had not easily forgiven him for what she considered the cowardly and avoidable indiscretion of having given her Bournemouth address to the police.

Acrimonious correspondence had led to a position in which they had passed each other this morning in the corridors of the court with no more than a cold and formal greeting, and he was as yet unaware that the publication of the report of Monday's proceedings, which had involved him in such difficulties of explanation, had been even more momentous in their consequences to herself, having led to the breaking of her engagement on the previous day.

It is a common experience of life that those events which are approached with the greatest apprehension of evil are seldom as sinister as imagination will have foreshadowed, and those from which the keenest pleasures are anticipated will not reach the measure of the expected ecstasy.

Mr. Berry experienced the truth of this aphorism. The questions which Mr. Bigland-Buffitt addressed to him related only to what he had seen on the height above, and his distance from the struggle. He answered these in a manner which left no doubt in Mr. Willerton's mind that he must admit the truth of the event, at least to the point to which he was satisfied that he had himself been fully informed, and his cross-examination was addressed to a single point, the full significance of which would not become evident until he should disclose the nature of the defence which he had been instructed to set up.

"You have told the court," he began, "that you saw a struggle between two men, one of whom subsequently passed you, and whom you are now able to identify as Mr. Cuthbertson, and that the other disappeared as though he fell over the edge of the cliff. I understand that you did not afterwards approach more nearly to the place where this incident occurred?"

"No, we—I turned back."

"A rather singular thing to do?"

"I don't know that it was."

"No? And you did nothing to give the alarm that a man had been cast, perhaps, to his death?"

"No."

"You took no steps to inform the police?"

"No."

"You did and said nothing whatever until Sergeant Poole called upon you, and the idea that a crime had been committed was suggested to you? Any explanation of that?"

"No. I don't know that I have."

"May I suggest one to your mind? You have spoken of a man being apparently thrown over the edge of the cliff, but, if you had never climbed to that height, can you tell me how you could know that there was an edge there?"

"I couldn't say for sure."

"Of course not. And if I tell you that there is, in fact, a lower level, a mere few feet below, at the spot where this incident occurred, you cannot deny it?"

"No."

"So that the idea of a fatal tragedy having occurred is rather one that was subsequently suggested to you, than a spontaneous deduction of your own mind?"

The witness, rather surprised by this process of reasoning, had the sense to answer, "Yes," and no more.

"Thank you, Mr. Berry. I think that is all."

Mr. Bigland-Buffitt said that he had no further questions to ask. Having no clue to the nature of the defence, it appeared to him to be of little importance to explore the processes of the witness's mind, or to consider the possibilities of lower ledges from which the victim of Alfred Cuthbertson's violence might or might not have bounced into the sea.

Also, he recognized it to be a fact, for what it was worth, that Mr. Berry could not have known with certainty what was below that apparent edge. It was a legitimate point for Cuthbertson's solicitor to make, though it might be of little avail, in view of the subsequent disappearance of Thomas Birchall, and the dead body that was to be quietly buried on the next day at his grandfather's charge.

Mr. Berry stepped down, feeling that he had had a very fortunate and narrow escape. He knew that the true reason for his silence had been quite different from that which Mr. Willerton had so obligingly suggested for him; and that, had he been pressed for more than monosyllabic answers, they would have been very difficult to give without disclosing his embarrassing companionship, or causing him to appear to have shown an attitude of unnatural callousness, such as would have brought him under the condemnation of the millions of his fellow countrymen whose minds and tongues were busy upon the circumstances of the alleged murder.

He had still to endure the ordeal of listening to the examination of Clara Mills, who was now called, and entered the court, a pretty, demure figure, very carefully dressed and toileted in anticipation of the coming publicity, and with an outward composure which did not suggest that she had anything either to conceal or fear.

She gave an account of what she had witnessed sufficiently similar to that which the court had already heard to supply a strong argument for its truth, which Mr. Willerton had, in fact, no further disposition to challenge As neatly as though she had heard the cross-examination of the previous witness, she answered Mr. Bigland-Buffitt's somewhat leading question with: "He fell back out of sight; of course I couldn't tell how far," and Mr. Willerton, seeing that she had presented him with the one point which he had been intending to make, let her go without any cross-examination at all, after which she found a seat beside an old gentleman whom those who had attended the previous hearing recognized as Eli Birchall, the grandfather both of the accused and the murdered man.

The next witness was a stout and nervous counter assistant from the post office at which Thomas Birchall had handed in the telegram, who was called to prove it in the formal way that the law required.

It was a moment at which Mr. Willerton could fortunately relax his watchfulness, for an urgent whisper from Mrs. Cuthbertson had caused him to leave his place to speak to Bertha for a few hurried moments in the comparative quietude of the corridor of the court.

He listened to a surprising statement, which, if it could be believed, raised her into the position of a witness of the first importance, and gave him his first genuinely hopeful feeling in regard to the fantastic defence which Alfred Cuthbertson had urged upon him. He said no more than: "You are quite sure? It will do us no good—may do us actual harm—if you should afterwards be shown to be wrong?" And received a quietly confident answer: "Oh, yes, I shouldn't make a mistake about that."

"Bertha," Dorothy added, with a new note of hopefulness in her own voice, though the girl's assertion had rather deepened than resolved the mystery of the case, "is very observant of such matters. She wouldn't make a mistake about that."

He went back into court in time to hear Bigland-Buffitt say that that was his case, and that he asked that the accused man should be convicted on the capital charge.

CHAPTER XXXIV.

MR. WILLERTON was brief in reply. He was unperturbed by the knowledge that he faced a bench of magistrates who had already concluded that the committal was no more than the routine preliminary which would launch his client on the short road to the scaffold or a life of penal servitude till his best years should be past.

It was his client's right to have his defence recorded upon the depositions if he should prefer to disclose it, and his solicitor knew that it would include one or two unexpected revelations, which could not fail to influence the public judgment, and perhaps ultimately a jury's decision, upon the case.

But he considered that those disclosures would be heightened in their dramatic effect if they should come first from the mouths of the witnesses, rather than in a preliminary statement from him, and—of greater importance—that he was still able to do no more than feel his way forward on a road which was hard to see.

"My client," he said, "protests that he is not only innocent of such a charge, either in intention or fact, or of homicide in any lesser degree, but that he has no responsibility whatever for the death, from whatever cause it may have arisen, of the unfortunate man whose body has been identified, rightly or wrongly, as that of Thomas Birchall.

"I will say no more at this stage than that, while the evidence of the three witnesses who have described what they believe they observed upon the edge of the cliff, will not be contested in so far as their veracity is concerned, I propose to show, by the evidence of several others, including that of Mr. Cuthbertson himself, that they were entirely, though quite excusably wrong, both as to what occurred, and the circumstances from which it arose.

"I shall have to ask for an adjournment of a few days, as there are enquiries still to be made for which the time has not been sufficient, but I have one or two witnesses whom I can call at once, if you will be able to hear them today."

Sir George had a whispered consultation with Mr. Waites. He asked: "How long do you suppose that Alfred Cuthbertson's evidence will be likely to take?"

"I should suppose that it will occupy some hours, if not more. But, with your permission, I think it will be the more convenient course if I call two other witnesses first, whose evidence will be of a briefer character."

There was a further consultation among the magistrates themselves, and again between the chairman and the magistrates' clerk, after which Sir George announced: "We will sit today until three-thirty, or later if necessary. After that the court will adjourn until Tuesday next, by which time I hope, Mr. Willerton, that you will be ready to go on, as we shall then be prepared to sit from day to day until the case is finished."

Mr. Willerton said: "Thank you, Sir George. I think that will be quite convenient. I call Bertha Gale."

The parlour maid took her place and the oath with the same self-assured and yet deferential detachment that she had been trained to show in the execution of her domestic duties.

"You have been employed," Mr. Willerton asked, "as parlour maid at Highview House for about eighteen months past?"

"Yes, sir. I went there in October, 1934."

"During that time you have waited at table, you have been constantly in and out of the rooms in which your master and mistress have been living, you have had exceptional—I may say unique—opportunities for observing the circumstances of their domestic life?"

"Yes, sir, I've been in and out, of course."

"Have you observed, either recently, or at any other time, any serious quarrel between them, or any lack of the normal intimacy of people who are happily married?"

"No, sir, not at all."

"Have you observed, at any time, that Mrs. Cuthbertson showed any preference for, or familiarity with, any other man?"

"No, sir, not at all."

"Her affections have always appeared to be fixed upon her husband?"

"Yes, sir, she's looking after him all the time."

"Now we will come to the visits of Mr. Birchall. He came first at Easter? Can you say on whose invitation that was?"

"The master asked Mrs. Cuthbertson to write."

"It was Mr. Cuthbertson's suggestion?"

"Yes, sir. I didn't think the mistress liked having him over-much."

"And the second time that he came was about two or three weeks ago?"

"It was the same then, sir. The master had some business with him, I understood."

"Did you know what it was?"

"Not to understand, sir. It was something about the sale of the master's books."

"And did you notice any familiarity on either of these occasions between Mr. Birchall and Mrs. Cuthbertson?"

"No, sir, there wasn't any, I'm certain about that. The mistress was just polite to him, nothing more."

"You mean nothing that came under your own observation?" Mr. Bullows interposed from the bench.

"I mean there wasn't anything, sir. You can always tell if there is."

She made this statement, not as one who expresses an opinion (which it would not have been her place to do), but as one giving information of fact for which she was asked, as though she had said that the coal would last till the end of the week.

Mr. Bigland-Buffitt saw that the question had been intended to help the prosecution, and had had a directly opposite effect. He wished that the magistrates would leave the examination of witnesses in his more capable hands.

Mr. Willerton went on: "Now we come to the evening of the 13th. Do you remember waiting at dinner on that night?"

"Yes, sir. Quite well."

"And how do you identify it?"

"I kept the dinner back about five minutes, because Mr. Birchall had gone to the post office. The mistress told me not to ring the gong till he'd had time to wash after he came in."

"For which five minutes was sufficient?"

"Yes, sir. He didn't dress for dinner. He'd only come with the one suit."

"Never mind that now. I shall come back to that. Did you notice any difference between your master and mistress and Mr. Birchall from their normal relations?"

"No, sir, not to notice. I thought Mr. Birchall was a bit quiet; but that was no more than he often was. Rather sulky, as you might say."

"Did you hear anything they said to suggest a cause?"

157

"No, sir, I don't know that it was anything more than his natural way. I thought I understood that he was wanting some money that the master wasn't very willing to let him have."

"Well, that mayn't have been very far wrong. And Mr. Birchall remained a guest in the house for another week before the day when he disappeared?"

"Yes, sir, just about that."

"And there was no sign of any quarrel between him and Mr. Cuthbertson?"

"No, sir, not at all."

"Nor of any difference in the relations of Mrs. Cuthbertson and her guest?"

"No, sir, not at all."

"Neither a quarrel of any kind, nor any noticeable intimacy?"

"No, sir, not at all. I thought the mistress spoke once or twice as though she would be rather glad when he was gone, but of course that wasn't for him to hear."

"I suppose it's nothing unusual to hear a mistress speak in that way of a guest, as though he may have outstayed his welcome?"

Bertha permitted a slight smile to cross the seriousness of her face, as she answered: "No, sir, I shouldn't say that it is."

"And now returning to the evening of the 13th. You have heard the tale that Ethel Harding has told of what she says that she saw as she came in?"

"Yes, sir."

"Do you believe it?"

Mr. Bigland-Buffitt rose before the witness had given the "no" which it was not possible to stop.

"I object to that question."

Mr. Willerton anticipated the magistrates' decision, and the fact that the answer had been given, though it might not be destined to the dignity of a written record. He said: "I will withdraw it. Let me ask you this: is it possible to see into the lounge as you come up the path?"

"Yes, it is, when it's lit up after dark, if the curtains are not drawn."

"How much can you see?"

"The wall between the window and door, and anyone passing in or out."

"The fireplace, or anyone standing by it, could not possibly be seen from that position?"

"No, nothing near."

"How do you know that?"

158

"Cook and I tried it after what Ethel said."

"Are the curtains usually left open?"

"The mistress isn't careful one way or other. I draw them most evenings before they come in from the dining room, and they're left open till then."

"And this room—the lounge, the curtains of which were not drawn—could have been entered at any moment from the hall? You might have entered it yourself without knocking?"

"Yes, I knock at bedroom doors, but not those on the ground-floor. That's the rule in all good houses that know how things ought to be done."

"I daresay it is. Anyway, it is the custom at Highview House? So that the suggestion is that though you had never seen the slightest evidence of familiarity between Mrs. Cuthbertson and Mr. Birchall, they were so utterly careless of what they did that they were 'embracing'—that is the word that has been used—in a lighted room of which the curtains had not been drawn, and one into which you might enter at any moment, and into which Mr. Cuthbertson, if we are to believe the tale, actually did enter, so that he was able to observe them while so engaged?"

Mr. Bigland-Buffitt looked restless while this question unfolded its somewhat involved length, but he did not interpose before the girl gave her answer with a faint sound of contempt in the discreet respectfulness that characterized her replies: "We told Ethel that anyone who'd believe that tale must be rather soft in the head."

"Well, the police didn't know all the facts as clearly as we've heard them from you. Now I come to another matter."

Mr. Willerton turned his eyes upon the garments, tattered and shrunk from their five-days' ordeal as the sport of the Channel tides, as they were displayed on the table before the seat of the magistrates' clerk. "I should like the witness to inspect the suit carefully, and state whether she can identify it as Thomas Birchall's property."

The usher passed the remains of the coat, from which a large part of the right side had been torn away, to the witness, who looked at it with sufficient care, but as one whose mind was already settled.

"Yes," she said, "it's the one that Mr. Birchall used to wear when he was here at Easter."

"You are certain of that?"

"Oh, yes, quite."

"And on the last occasion when he came to Highview House?"

"He wasn't wearing that suit. It was the one with a white stripe in the blue."

"A different colour?"

"No, but the one he wore the last time had the stripe."

She answered these last questions in the dead silence of a court which had become aware that it was confronted by some unexpected evidence, such as might alter the presumptions of that which had gone before, though uncertain as yet of what its significance would be likely to be.

Sir George Hawler interposed: "Do you mean to say seriously that Thomas Birchall was not wearing this suit on the morning of his disappearance? Or may there not be a genuine error of memory on your part on a matter which you can hardly have regarded as of importance at the time?"

"No," she answered. "He wasn't wearing this one. He didn't bring it."

"Didn't bring it?" Sir George continued incredulously.

"No, he didn't bring any suit with him either time, except the one he was wearing, and it was this one the first time, and another one when he came again."

"You say the two suits were almost exactly alike?" The magistrate's voice was still sceptical, approaching that with which he would address a prisoner who made lying pleas to lessen the penalty his fault had earned, but there was no change in the placid deference, or in the decision, of the witness's quiet replies.

"Yes, but you could tell one from the other."

"You remember that you are on oath?"

"Oh, yes." There was a faint tone of surprise in the respectful assurance of the reply.

"And that you are asserting an extremely improbable thing?"

"I thought it might be important for you to know."

Mr. Bigland-Buffitt, silently and alertly watchful, his mind a lively note of interrogation as to where this unexpected evidence might lead, and whether he were listening to error of memory, unlikely truth, or a deliberate almost equally improbable lie, had occasion to think, for a second time, that the magistrate would be wiser to leave the witnesses to him.

Sir George Hawler said no more, and Mr. Willerton resumed: "When did you first become aware of this difference?"

"When I was in court this morning. I could see from where I sat that it wasn't the suit he'd been wearing the last time he came."

"And you thought it was a sufficiently curious fact to inform me of it at once?"

"Yes. I thought that if he had fallen off the cliff that morning he must have been wearing the other suit at the time."

"Very well. Now with regard to this knife." Mr. Willerton turned again to the exhibits in the case, and took up the knife which had been found in the trousers pocket of the dead man. "Can you identify this as being Mr. Thomas Birchall's property?"

"Yes, he had it with him when he was with us at Easter."

"And on the last occasion?"

"I'm practically certain he hadn't."

"How can you know that?"

"He used to empty his pockets at night, and put the contents on a little table at the side of the bed."

"How do you know?"

"I used to see them there when I took in the early morning tea. I usually had to move them aside to make room for the tray."

"And you remember that the knife used to be among them when he came at Easter, but not on the second occasion?"

"Yes."

"Absolutely sure?"

"Yes, quite."

Mr. Willerton sat down, satisfied that he had been able to drop an unexpected bomb into the case for the prosecution which had seemed to be so securely established when the witness entered the box, and Mr. Bigland-Buffitt rose. He was not unused to such disconcerting emergencies, nor inexpert to face, and perhaps to foil, them.

"You have a most remarkable memory, Miss Gale?" he began. "And a most remarkable gift of observation?"

"I don't often forget what I see."

"And you would not be sorry to assist either your master or your mistress in their present difficulty?"

"No, sir, I am glad that I am able to help them."

"How do you know that Mr. Birchall did not have both of these very similar suits with him on his second visit?"

"Because he only brought a small suitcase with a few odds and ends of underclothing. I don't think he expected to have stayed as long as he did."

"Do you mean that your observations extend to inspecting the interiors of the suitcases of the gentlemen visitors to the house?"

"The mistress told me to pack it, and send it back to him when he didn't return."

"So that all you can really say is that you didn't pack this, or any other suit, and return it to Mr. Birchall's address?"

"No, sir, what I say is that Mr. Birchall didn't go out in the suit on the morning that you say he fell into the sea."

"And you are prepared to swear to that, in spite of the fact that he was wearing it when he was fetched out?"

"Yes, I know it's true."

"Although, at that time, you could have had no occasion to notice it particularly, one way or other?"

"I know I did notice it."

"And though the two suits, by your own account, were so very nearly alike?"

"They weren't so that you couldn't tell them apart."

Mr. Bigland-Buffitt recognized that, whether the witness were right or wrong, she was of a settled mind, and was not of a disposition to concede the ground she so firmly, though respectfully, held. He sat down, seeing that the point must be attacked on the ground of its inherent improbability rather than by endeavouring to shake the girl's quietly confident testimony.

Sir George Hawler looked at the clock. He had allowed the usual hour of adjournment to pass rather than interrupt this unexpected testimony. "Will your second witness take long, Mr. Willerton?" he asked. "Because, if so, it might be convenient to defer it to the next sitting."

Mr. Willerton had been in some doubt of the importance of this witness, and even of the expediency of calling him until he could see more clearly the direction in which his defence might most profitably developed; but Bertha Gale's evidence had driven this doubting reluctance finally from his mind. For the first time, he gave more than professional belief to his client's angry assertion that he had seen Thomas Birchall walk away after the mock tragedy that he had staged to such unforeseeable realism as had trapped him now. He said that he thought half an hour would be sufficient, or perhaps less.

Sir George consulted his colleagues, among whom some difference of opinion became evident. Miss Grigson Lait could be heard to say: "And find it's nearer two hours, more likely than not." In the end, the chairman announced that the court would adjourn for thirty-five minutes, after which Mr. Willerton's second witness would be heard.

CHAPTER XXXV.

MR. BERRY heard the announcement as the court rose that the attendance of the witnesses who had already given evidence would not be further required that day, with the relief of one who could attend, at last, to his own (he would have said) more urgent, if not more important affairs. He knew that it was nearly two hours before the next train for Bournemouth would leave, and he calculated that the time should be sufficient for a leisurely lunch with the lady whom he had led (unless we say, looking more deeply into the origins of human events, that she had led him) into this annoying entanglement, and for a subsequent walk, either toward the shore, or upon the Osbury hills.

He had been conscious of a great relief since both Miss Mills and himself had left the witness box without their personal affairs becoming bare to the immense publicity which the reports of such legal proceedings receive. He felt that the danger of any serious trouble with his firm had disappeared—unless, which he would not anticipate, they should be subjected to a different manner of examination at the trial itself—and he had some reasonable ground for expectation that Clara would be relieved in the same degree.

He was abruptly disconcerted to observe her leaving the crowded court, somewhat in advance of himself, in the evident company of the elderly gentleman who had been seated beside her. He did not recognize Mr. Eli Birchall, not having been present at the previous hearing, and having had no disposition to study the report of the trial, or the portraits of the witnesses which had been so generally printed, apart from those portions which had been of immediate concern to him. He wondered now if he might be some aged relative who had come to escort her home.

He saw that that was not a probable supposition, knowing that she had arrived alone, but he could think of no better. He saw them cross the road, still in advance of himself, and enter Crosbee's Restaurant together.

He followed them in, but could not have joined them, even had he been invited to do so, for they sat down at a table which was only set to accommodate four, and the other two places were already occupied.

He took a place as near to them as he could, which was about three tables away, but though he was certain that the girl's eyes had been upon him on one occasion, she gave him no second glance; and when she rose and went out, still in the old gentleman's escort, she was now followed by a miserable and by this time very puzzled and angry man.

From the window of the first-floor room in which they had dined, he watched them cross the road, as though returning to the court, instead of which they went on to the taxi rank which is at that side, and entered the foremost vehicle, which drove off toward the sea.

He decided that his best course was to be on the platform when the Bournemouth train should go out, when he might either see her alone, or discover who the old gentleman was. But he did this with no better result than to ascertain that she did not leave by that train, and he reluctantly faced the fact that he must return to London unless he would be blamed for lingering in Osbury without excuse for a second time.

He took what consolation he could from the fact that Miss Mills was unlikely to have transferred her affections from him so suddenly in favour of a man who, at the least, had said goodbye to his seventieth year, and he invented explanations of her conduct with the theory that she had wished to demonstrate to the public that he was nothing to her, which in that atmosphere of photographers and reporters, it might be no more than prudence to do. It would certainly have done him no good with his firm had there been a snapshot in tomorrow's papers showing them leaving the court together.

Accepting this theory, he saw that she might have resented the fact that he had followed her into Crosbee's, as a further instance of the clumsiness from which she already suffered, and that this resentment, and the policy she had adopted, would unite to incline her to cut him there, as he was sure that she had deliberately done.

He even felt disposed to bless her discretion on the following day, when, in discussing the case with one of the departmental managers, he was able to say: "Oh, Miss Mills? The fact was I didn't get a chance to speak to her. She was with an old gentleman—some relative, I suppose—and they went off together."

But the truth was quite simple and quite different, though it may be accepted as probable fact that Clara Mills was quite willing to give her lover an uncomfortable afternoon in return for the mess into which (she considered) he had got her.

Being a more diligent student than himself of the illustrated daily press, she had recognized Eli Birchall, even before, by no more than the chance of a vacant place, she had sat down beside him.

He had followed the evidence with a mind which certainly suffered from no weakness of senile decay, and with no purpose but to learn what the truth might be. Although he gave no credence to the fantastic suggestion that the body which he had himself identified was not that of Thomas Birchall, he had been genuinely puzzled by the evidence of Bertha Gale, the sincerity of which he saw no occasion to doubt, nor, being a man of acute observation himself, did it seem improbable that she should be conscious of the difference between two suits of the same colour.

He felt that it is less objectionable to be the grandfather even of a writer of criminal fiction, than of a man who would not scruple to throw his cousin over a cliff without subsequent effort to save him, and he recognized that the evidence of the parlour maid threw a suggestion of doubt, or at least of mystery, upon the otherwise obvious theory of how Thomas had met his death. And the attitude of aloofness which he had hitherto maintained toward his remaining grandson was not one which he would wish to continue if his innocence could be reasonably presumed.

When Miss Mills took a seat at his side, he introduced himself with the ease which his years permitted, and asked her if her leisure would allow her to do him the service of showing him where she had been when she had witnessed the scene which she had described that morning.

He felt that he would be better able to judge the value of whatever evidence was to come, if he should himself have inspected the site of the alleged tragedy.

Miss Mills, easily appreciating his interest in a case in which he was so nearly concerned, had assented readily, and so they had very naturally gone to lunch together.

The incident, and any deduction which Mr. Birchall senior may have made from his visit to the cliff side in Miss Mills's attractive company, had no influence of importance upon the subsequent course of the prosecution, and would have been needless to chronicle had it not had most momentous consequences for four of the people with whom this narrative is concerned in quite separate ways.

So it came to be that John William Berry paced disconsolately the western departure platform of Osbury station, and Eli Birchall, shivering somewhat in a chill wind, but enjoying the vitality of his young companion, climbed a steep upward path, while Mr. Willerton, having returned to court to await magistrates who were again somewhat less than punctual, was questioning Lieutenant Penrose, R.N. (retired wounded in the Battle of Jutland and now attached to H.M. Coast Guard Service), upon the course of the Channel currents and the force of its moon-led tides.

Lieutenant Penrose, though called by the defence, was clearly not one of those very numerous experts whose minds appear to reach any conclusion which may be required with the aid of a sufficient fee.

To the question on which Mr. Willerton had consulted him—would a body falling into the sea at the place at which Alfred Cuthbertson was alleged to have thrown his cousin, be cast ashore two or three miles farther westward along the coast, as that which was the subject of the present charge had certainly been?—he did, indeed, give a decidedly negative answer, but that was qualified or confused by the further statement that he was unable to understand how anybody falling into the sea along that coast could remain five days in the water before being washed ashore, as it appeared certain that Thomas Birchall had been.

He discussed currents and tides, and he was detailed regarding the winds of the previous week. The most that Mr. Willerton could make of his evidence was that he was unable to understand what had occurred. He said, indeed, that the facts rather indicated that the man had been drowned at sea—or at least cast into the water at some considerable distance from land, if the medical evidence showed that drowning was not the cause of death.

Mr. Bigland-Buffitt recognized that he listened to a witness who understood his subject and who was genuinely trying to assist the court. His evidence required consideration, and perhaps submission to other experts, but its significance was uncertain, and cross-examination might well be delayed until the case was before a jury. He said that he had no questions to ask.

CHAPTER XXXVI.

MR. WILLERTON, feeling that he had had rather a good day, though the end of the road might still be distant and hard to see, paid his client another visit after the court adjourned, to discuss the effect of the evidence which Bertha had given.

He found him to be more confident in manner than he had appeared since the first day's hearing had disclosed the strength of the case which he had to meet, but this recovered confidence did not appear to have improved his temper, but rather to have intensified the exasperation with which he regarded the position into which his own folly had led him.

"Perhaps," he said, in a tone which was at once nervous and savage, so that the solicitor found it hard to endure patiently, "you'll believe now that I didn't pitch Tom over the cliff and walk quietly away?"

"I'm prepared to believe or disbelieve almost anything in this case, but perhaps you'll tell me now what actually did occur, and we may be able to present a defence which will bring us home."

"I've done that till I'm tired already: I've told you I saw him walk off by the path that trends away from the edge."

"Very well, I accept that. But I'm sorry that you can't tell me a bit more, or something a bit different. Do you agree with Bertha that when he left you he wasn't wearing the suit in which the dead body was washed ashore?"

"I couldn't answer that if it would save my life. I can't remember his rotten suits. But I expect all the women will."

"Mrs. Cuthbertson does. She blames herself that she hadn't thought of it earlier. But I don't know whether it has occurred to you that this evidence doesn't only make confusion for the other side—though of course it does that—but it also rules out more than one of the most plausible theories that we could have advanced on the basis of it not being Thomas Birchall's body at all."

"I've always understood that it's necessary for the prosecution to prove their case, not for the defence to prove that it didn't happen. I don't see why we need worry with any theories at all."

"So, in strict law, it is. But it doesn't work out in practice quite that way, especially in murder trials, in which it has become customary to admit a lot of what I may call secondary evidence on both sides, especially on the questions of motive and opportunity, which would be redundant if a case were properly proved, as that they must be considered as substitutes for proof, or they would not be required at all.

"Then you are up against the difficulty that the jury's decision is considered final on all questions of fact, unless it be perverse, and no one can look into their minds to see by what process their conclusions are reached."

"Well, I know all that. But I don't see that we've got much to worry us, all the same. We've got Dorothy's evidence and mine as to the silly plot that we had made, and my evidence that I only pretended to throw him over, and saw him walk off safe and well; and against that they've got to persuade a jury that I threw him over the cliff in one suit and he was fished out in another! Will they make out that he may have changed while he was in the sea, or had a second suit under his arm?"

"Of course, it sounds absurd when it's put like that. And, for that matter, we know that something very unusual *has* occurred. That's our own contention rather than theirs. But there are other aspects of the matter which you may not be equally willing to see. There is—"

"I see," Alfred Cuthbertson interrupted sharply, "that from the moment I parted with him, when he was wearing the other suit, there are plenty of witnesses of where I was every minute for the rest of the day; and it seems to me that that alone should make an end of the case. Their own witnesses help us there. They saw me leave him and going home."

"So they did. We shan't overlook that. But will you listen while I put the case from another angle? The jury will know—any jury will know—that you are a specialist in criminal fiction. They will regard you, with reason, as having a mind capable of constructing a crime calculated to baffle any ordinary investigation. And on the top of that you will advance an explanation of what was seen to occur which, whether they believe it or not, will exhibit you in the same character of a most ingenious plotter. Will it not be put to them by the prosecution—or, if it were not, would they not put it to themselves—that this puzzling point of the suit, and other mysterious aspects of the case, are all cunning contrivances of your own for making away with a cousin of whom you may or may not be jealous, but who certainly stood in the way of a possible inheritance, in such a manner as to throw dust in their eyes? Will they not be asked to put aside all confusing details and keep their minds fixed as sensible men, as men of the world—that is the phrase most commonly used—on the central fact that three witnesses saw you throw a man over the cliff, who was afterwards washed up dead by the sea?"

"And what," Mr. Cuthbertson replied, in a tone of sarcastic bitterness, for which he may be excused, whether he were innocent or guilty of his cousin's death, "am I to understand by this eloquent speech for the prosecution? Are you suggesting that it would be better for us to withhold the true explanation of what happened? And, if so, what other one am I expected to give?"

"I don't suggest anything of the kind," Mr. Willerton answered, keeping his own temper with more success. "The truth, whatever it may be, is the safest ground for us to keep to in such a case, even though it mayn't look as sound as we should like it to be.

"All I was trying to say was that, important as this evidence regarding the suit may appear to be, it mayn't be much use to us unless we can support it with something more. It won't take us far—and may be utterly disbelieved—unless we can supplement it with other evidence of what did occur, concerning which I own that I find it hard at present even to make a plausible guess.

"In other words, the fact that Bertha is sure that he was wearing a different suit is less important in itself than in its indication that there really is a solution to be found which will clear you from the charge, if we can only find it without delay."

"Well, that's sense," the accused man replied, in a more reasonable voice. "And I'm sorry I got a bit roused. But if you knew what it is to be cooped up here! What do you think we can do?"

"I really came to talk it over, in that hope that you might have some suggestions to make, and that you might possibly have some explanation to propose of how the suit could have been changed which mightn't occur to me. But I've already started enquiries as to whether anyone resembling Birchall was seen after he left you, either in the clothes he then wore, or those he took in the case. And we can hope something from the reward that the *Record* will offer on Sunday. It's large enough to tempt most men to open their mouths, if they are in a position to claim it. Of course, that's on the assumption that he's still alive, on which point I can't say that I've got much confidence myself, though I may be wrong. As I said before, I'm ready to believe almost anything now and we mustn't let assumptions stifle enquiries in any direction.

"I think enquiries ought to be made in London also, and in that connection I thought of seeing your grandfather and having a frank talk with him. And there's that Mr. Bevan, to whom the telegram was dispatched. He must have been on a friendly footing, and he was a neighbour. It's a poor chance, but I thought of going to London myself to see them both. They might say more to me than they would if they were interviewed by private enquiry agents or the police.

"Well," Mr. Cuthbertson said, "they both seem chances worth trying, though I should suppose that the local enquiries are more likely to bring the kind of information we need.

"There's one thing in our favour. The whole country will be talking about the new evidence tomorrow, and those who know anything won't find it easy to keep their mouths shut, especially if they find they will be paid if they open them.

"Then, if you agree," Mr. Willerton concluded, "I'll get up to London as soon as possible. I can't go tomorrow, because Beecher's to be here from the *Record*, and I shall be busy on what he's to publish. But I'll get there on Saturday, and stay, if necessary, over the weekend."

CHAPTER XXXVII.

MR. WILLERTON had only just reached his office on Friday morning when he received a telephone call from London. Mr. Beecher, who was due to wait upon him in twenty minutes, asked to be excused, and hoped it would not cause inconvenience to anyone if the appointment should be deferred to the following day. The fact was, he said, that when he got back late last night with his report of the day's proceedings before the Osbury magistrates, his editor had asked him to undertake some enquiries in connection with the case which might occupy most of the day. He was quick to add that the delay was no indication of any wish to withdraw from the agreement. The next issue of the *Record* would spread itself over the case so that it would not only be front-page news, but the main substance of the paper. It would offer the promised reward for the discovery of a living Birchall, which would be likely to attract a livelier interest now that Miss Gale's testimony about the clothes had raised a confusing doubt as to how they could have got on to the body of the dead man, whoever he might be.

"I want to be sure," he said, "that Mrs. Cuthbertson's story will contain a statement that she is convinced that Thomas Birchall is not dead, so that we can make that assertion the reason for offering such a reward."

"Well," Mr. Willerton answered doubtfully, "she may consent to that now. I'll get it in if I can. You don't think you're leaving it rather late?"

"Not if you don't mind doing business on Saturday morning."

"I don't object when it's as important as this. Mind telling me what you're trying to get hold of today?"

"I don't think I ought to do that. Not now, anyway. If I dig up any nuggets, I'll probably have the editor's permission to tell you tomorrow."

"Thanks. That will do for me. Some time tomorrow, and I'll probably have Mrs. Cuthbertson here when you arrive, so that we can get at it right away."

He rang off and got up in the same action. He said to Riddell, the clerk to whom he had been giving some instructions when the call came through, and who had been standing waiting beside his desk: "I can't stop now. Ring Mrs. Cuthbertson up, and tell her that everything's all right, but the appointment's put off till tomorrow. I've just got five minutes for catching the London train."

The train was caught with a margin of several seconds, but Osbury, as its residents will testify, is not favoured with an express service, and it was past the hour of lunch when Mr. Willerton arrived at Thames Mansions, and asked the lift attendant to take him up to Dr. Bevan's flat.

"I've just taken a gentleman up there, sir," the man said, shaking his head. "I told him the doctor hadn't been here today, but he would go all the same."

"There's no one in the flat above—Thomas Birchall's flat—I suppose?" the solicitor asked, reluctant to be turned away, and willing to learn anything he could from a man who must have had opportunities for observing the two tenants in whom he was interested.

"No, sir. There's no one been there since the poor gentleman left. Except the police gave it the once-over on Wednesday morning, and Inspector Monkhouse was here again last night."

"Monkhouse on the job?" Mr. Willerton said, with some surprise, the name being that of one of the best known of the Chief Inspectors of Scotland Yard.

"Yes, sir," the man replied, being quite ready to talk on a matter which had been little out of his mind during the past week. "I don't think they found much when they searched on Wednesday. I heard one of them say as they came down that he couldn't have left it much different if he'd been expecting them to be looking in."

"Well, perhaps he did," Mr. Willerton said, adding a detail of confirmation to the tale which the Cuthbertsons had told him.

The man looked puzzled. "I don't see how he could have done that, sir. Not when he went away."

Mr. Willerton decided to be confidential. He produced a card. "I ought to tell you," he said, "that I am Mr. Cuthbertson's solicitor, and I'm quite sure that all the truth hasn't come out yet, whatever it may prove to be. I want to ask you to help me, if there's any way that you can, remembering that it is the truth, and nothing else, that I'm trying to get at."

He took out a ten-shilling note to support the request he made, and the man accepted it in a mechanical manner, but held it uncertainly in his hand as he answered: "I don't mind telling you anything that I know, sir. But I don't know that I ought to take this. I don't know anything that could be any use to you."

"Well, I'll risk that. Do you think that Inspector Monkhouse found out anything more when he came again yesterday?"

"I don't know that he did, sir. He asked me to run him up to the top floor, but he rang to be fetched down almost at once, and then he'd gone down to Dr. Bevan's floor, and found that he wasn't in. It was about him that he questioned me most, as to what time he'd most often come, and how long he'd stay."

Mr. Willerton was not surprised to hear this, concluding that the police had been prompt to follow up the trail that had brought him to the same door. He asked: "Then Dr. Bevan doesn't live here all the time?"

"Oh, no, sir. He's a real gent. His house is in Portman Square. He comes here when he's working, sometimes every day, and sometimes not more than once or twice a week. And other days I do the feeding for him."

"Feeding?"

"Yes, sir. Mice and rabbits and rats. He's mostly got two or three dozens here, and hundreds at times, and then he'll clear a lot off. He doesn't do much of the killing here now, because the other tenants and then the landlords made too much fuss, but he does a bit on the quiet still. I've known times when he'd go on so that the place would smell like a butcher's yard. And the cleaning up! But he says it's science, and we ought to look at it in the right way. It wasn't I who made any complaint. He doesn't mind what he pays, and I should be sorry to see him go."

"When do you think he's likely to be here again?"

"I couldn't rightly say, sir. It isn't often that he misses more than a few days. Not unless he's on holiday somewhere. He goes yachting a lot. But he always tells me before he goes."

"Then I'd better try for him at Portman Square?"

"Yes, sir. That might be best. But I ought to tell you," the man added, conscious that he had not yet done much for the ten-shilling note, "that from what Inspector Monkhouse said he'd been there yesterday himself, and only came here when he couldn't find him at home."

"Well, I must chance that," Mr. Willerton answered, and was turning away, thinking that his time might be better occupied in seeking Dr. Bevan than in further gossip with a man who said frankly that he had no useful information to give, when he became conscious that Mr. Beecher was standing behind him.

The journalist must have been there sufficiently long to have heard at least the concluding words of the conversation, for he interposed with: "You won't find it's much use doing that. Dr. Bevan hasn't been home since Wednesday. I suppose he's keeping out of the way of this fuss."

Mr. Willerton smiled. "We seem to be on the same trail. I suppose it's really no use going up?"

"Not the least, unless you've come with some skeleton keys. I've just come down. Both the flats are locked and seem empty."

"Well, I'm wanting lunch more than anything else now. Would you care to join me?"

Mr. Beecher said that it would be a pleasure. He had had a hurried meal about an hour before, but his opportunities for refreshment were irregular, and he made it a rule of life not to refuse an invitation on any such trivial pretext.

They went together to the *Boatman's Head* in Horseferry Road, where they found a parlour, quiet and clean, in which they were served with a plain but well-cooked meal of pork chops, with an apple tart following; and Mr. Beecher, with the help of two glasses of beer, put his portions away, without visible protest from the location of his earlier lunch, while he made due payment by giving his host the benefit of the knowledge which he had acquired since their telephone conversation of the earlier morning.

Unfortunately, it was not much. He had ascertained from the *Medical Register, Who's Who,* and other sources of information, such as are readily available in newspaper offices, that Dr. Edward Bevan was of good family, ample means, and established reputation. The eldest son of a famous surgeon, he was himself an expert operator, but the wealth which had come into his hands at his father's death five years before had enabled him to devote himself to research work, with results which were already regarded as brilliant in professional circles. His age was thirty-eight. He was unmarried. His recreations were golf and yachting.

He appeared, from these evidences, to be a man whose witness should be of a reliable kind, and Mr. Willerton felt it to be of increased importance to ascertain why Thomas Birchall should have considered it necessary, and indeed urgent, to inform him that he would be at Highview House for a week longer than he had expected.

Returning confidence for confidence, he mentioned this point to Mr. Beecher, who was quick to see its indication that the telegram must have had some exceptional cause.

"The point," Mr. Willerton said, "which struck me from when I first heard about it, and which made me determined to follow it up, was that Birchall was so anxious to get it off on the night of the 6th. It was something he didn't want anyone else to see, and which he was so particular to get off that night that even the episode with Mrs. Cuthbertson didn't take it off his mind for a single minute.

"When I read how little there was in it, I didn't think it simple at all. I thought it made it more important, and more difficult to explain.

"The fact that the date on which Cuthbertson's scheme was to be put; into operation was set forward for a few days might, or might not, affect the time at which Birchall would ultimately reappear, but it couldn't make any difference to the fact that *in any case* he wouldn't be returning to his flat for some time, and certainly not during the next week.

"I don't say that there may not be a simple explanation—probably there is—but, if so, it's one that Dr. Bevan could give us, and I should very much like to hear it. Do you think he can be keeping out of the way because he knows more than he wants to tell?"

Mr. Beecher considered this, but thought it unlikely that Thomas Birchall, dead or alive, would be of sufficient importance to affect the movements of the more affluent and more successful scientist. Of course, he might have cleared out for a few days because he didn't want to be bothered by reporters and other curious persons who (like himself) would be round his door as soon as his name was mentioned in connection with this notorious case.

He said that he should not be able to do much more himself in following up Dr. Bevan now, having, like Mr. Willerton, to be in Osbury next morning. Probably the editor would put someone else on to the search, which was sure to be one of Fleet Street's principal occupations now, and in which the *Record* might be disposed to make an unusual effort, as it had already made the case so triumphantly its own. But there was one thing he could do. He could ring up Inspector Monkhouse, and ask if the police had knowledge of Dr. Bevan's present address which they would be willing to share. He had been able to do the Inspector a good turn two or three months before, and these services were remembered between Fleet Street and Scotland Yard, and frequently paid in kind. If he should learn anything, Mr. Willerton should have the benefit when they met in the morning.

They rose to go, Mr. Willerton paying the bill, and remarking as he did so that he had still another call to make, and was anxious not to miss the 5:10. But a taxi would soon get over the ground—

"Not my way?" Jimmie Beecher asked. "I'm straight back for the office now. If I could give you a lift?"

"No. I'm afraid it isn't. I thought of having a talk with Birchall senior. The address I've got is north London—Hampstead way."

"Then, if that's what you were meaning to do, I can save you a useless journey. The boys have been round his door ever since he got back yesterday evening, and he won't see anyone. I tried myself this morning, or I should have been on Dr. Bevan's track earlier. A woman came to the door—a housekeeper, I should say—who was going to shut it again without speaking, but I got a pound note under her eyes just in time.

"After that, she told me that the old gentleman seemed to have taken a chill, beside being rather excited, and she had thought it prudent to keep him in bed.

"I don't know whether it's a real cold, or the sort of illness that politicians get at the right times, but if you can get over the doorstep you can say that you've beaten me."

Mr. Willerton considered this, and decided that he would go home. He had had a very hard and anxious time for the last five days, and he saw that the kind of investigations which he had undertaken might be pursued more successfully by those enquiry agents, journalists, or police who specialize in such activities.

He had done something in securing Mr. Beecher's promise that he would give him the benefit of any information he might be able to gain, and a calculation of his remaining time showed that it had been a sanguine hope rather than a mathematical probability that he could have visited Hampstead and returned with sufficient speed to have caught the last train which would have landed him in Osbury before midnight.

Reflecting that he could come up again on Monday, if necessary, he accepted the journalist's invitation, and shared his taxi as far as Piccadilly Circus, where he indulged himself with the latter half of one motion picture and the commencement of another before returning to Waterloo.

CHAPTER XXXVIII.

MR. BEECHER, on regaining the offices of the Sunday *Record*, rang up Scotland Yard, and was informed that Chief Inspector Monkhouse was out, but might return at any moment. It had been his intention to leave early that evening, having, like Mr. Willerton, had a busy week, and having to get up in time to catch the 6:35 A.M. for Osbury on the following day; but he was not of a disposition to be easily turned from anything on which he had set his mind, and he remained in touch with the telephone for a further two hours before he was rewarded with a sound of the Inspector's voice.

"That you, Jimmie? What are you wanting us to do now?"

"I thought you mightn't mind giving us Dr. Bevan's address."

"Edward Bevan's? Sorry, but that's just what I'm wanting to know myself." And then, after a moment's pause: "What made you think we should be likely to have that?"

Excepting he saw an evident reason for more circumlocutory methods, Mr. Beecher allowed his natural frankness to have its way. Now he said: "I thought you might be curious to know why Birchall sent him that wire. And I heard that you had a try at his door, after you'd found that Birchall wasn't in on the floor above."

"You don't miss much! But I'm wanting a few words with Dr. Bevan about another matter, and when you mentioned him, I wondered if you'd got on the track of that."

"Sorry I can't oblige. I'm full up with the Birchall case for the next few days. We're going to give you some fresh ideas about that when we go to press tomorrow night."

"Well, that's not our funeral. It's for the County Police to lose weight, if you've caught them barking under the wrong tree. Ring me up on Monday, and if we've caught up with Bevan I'll let you know. By the way, if you think he's mixed up with the Birchall murder, I should be rather interested to hear."

"But I don't think anything of the kind. For that matter, I don't know that there's been a Birchall murder at all. And I don't connect

177

Bevan with what happened in any way, except that I'd like to know why Birchall wired him that he was staying at Osbury."

"That all? Then I should say that it isn't much. I want to see him for a better reason than that."

Inspector Monkhouse rang off, feeling that he had said as much as it was prudent to do at that moment, and by that medium of communication; but he might have been more explicit, to the serious detriment of Dr. Bevan's plans, had he known that that gentleman was then heading for the office of the *Sunday Record* as rapidly as the car of his most intimate, but now rather nervous friend, Sir Isaac Thuster, could bring him through the stream of the Fleet Street traffic, which is particularly heavy on Friday evenings.

Mr. Beecher abandoned the idea of interviewing Dr. Bevan, and decided that he must concentrate upon the material he already had, and the statement which he was to obtain from Mrs. Cuthbertson in the morning. His immediate need was a sufficient interval for rest before he would have to rise for the early-morning train. But his journalistic instinct was too keen to enable him to put the conversation with Inspector Monkhouse out of his mind. He speculated vainly as to the urgent occasion that the Inspector could have for wishing to meet with a medical gentleman who had become so difficult to find.

Presuming that some criminal business was indicated, he saw that minor offences must be excluded from consideration, as they would be unlikely to attract the personal attention of a Chief Inspector. He must also eliminate other more serious felonies or misdemeanours, such as burglary, arson, or baby-farming, on grounds of inherent improbability.

It appeared most likely that Dr. Bevan had been engaged on one of those illegal operations which the law regards with occasional seriousness, if they result in the death of the female conspirator, instead of that only of the unborn child; or perhaps he had allowed his name to be used as the director of some fraudulent firm.

But when he recalled the status and antecedents of the missing doctor, as he had ascertained them during the earlier day, he was obliged to discard these theories also. The crimes of procuring abortion, or of drawing director's fees from fraudulent companies, are the temptations of impecunious greed, into which a doctor, well connected, independently wealthy, and engaged in research work for his own gratification, would be unlikely to fall.

Finally, he approached nearer to probability when he decided that Dr. Bevan must have been involved in a motor accident which had resulted fatally, probably having driven on without stopping, but not before his number plate had come under the notice of some sharp-eyed witness.

These speculations were matters of moments only, as he was on his way to the editor's room, where he was to make report before leaving, and to receive the cheque for one thousand guineas which would pass into the bank account of Mrs. Cuthbertson's solicitors on the following day.

But when he entered the room, the editor had an opened envelope on the blotting pad before him, and a slip of paper in his hand, which he threw across the desk, with the words: "You've come at the right time. What do you think of this?"

Jimmie Beecher picked up the slip, on which was written the name of Dr. Edward Bevan, as seeking an interview with the editor, "urgent and important," in connection with the Birchall case.

"It looks," he remarked, "as though today's evidence has brought him here with a run."

"That's how it seems," the editor agreed. "But we're likely to have to take what he says on trust, without mentioning how we get it. He was so particular about not being observed that he wouldn't give his name downstairs, nor fill in the slip you've got till the porter had promised it should come up here under cover, in an envelope he addressed."

"Shall I see him, or will you have him up here?"

"You'd better deal with it. You know the case better than anyone, and I've got Lord Hillsdale coming in any minute now. You must make the best bargain you can, when you find out what he's got to sell. But you must remember that we pay nothing except for statements written and signed."

"I don't think he'll be out for money. He's too well off."

"Then I needn't tell you to get all you can on a free basis. But he must have some motive in coming here, and you know it's cash a great deal more often than not."

Jimmie Beecher did not dispute that. He replied only: "Well, if that's it, he's come to the right address." He gave instructions for the caller to be taken to the waiting room on the fourth floor, where he joined him a few minutes later, after completing the business which had taken him to the editor's room.

He met a man well, though not carefully, dressed, who looked at him with black, intelligent, but suspicious, unfriendly eyes, under a high forehead, showing scanty receding hair. He had strong teeth, a fleshy brutal jaw, and large sensitive hands.

"Dr. Edward Bevan?" Mr. Beecher enquired.

179

The doctor did not give a direct answer. He asked bluntly: "Would you like to know the facts of the Birchall case?"

Hearing this question, Jimmie Beecher forgot that he had been thinking of going home, or that he had an early train to catch on the following day. He said: "Won't you sit down?" And then noticing, with a trained observation, evidences of haste or discomposure in his visitor's manner, which it must be his first aim to soothe, he went on easily: "Yes, we should be glad to know that, especially if it's more than we do already.

"As a matter of fact, I was trying to get in touch with you this afternoon. I thought it might be interesting to know why Birchall sent you that telegram when he found he'd be at Highview House longer than he had expected when he left London."

"Oh, you spotted that? But I'll bet you didn't guess what the answer is."

"We've had one or two guesses. I won't say that we've guessed right."

"Would you give £500 cash down to know?"

"It might depend upon what the answer is."

"You'd have to trust that to me."

"I'm afraid I couldn't promise without knowing more."

"Then I must try whether the *Sunday News* will."

Dr. Bevan, who had consented to sit, rose as he spoke.

Jimmie did not appear to notice the action. He kept his own seat as he answered quietly: "Five hundred pounds is a large sum."

"It's a lot less than the tale will be worth to you."

"Then you can trust us that we shan't haggle at the amount."

"You'll have to take my word about that. I should want the cash down, and the statement kept sealed for forty-eight hours, or a bit more."

"You mean actual cash?"

"Yes. One-pound Bank of England notes. I suppose you wouldn't find that impossible at this time of day?"

"It's a bit late. But we have done such things before now. Don't you think you might explain rather more fully?"

Dr. Bevan resumed his seat. He said: "I'll trust you as far as you can expect, and perhaps as far as you'd wish me to do. I'm not sure that I'm not in trouble with the police—"

"Then I think I can remove any uncertainty about that. Inspector Monkhouse is making it a personal matter, and that means it's likely to be something important for you, as well as for him."

Dr. Bevan scowled at this information, but did not appear surprised. He asked: "You're not in with them, are you? You wouldn't give me away?"

"We don't work for the police, if you mean that. We shouldn't be likely to do anything to help a criminal to escape. If you tell me anything in confidence, I shan't give you away, unless it's of such a nature that—well, I must leave that to your own discretion."

"Well, I'll say this. I'm not a poor man, as you probably know, but I want to leave London at once, and, for reasons I needn't go into, I didn't think it wise to call at my bank this afternoon to get the cash I require.

"I've got something to sell that must be worth a large sum to you, and, apart from that, I may be away for some time, and I should like to give my own account of the matter, rather than leave it to that little swine Birchall to—"

"You mean that Birchall's really alive?"

"Did I say that? I didn't mean to tell you anything till we'd fixed the deal. But if I did, it isn't much of the whole tale."

"Possibly not. But if you tell me definitely that Thomas Birchall's alive, and you can put us in touch with him, I'll go to the editor now and ask him about buying the story."

"I didn't say I could put you in touch with him. I'll tell you this much. He wasn't the body they fished up."

"Well, I'll see what I can do. But you can't expect that we shall pay for something we haven't heard. I shan't keep you five minutes."

He rose to go, but Dr. Bevan rose also, with a motion to delay him. He said: "Look here, I don't want to lose time. I'm in a hurry for several reasons. I'm not a poor man. My cheque's good for £500. If you'll cash it for me tonight, I'll give you the tale, and you can send me what you think it's worth after you've read it—say, not before Monday midday."

"Well, that sounds fair. I'll see what the editor says."

Jimmie hurried back to the editor's room, feeling that he had struck oil again. But he found that his tale was received in a very sceptical way. Indeed, as he told it, without the support of Dr. Bevan's presence, he was aware that it sounded thin.

Mr. Garbett was not one who shirked such risks as his judgment endorsed, as may have been demonstrated by what he had agreed to stake already on the Birchall case, but he had learned to be wary also; and the present position was that, because Jimmie Beecher had obtained exclusive news of the arrest of Alfred Cuthbertson a week before, he had allowed him a very free hand with the case subsequently; and that policy had involved him in a liability of £1,000 for an interview he had not yet had, and a potential payment of another £1,000 for the discovery of a missing man.

"You don't want me," he asked, with a smile which reduced the sarcasm of the words, "to hand over the whole capital of the firm? Lord Hillsdale has just been asking me whether I'm sure that you know the difference between pounds and pence. As to this cheque business, it's impossible for several reasons. Besides, it sounds too much like our old friend the confidence trick to me. How do you know that the man's Bevan at all?"

"I've not much doubt about that."

"No? Well, I prefer to know. I telephoned Hatch & Welfords for a photograph of the doctor as soon as you went to speak to him. Luckily, he's on their file, and they promised to have it here in ten minutes. By the way, they supplied one to Scotland Yard a few hours ago."

Even as he spoke, his secretary entered, and laid a photograph on the table before him.

He passed it over to Jimmie, with a laconic: "This he?"

Jimmie looked at it with a moment's dismay, after which his face cleared. "Yes," he said, "that's the man. But he's done some shaving since then."

"Yes? That sounds as though he may have got in a tight squeeze. Now just listen to me. We can't cash the man's cheque, after what you heard from Inspector Monkhouse. It would be too much like helping him to escape from justice, and we don't know what he's been at, or how important it may be to Monkhouse to trip him up."

"Monkhouse didn't even say that he'd got a warrant out for him. He only said he was anxious to run him down."

"So I understand. You may have to remind him of that. But there's no reason we shouldn't buy this tale from him, even if he's just murdered his godmother. That's quite different from cashing a cheque. The only question is whether the tale's worth the amount. If he really knows that Birchall's alive, and can explain how the whole thing has happened, it might be cheap at the price. That's a big if. And you mustn't forget that we've bought a narrative from Mrs. Cuthbertson that we haven't yet had. We don't want to pay twice for the same tale."

"I don't think there's much fear of that. Whatever Mrs. Cuthbertson knows, it isn't that Thomas Birchall's alive. That's what they're so anxious to be able to prove."

"Very well, you can do this: if you're satisfied he's the man, and if he convinces you that he's got the goods, you can say that we'll give him cash, but he's to give you his cheque dated a week ahead for the same amount. If we decide not to use the story, we bank his cheque and repay ourselves, but if we use the story we tear it up. It may be a good thing that Monkhouse didn't say more than he did."

Jimmie went back to continue the negotiations on these terms, leaving Mr. Garbett little less excited than himself. He saw that if he could publish two statements in successive weeks, complementary to each other, sensational in themselves, and combining to prick the prosecution's confident bubble, he would have pulled off the scoop of the year, and even Lord Hillsdale himself would regard the cost as of no more importance than a matter of petty cash.

He put it out of his mind next moment, for Friday evening is a busy time in the editorial rooms of a Sunday newspaper, and it was half an hour later when Jimmie re-entered his room in a mood of triumph, and laid a sealed foolscap envelope on his desk.

"There it is," he said, "and here's the cheque, and Bevan's only waiting to pouch the cash, which I've told him he shall have in about three minutes."

Mr. Garbett handled it doubtfully. The sealed envelope again reminded him forcibly of the devices of the confidence trickster, and of the vendors of the golden brick. He hoped better things, but might it not make him the laughter of Fleet Street if he were wrong? Or even lead to the vacating of that comfortable editorial chair?

"It didn't," he said, "take very long to write."

"He hasn't written it here. He had it ready, and pulled it out when I told him he could call it a deal."

"You feel sure we're not being fooled?"

"I'll risk being fired. He's told me enough of the truth in confidence, both about this and the jam he's in, to make me sure that it's true. He's a filthy dog, but he's not lying now. It fits in too well with the facts we know."

"Very well. I told the cashier some time ago to have the money ready if it should be required."

Five minutes later, Dr. Bevan left the offices of the *Sunday Record* by the side-street exit, and sought the shelter of a passing taxi.

He twice changed his vehicle, walking a short distance in the intervals, and, being satisfied that he was not followed, he then entered a fourth, instructing the driver to take him out to the country residence, beyond Camberley, of Sir Isaac Shuster, who was giving him a temporary and nervous shelter, his mind divided between the claims of friendship, loyalty to what they considered to be the ethics of their profession, and a timid dread of the possible consequences of sheltering a man who had broken his country's laws.

CHAPTER XXXIX.

IT is a fact which we may regard as very strange, or very natural if we will, but it remains a fact which we cannot deny, that many of the world's greatest books were written in jails by convicted men. It is true that such happenings were in uncivilized times, and they would be as impossible as for Nelson to enter the Navy now, but Alfred Cuthbertson, not being even committed for trial as yet, was allowed paper and pens.

He used them for the working out of solutions to a problem of crime, or suicide, or what else it might prove to be, which might owe its inception to himself, but had passed beyond his design, and now declined to adapt itself to any plausible theory of explanation.

He must now use the wits which had previously enjoyed the ingenuity of their own inventions to formulate some reasonable sequence of events which could have put the clothes of the cousin whom he had feinted to kill upon the body of another man who had come in reality to that violent end; and he had occasion to realize the wide difference which separates fancy from actuality, the greater difficulty of persuading theory to accept fact, when compared with the facile adjustments of a self-invented story.

Yet he did, in fact, work out not less than twenty-seven logically possible, if not probable theories, of which three of the more fantastic were not entirely different from the truth; and though he remained in a state of nervous exasperation over the weekend, this feeling was grounded on the discomforts of his present experiences, rather than in anticipation of a possible worse to come.

So far as the object was concerned which had first attracted his mind, he had no ground for dissatisfaction. The doubts raised at the last hearing concerning the clothes and identity of the dead man had intrigued every newspaper reader within the British Isles, and he had consequently become, in a single week, the best known of all British writers of detective fiction. And then on Sunday the public were stirred to additional extremities of excitement and speculation by the publication of Dorothy's account of the plot which had achieved such super-successful realism, and by the £1,000 which was offered for the production of a man whose death has been the common assumption, not only of the prosecution, but of many millions of readers during the previous week.

But Alfred Cuthbertson, working out ingenious, improbable theories, and discarding them one by one as he stumbled over some awkward fact to which they refused to bend, had ceased to fear the ultimate issue of the accusation which had been made against him. He kept his mind steadily on that one logical argument, that if he had cast a man over the cliff, he must have been washed ashore in the same suit as that in which he had commenced his descent, and not (paradox of ultimate improbabilities!) in another which was also his property and had been on his back a few weeks before. It seemed to him that it could only be necessary for his counsel to hold firmly to this narrow but yet impregnable ground, and the most perverse of juries could not refuse him the freedom which was his due.

But Mr. Willerton felt differently. Being more in touch with the outside world, he was able to observe the reactions of many minds to Mrs. Cuthbertson's revelation of the conspiracy in which the present charge had its root. Various as their opinions were, there were few who accepted it as conclusive evidence of the innocence of the accused man, and to many it appeared to remove the homicide definitely from the categories of accident or impulsive violence to that of pre-calculated murder.

They said with reason that there was "some funny business somewhere." There was incontestably a dead man, which is always difficult to explain away! And who more likely to be the originator of funny business than the man who made a living by the invention of ingenious mysteries which were saturated in crime? And now Mrs. Cuthbertson had come forward, and had actually told a story in which her husband appeared in his expected character. That she believed in his innocence might be natural enough. He would be a poor plotter of criminal mystery who could not deceive his wife! But the most common reaction was to conclude that Alfred Cuthbertson, contemptuously underrating the intelligence of his fellow men, had had the audacity to murder his cousin in full view, so to speak, of the whole world, relying upon the confusion he had first established by telling his wife that the deed would be an affair of pantomime only, and then upon the second ingenuity (but was it more ingenious, more improbable, than that of *The Clue of the Twisted Spoon?*) by which he had somehow juggled the clothes of the missing man. But a British jury would be unlikely to be bamboozled by such devices! As men and women of common sense, "of the world," they would know that when one man is seen to throw another into the sea, who is afterwards fished out dead, there is an obvious inference to be drawn.

Alfred Cuthbertson might wriggle and twist, as no doubt he would, and it would be diverting to watch, but British Law (which is an example to the whole world!) would put his nonsense firmly aside, and deal with him as his crime required.

Mr. Willerton, considering that Tuesday, when he must put the Cuthbertsons into the witness box, was now very near, and the unfortunate fact that he could only propose a mystery to the magistrates to which he had himself no plausible solution to offer, must find what hope he could in the magnitude of the reward which had now been advertised, and from a hint that Mr. Beecher had given that he knew something more than he yet had freedom to say.

CHAPTER XL.

IT was on the day of publication—Sunday, May 26th, 1935—and on a bench in a Dublin park, that Thomas Birchall read in the *Sunday Record* the announcement of the substantial sum which might at any moment be his, at no further cost than a journey to London to collect the cheque.

Of whatever other obliquity of conduct he may be charged, it would be unfair to condemn him because he was not in a remote village, such as he had promised that he would seek, and to which he had actually proceeded.

He had discovered that to be inconspicuous in Ballymolly (Galway) was, for him at least, an impossible thing. It was particularly so after he had announced that the object of his visit was to fish its mountain streams, but that his nets had been unfortunately lost on the rail.

He did nothing to reduce curiosity by ordering a large number of English newspapers, which Ballymolly does not ordinarily import. At the end of the third day, and after noticing that the papers he was receiving were attracting the surreptitious attention of his landlady's daughter and her two sons, he came to the sound conclusion that he would be less conspicuous in a larger place. He announced that the loss of the nets was an irretrievable calamity, and returned to Dublin.

He put up there at a small hotel at the back of the railway station, and might not have attracted the attention of Mr. de Valera's energetic police had he not again felt it necessary to assume a fictitious character, for which he selected that of a dealer in Irish cattle, having observed the existence of such gentlemen as he had come over in the Holyhead boat.

But the chaotic ignorance of matters beyond the range of his own specialized studies which is the prerogative of the modern scientist, and which had already led him to the assumption that English visitors fish with nets in the Galway streams, was to betray him again.

After somewhat puzzling his host by informing him that his occupation was the purchase of "beeves on the hoof," which he supposed to be the vernacular of a dealer in Irish cattle, he completed bewilderment by unconsciously disclosing his ignorance of Mr. J. H. Thomas's enterprising method of collecting the Irish annuities. Mr. Doolan felt that so singular a cattle dealer might be of interest to the police, to whom he therefore made a report.

This occurred on Saturday evening, and when he strolled through the city streets on the following day, waiting for the hour when the English Sunday newspapers would be on sale, and being nervously watchful of any sign that he was attracting the observation of those around him, he became uneasily suspicious that he had engaged the interest of more than one of his fellow loiterers.

So, in fact, it was. A plainclothes policeman had been detailed to watch the movements of this exceptional cattle dealer, and to invite him to accompany him to the police station if they should appear to be inconsistent with the occupation which he professed. And Mr. Theophilus Fairbrother (commonly known in Fleet Street as Phil) was observing him with an even keener interest.

Mr. Fairbrother considered that he had good reason for hating the name of Cuthbertson, and that of Birchall was one that he did not love. A fortnight before, he had committed the error of leaving Osbury on a Saturday afternoon when it had seemed that the prospect of securing copy of any value for the issue of the *Sunday News* which was then being prepared for press had become negligible in its improbability, with the result that his despicable rival, the reporter of the *Sunday Record*, had made an exclusive scoop. Jimmie Beecher, passing him in Tudor Street, had smiled in a way that he did not like. And his editor (whose manners were frequently deserving of condemnation) had been plainly rude. He had not taken him off the case. He had told him to stick to it, and give Jimmie one in the eye if he wasn't anxious to lose his job. With that attractive object in view, and with the instinct of self-preservation sharply aroused, he had seen, on the first suggestion being made by Mr. Willerton, that Thomas Birchall might still be alive, the faint but solitary possibility that he might, by one brilliant stroke, overshadow the success into which the dull-witted Jimmie's infernal luck had caused him to stumble.

Aided in Dorchester by something which an impartial tongue might have called by the same name, but which he rather ascribed to his natural genius, he had got, almost immediately, upon the track of the flying man, and had obtained a description of the disguise, including a top coat of emphatic colour, which Thomas had purchased there. He had followed a trail which became plainer as it proceeded, arriving in Ballymolly in time to see Mr. Birchall, if it were he, clad in that unmistakable coat, seated at a window of the train which left for Dublin as he had alighted on the opposite platform.

He had made enquiries during the eight hours that he had waited there till the next train should leave, which had convinced him that the eccentric fisherman was the missing scientist; and having ascertained with little difficulty, and at a cost of only two shillings, from the booking clerk, that the English gentleman had taken a Dublin ticket, he had returned to that city in time to discover the hotel where he (or, more exactly, where the emphatic overcoat) had put up.

Now he stalked him with the triple objects of observing his occupations, comparing him with the newspaper photographs in his possession, and taking a snapshot of him with the pocket camera which he always carried. It had occurred to him that a picture of "Thomas Birchall in Dublin Yesterday" as a headpiece for the account of next Tuesday's proceedings against a man charged with his murder, might be something which his editor would be pleased to have.

Thomas Birchall bought several papers. He found a seat, and commenced upon the *Sunday Record*, as the one which had had exclusive news on the previous week concerning that which he wished to know. He read the offer of £1,000 for evidence of his own existence, and, like Dante's lovers, he read no more. He rose up, tearing out the momentous page, and went back to his hotel. Or, at least, he started to do so. But he had not gone many yards before he was stopped by a man who said that he was a police officer in a tone that suggested that it might be unhealthy to doubt his word, and invited him to accompany him to a place where they could have a more intimate talk.

Mr. Fairbrother strolled up to the vacated bench. He observed that it was the *Sunday Record* to which the suspected man had directed his first attention. He could not read a page which was no longer there, but the inferences were obvious.

He quickly procured another copy, and the matter passed beyond the realm of probability into that of ascertained fact. He went to the telegraph office, and then took a ticket to return to London by the next boat.

CHAPTER XLI.

MR. BIRCHALL had an unpleasant time at the police station. He commenced with falsehoods, and then, finding them hard to sustain, took refuge in a stubborn refusal to answer any questions whatever. He was resolved not to admit his identity, and, as he was not searched, the Dublin police missed the opportunity of collecting the substantial reward which an examination of the abstracted page of the *Sunday Record* would have put so nearly within their grasp.

He gave the name of Richard Mortimer, which he had adopted since leaving Osbury, and though they saw no reason to believe his word, they had no suspicion of who he was.

Having nothing against him beyond the two evident and almost equally sinister facts that he was an Englishman and had a mendacious tongue, they let him go with a warning that if he were a wise man he would return to his own land by the next boat, which he willingly undertook to do.

The episode had, indeed, the effect of deciding his course of action with less consideration from himself than it might otherwise have received. He had been increasingly uncomfortable, as the enforced leisure of his stay in Ballymolly in the passive role of a fisherman who had lost his nets had given him time to consider various possible or even probable sequels, if he should remain hidden there until Alfred Cuthbertson should be irretrievably hanged. As Alfred had discovered from his own angle, that which is satisfactory in anticipation may be less pleasant when it has become experience of an unavoidable kind.

In any case, £1,000 to a man of very limited means is a sum which it is worthwhile to pick up. He felt that he was being pushed by the police in the direction in which he would probably have chosen to go, and returned to the hotel to pack his very limited luggage, and to leave for England practically at the same time, though not actually by the same boat, as the representative of the *Sunday News*.

He was not aware that it is the custom for the editorial staffs of Sunday newspapers to take holidays on Monday, as compensation for their strenuous exertions during the latter part of the week, and so arrived at the offices of the *Sunday Record* without the hesitation which might have come from fuller knowledge; for which there was, in fact, no occasion, for it is a custom which will give way to sufficient urgencies, and Mr. Garbett was in his room, with Jimmie Beecher in attendance, and about half the full clerical staff, who were dealing distractedly with an overwhelming bombardment of telegrams, telephone conversations, and personal calls from the large section of the population who had seen Mr. Birchall since yesterday, and were anxious to collect the reward as promptly as possible.

Through this miscellaneous hubbub, the preference given to the police had enabled Chief Inspector Monkhouse to get a call through to Mr. Beecher about half an hour before the authentic Birchall appeared on the scene.

The Inspector spoke as an aggrieved man. "I hear," he said, "that you had Bevan with you on Friday and let him go."

"Well, what else did you expect me to do? I hadn't got a warrant for his arrest!"

"No, but I had."

"You didn't tell me that. I don't think you even said he'd done anything wrong. You said you'd like to have a talk with him, which might have meant anything."

"I suppose you told him I'd said that?"

"I think I did. But it wasn't much news to him. He seemed to be expecting trouble from you."

"Did he tell you what he'd been at?"

"Not as much as I should have liked to know. But he's left us something to open at noon today. I hope there'll be more in that."

"I shall have to ask you to open that now."

"I don't think the editor would allow that. Why do you ask?"

"The man's bolted, and we want any clue we can get as to where he's most probably flown to."

"Flown?"

"Yes. That's the right word. He stole Sir Isaac Shuster's private plane, and got off in the night."

"I don't see how the statement would be likely to help you. It's supposed to be confined to the Cuthbertson case."

"Yes? I'm not worrying about that. Not at present. But I should like to see that statement as soon as I can. I'll be with you in half an hour, or perhaps less."

"Very well, come along, of course. But I can't promise any-thing. It's not exactly a public document. We had to pay a good price to get it."

"You mean you gave him the money to get away?"

"Not at all. We gave him money for something we were very anxious to have."

There was a moment's pause, and then the Inspector's voice said curtly: "Well, it's no use saying more. I'm coming round."

But he happened to be delayed after that by some other matter of equal urgency, so that he had not arrived when Thomas Birchall entered the enquiry office on the ground floor, and, a moment later, Mr. Fairbrother followed him.

The reporter had arrived in London at an earlier hour but had been delayed by the necessity of getting his own editor on the phone, and obtaining his authority for that which he wished to do; for he could not overlook the fact that whatever information he had gained was the property of the *Sunday News*, and, even for a reward of £1,000, he had no right to disclose it to a rival periodical. The editor, having left his home for an early round on the golf course, had not been immediately available, and had then declined to dis-cuss the matter until he had returned from the club room to his own house, the position being sufficiently unusual to justify a delayed decision, and (which he did not think it necessary to mention to Mr. Fairbrother) a reference to the proprietor for his advice.

So it happened that it was almost at the same instant that Tho-mas Birchall and Theophilus Fairbrother passed the swing doors that give entrance to the offices of the *Sunday Record*. Thomas was in advance, and the porter should, and doubtless would, have given him the prior attention which was his right. But Mr. Fairbrother had two advantages. He knew Thomas, whereas Thomas did not recog-nize him, and he knew the offices into which he came.

Seeing Thomas, he guessed his purpose, and he saw that the price of precedence might be a four-figure cheque. He said breezily to the porter, of the strictness of whose orders he was well aware: "It's all right, Jack. I only want a few words with Jimmie. I guess I know the way up," and as the last words were said, he ignored the closed door of the lift, and ran lightly up the stairs on the farther side.

The porter glanced after him in a moment's hesitation, and turned to Mr. Birchall, who submitted without protest to fill up a form which was conveyed by the lift boy to the editor's floor in the usual manner.

Meanwhile, Mr. Fairbrother had run upstairs in some doubt as to whether he might not have spoiled his chances by the unauthorized manner of his approach. He remembered that it was Monday, and that it was uncertain what rooms would be occupied. He knew his way about, but even his audacity might have hesitated to penetrate among the probably-vacated rooms of the opposition newspaper offices. Fortunately for him, the occasion for solving this problem of ethics did not arise.

As he gained the fourth landing, he saw a figure he knew, that of Mr. Garbett's secretary, Miss Margaret Bailey, a sharp-witted, sharp-tongued girl, who had been at one time on the staff of the *Sunday News*, receding down the corridor, and he was swift-footed in her pursuit.

She turned in surprise at the sound of his hasty approach, which was not lessened when she recognized who he was.

"I suppose," she said, with a sarcasm natural from one who had been on the editor's telephone for the last two hours, "you're going to tell me that you've got Thomas Birchall in a taxi outside."

"You're middle-stump," he said, "with the first ball. He's sitting kicking his heels down below now. I'll give you five pounds if I'm in Mr. Garbett's room within thirty seconds."

He pulled out his watch as he spoke.

"Honest fact?" she asked bluntly, ignoring the watch, and the offered bribe.

"Should I be here if it weren't? I don't exactly want to be kicked downstairs."

"Wait a moment," she said, and passed on to the editor's door, leaving him in the corridor, which was, at least, better than being shut away in the waiting room at the end of the passage, where he could not have seen if anyone had had precedence of himself.

A moment later, she appeared at the open door. "Mr. Fairbrother, Mr. Garbett will see you," she said formally.

He went in, with some reason to think that the game was won.

CHAPTER XLII.

MR. BIRCHALL was kept waiting for about twenty minutes, during which time he saw Inspector Monkhouse, whom, being in civilian clothes, he did not recognize as an officer of the Metropolitan police, go up before him.

He had not introduced himself in his own name, but, retaining that which he had adopted in Ireland, and which he had already found himself becoming accustomed to use, he had written, on the slip of paper that the porter had invited him to fill up, that Mr. Mortimer wished to see the editor on important business. He had no suspicion either that Mr. Fairbrother had already betrayed him, or that his identity would be otherwise guessed, as he was, at last, invited to enter the lift, and conducted politely to the editor's room.

Being unfamiliar with the interior of newspaper offices, he was not surprised when he found himself the centre of about half a dozen men, one of whom sat at a wide desk by the windows, while the others were scattered sitting or standing about the room. There was one young lady, Miss Bailey, seated at a desk on the farther side, who did not look up from her work as he entered.

Mr. Garbett spared him the awkwardness of introducing himself by his true name. "Mr. Thomas Birchall, I believe?" he enquired smoothly.

Mr. Birchall was surprised by this reception, though he did not immediately realize all that it implied.

"Yes," he said. "I expect you thought I should soon be here when I read about the reward."

"We did have that idea. And it can't be said that you lost much time. It's a pity you couldn't have managed to be half an hour earlier. As it is, Mr. Fairbrother here claims the reward."

Mr. Birchall turned indignant, astonished eyes upon the reporter of the *Sunday News*. He recognized him at once as the young man who had entered behind him, and run up the stairs with the familiarity of one on accustomed ground. "Why," he said, his wits sharpened by the magnitude of the stake at issue, and seizing the one point which could be urged for his own claim, "I came in before him!"

Mr. Garbett looked at Mr. Fairbrother. "That so, Phil?" he asked.

Mr. Fairbrother did not deny it. "He may have come through the door first. I don't see that there's much in that."

Mr. Garbett turned his eyes to Mr. Hudson, the solicitor to the group of syndicated newspapers to which the *Sunday Record* belonged, whom he had requested to be present. He asked: "Any point there?"

He had no love for Thomas Birchall, but he would have welcomed almost any development which would have provided an adequate reason for refusing Mr. Fairbrother's claim. He had bitterly realized (as had the proprietor of the *Sunday News* when he had given ready, even jubilant consent to the claiming of the reward) that it would be the joke of Fleet Street, and an enormous advertisement throughout the country, that the reward should have been claimed by one of the staff of the rival newspaper.

But Mr. Hudson, looking with disfavour upon Thomas Birchall, of whom he had heard much evil during the last twenty minutes, and having no doubt of the legality of the position, was discouraging in his reply. "There's nothing in who came through the door first. It's Birchall's fault for not sending up his own name."

Mr. Birchall had sufficient sense to see that it would be useless to argue the point at that moment, and in an atmosphere of obvious frigidity. He said: "I guessed you'd try twisting me somehow. I'd better get a good lawyer on to the job." He rose up to go.

Mr. Garbett, regarding him as a source of interesting copy rather than a fellow man, declined to take offence. He said: "If your solicitor can show us that we are liable, we shall be quite willing to pay. But I should say you'll have something else to think about for the next few days. There's Inspector Monkhouse here, quite willing to listen to your account of how this trouble began."

Mr. Birchall's attention was directed to the Chief Inspector, who returned his glance in a coldly-professional manner very difficult to endure.

Had he been asked to make a statement without the threat implied in the wording of Mr. Garbett's invitation to do so, he might have been alert enough to stipulate for adequate payment first. But he was well aware that his conduct had not been such as those who administer the law would be likely to regard with indulgent eyes. It was that realization which had become increasingly insistent during the idleness of the last week; which had spoiled his pleasure in contemplation of his cousin's calamitous position; and which was largely responsible for the ease with which he had decided to disclose the fact of his continued existence, with the consolation of being able to claim the unexpected prize of the offered reward.

Now he remembered opportunely that the double sheet of the *Sunday Record* which he had brought away, in addition to the offered reward for himself, had contained a statement from Dorothy Cuthbertson, which he had naturally read with care. He resolved at once to be frank concerning such facts as were already beyond concealment. He said boldly: "Well, I don't mind telling anyone that. I've got nothing to hide."

He paused a moment, for there was an interruption from the telephone on Miss Bailey's desk, to which she listened and answered with decisive brevity: "Yes, quite right: send it up."

As she laid down the receiver, Inspector Monkhouse spoke: "I shall be pleased to listen to anything Birchall wishes to say. But he must understand that he speaks at his own risk."

The remark was not reassuring, nor was the significant fact that it was addressed to Mr. Garbett, not to himself; but Thomas Birchall had gone too far to recede, and was merely confirmed in his private intention of saying nothing more than was known already.

He commenced a somewhat prolix narrative, such as would have exasperated his cousin's faculty for concise or dramatic statement, which would be wearisome to record; as it only deviated from facts which have been already disclosed sufficiently to assert his own natural rectitude, and the reluctance with which, at the call of friendship, he had become a party to a plot which had not originated with him.

He was only once interrupted, when a page boy entered, and handed Miss Bailey a fragment of galley proof, which she laid silently on Mr. Garbett's desk.

The editor had glanced at it with a moment's raising of bushy brows, and had afterwards kept it in his hand, as though it waited its turn to divert the current of the events around it. "Of course," Mr. Birchall concluded, "when I got back to Dublin, I saw the newspapers, and I came home at once. I've no doubt I should have done that, even if I hadn't read about the reward. But I hadn't thought I should be wanted so quick. Alfred gave me the idea that he might wish me to stay away for two or three weeks, or even a bit more. He seemed most afraid that I should come back too soon."

"Do you mind telling us," Mr. Garbett asked, "why you sent that telegram to Dr. Bevan?"

The question seemed to discomfort Mr. Birchall, but he recovered himself quickly to answer: "I wanted to let him know that I should be longer away."

"Why should he need to know that?"

"He had promised to keep an eye on the flat, and to do other things for me while I was away."

"You must have been very close friends?"

"We were well enough."

"Perhaps I ought to tell you that Dr. Bevan has made a signed statement of what occurred. I might call it a confession. It seems to incriminate you about as much as himself."

Mr. Birchall went perceptibly paler as he heard this. He broke a moment's expectant silence to say: "Dr. Bevan could always tell a good lie. He could tell a lie in his sleep."

"Perhaps he could," Mr. Garbett allowed, trying to draw him out, "but the dead body wasn't a lie. It was a very serious fact."

"Well," Mr. Birchall replied, with obvious though ambiguous truth, "it wasn't mine, anyway."

There was curtness in this reply sufficient to indicate that the speaker was no longer in a talkative mood. Mr. Garbett changed the subject. "There's something here that you may be interested to know. It appears that your grandfather died at an early hour this morning."

He read the brief account of Eli Birchall's end which had been set up for the columns of the *Evening Mail*. It appeared that Mr. Birchall must have caught a chill in the keen sea air as he had stood on the cliff top four days before. Pneumonia had developed with the swiftness characteristic of its attacks upon the weak and aged, and Eli Birchall had died at ninety-four without admission that he had outlasted his youthful days. His grandsons' plot, by that remoteness of unavoidable consequence which makes a jest of the plannings of prudent men, had brought his death, at which they had cast no thought, and had given him a fortuitous and momentary publicity which might have come in no other way.

Thomas Birchall took the news, among that group of unfriendly men, with no indication of what he thought. He got up with the remark: "Well, I suppose it's no good saying any more now."

The words were received in silence, and in that hostile silence he withdrew, half-expecting to find that the movement would be signal for his arrest. He went with some satisfaction in the thought that he had not been pressed to admit the truth of Dr. Bevan's statement, the nature of which he was well able to guess, and with his chagrin at the refusal to admit his claim to the advertised reward almost forgotten in the excitement of the thought that his grandfather's wealth was about to come into his hands.

He could not know that he had no more withdrawn from Inspector Monkhouse's observation than if he had been a dog taken out on a lead, for the plainclothes man who had been detailed to keep him in view was too experienced in his work to allow suspicion to enter his quarry's mind.

Mr. Birchall delayed only for a frugal and hurried lunch, and then boarded a Hampstead bus. He had some reason for fear that his grandfather might have imprudently postponed making a will, in which case he knew that no evidence of his intentions, however clearly expressed, would be sufficient to shut out his cousin from an equal share of the now derelict wealth for which he had waited through such lengthened years, and it was a point on which Eli Birchall's housekeeper would be the one who would be most likely to be able either to dispel or confirm his fears.

The woman received him with sufficient politeness, and showed no reluctance to inform him concerning the last days of the old gentleman's life. Herself a mere quarter of a century younger, she had the attachment of long service, and the personal grief of feeling that the home of which she had long been the mistress in all but name must, in the natural order, be broken up.

She said that Mr. Birchall appeared to have realized at an early stage that his illness might terminate fatally, for even on Saturday morning, and before the most serious symptoms developed, he had been urgent to make a will, which she had never previously heard him propose. He had sent for Mr. Turnbull of Turnbull and Masterman, who had charge of his investments, who had come in haste, bringing two gentlemen to act as witnesses, and the will had been drawn and executed that afternoon. She knew, she said, nothing of its contents, which he had not discussed with her.

Thomas Birchall called a taxi, feeling that the importance of the occasion, and the impending change in his financial circumstances, justified an unusual extravagance. He arrived at the solicitors' offices in Bedford Square just as Mr. Turnbull was about to leave for the day, but he was good enough to take off his coat and grant an interview to the grandson of a deceased client who had been one of the most affluent and valuable on the books of the firm.

He congratulated Thomas on his appearance, having understood that he had recently suffered a violent death. Yes, Mr. Eli had made a will only two days ago. It was unfortunate that he had taken this step in the full belief that his favourite grandson was dead. He had, in fact, become anxious to make a will when he had considered that circumstance, and realized that if he should die intestate the murderer, if he were not hanged, would inherit the wealth which he had probably committed the crime to gain.

Faced with this dilemma, he had left his household effects to his housekeeper, together with an annuity of £500; and the remainder of his estate to a Miss Clara Mills, who had shown him kindness on the occasion of his last visit to Osbury.

Did Mr. Turnbull think that a will made under such a misapprehension could be upset? He was afraid not. He asked Thomas whether a glass of brandy would do him good.

CHAPTER XLIII.

THE court had opened. The three magistrates sat on the bench. The accused man sat in the dock. Mr. Frampton conferred with Mr. Bigland-Buffitt. Mr Bigland-Buffitt conferred with Mr. Willerton. Mr Willerton conferred with his client in the dock, and with Mrs. Cuthbertson at his side. Mr. Bigland-Buffitt, Mr. Frampton, and Mr. Willerton conferred together. They conferred, but they did not agree.

Their failure to agree became apparent to the whispering spectators, among whom excitement stirred, and copies of the *Morning Standard* could be observed to circulate. The *Morning Standard* was the daily newspaper which Lord Hillsdale controlled, and it had been arranged at a late hour last night that, in return for a substantial financial payment as between the funds of the two papers, the news of Thomas Birchall's return to London, and the very curious statement which the absconding Bevan had left behind him, neither of which could be advantageously held back till next Sunday, should be handed over to that journal from the *Sunday Record.*

Sir George Hawler became impatient. He conferred with his fellow-magistrates. He conferred with the magistrates' clerk. He said at last: "Mr. Willerton, I shall be obliged if you will go on."

Mr. Willerton rose. He said it was what he had been anxious to do, but the learned counsel for—

Mr. Bigland-Buffitt did not wait for him to finish. He interposed: "I have suggested that, in view of certain developments, a short adjournment, say for a couple of days—"

"Which," Mr. Willerton retorted, "I most strenuously oppose. My client has protested his innocence from the first, and I am prepared to continue a defence which I have already opened. Unless I am assured that such bail as can be promptly furnished will be accepted as satisfactory—"

"You must know, Mr. Willerton," Sir George interposed, "that it is unusual for bail to be granted in a charge of this nature."

"I submit that it is also unusual for the prosecution to object to the defence being heard, after their own case has been closed."

"It is possible," Mr. Bigland-Buffitt replied, "from information which has been received this morning, that, if a short adjournment be taken, the prosecution may be withdrawn. I cannot go beyond that. But I submit that it is a position in which it is pre-eminently desirable that a short adjournment should be agreed in the interests of all parties concerned."

"I am concerned," Mr. Willerton replied sharply, "for one party only. I am concerned for the liberty of an innocent man. If the accusation be not withdrawn, I am prepared to continue the defence, as I am entitled to do "

Mr. Bullows, who appeared to find some enjoyment in the dilemma of the legal gentlemen, turned to the chairman to say, in a voice audible through the court: "If the prosecution want to adjourn, why don't they apply properly, and say why?"

Sir George took the hint. He said in his more important manner: "If you desire to apply for an adjournment, Mr Bigland-Buffitt, I am sure you will recognize the propriety of informing the court of the grounds on which that application is made."

That was precisely what the learned counsel had hoped that it would not be necessary to do. He was well aware that the position was known to everyone in that crowded court, and he would have preferred to gain his end without public discussion, but now he rose to the inevitable.

"The position is," he said, "that there is a report that Thomas Birchall is alive, and has been seen in London. Against that, we have heard sworn evidence identifying the body which is the subject of the present charge. There is also a newspaper publication of an alleged statement by a Dr. Bevan which gives a fantastic reconciliation of these conflicting circumstances. Unfortunately, Dr. Bevan is not here, and cannot be called.

"I am told that he is a fugitive from justice, there being a warrant out against him in another matter.

"I submit that it would be improper for the prosecution to be withdrawn on the basis of such reports, without verification of any kind, and that it is a position in which a short adjournment is peculiarly desirable."

Sir George asked: "What have you to say to that, Mr. Willerton?"

The defending solicitor was very quickly upon his feet. He was naturally somewhat elated at the events of the last forty-eight hours, and he was conscious of Mrs. Cuthbertson at his side, urgent that he should procure her husband's instant release, and having a feminine confidence in his ability to succeed.

He readily understood Mr. Bigland-Buffitt's dilemma, and may be excused if he was not greatly concerned to ease it. The learned counsel had realized that there was nothing left for him to do but to withdraw from the case with such dignity as the position allowed. He saw that there were matters on which he could still cross-examine Alfred Cuthbertson with severity, if he should go into the box, but he was not sure that it would be wise for him to do so. Popular feeling, which might otherwise hesitate in its sympathy for the accused man, who could be said to have done much to bring his troubles upon his head, might resent any appearance of bullying him in the witness box, after it had become apparent that he was innocent of the crime for which he had been arrested.

Subordinately, Mr. Bigland-Buffitt was influenced by the fact that to go on would involve another day in that somewhat ill-ventilated court, in proceedings which would bring little gain to him, either in credit or cash, for he had a sound anticipation that it had become a case for which the county authorities would reward their legal satellites with a grudging, half-opened hand.

"I have to say," Mr. Willerton replied confidently, "that the defence does not rest upon such reports or confessions, or upon the evidence of witnesses who are not here. We have contended strenuously, from the first, before such confirmatory evidence had become available, that the body which is the occasion of this prosecution was not, and could not be, that of Thomas Birchall, and that he was still alive. I am prepared to put both my client and Mrs. Cuthbertson into the box at once, so that they may give the true explanation of the circumstances under which Thomas Birchall left Osbury, which would have been available to the police before the blunder of this arrest was made, had they conducted their enquiries in a more circumspect manner. And I may say further that Mrs. Cuthbertson, who has inspected the body, and who was, as we know, sufficiently acquainted with Thomas Birchall, will swear definitely that it is not his.

"I submit that, if the prosecution will not abandon the case, I am entitled to go on."

Sir George Hawler, after a whispered consultation with his fellow magistrates, announced that they would retire to consider their decision.

Amid the buzz of excited conversation which rose as they left the bench, Alfred Cuthbertson leant over the rail of the dock to confer with his solicitor.

His manner had regained much of its natural assurance, but impatient irritations of voice and gesture were still indicative of the nervous ordeal through which he had come.

"As my hotel," he said sarcastically, "did not provide me with a full selection of the morning papers, and I have not had an opportunity of reading the *Morning Standard*, I suppose that I am the one person in court who does not know what has come out."

"Well, it's a queer tale," Mr. Willerton replied, "but I got through to Scotland Yard this morning after I read it, and had a talk with Chief Inspector Monkhouse, and he's given me a few extra facts. He's quite satisfied that it's mainly true. The most important development, from our standpoint, is that the offer of the reward proved successful, and Birchall walked into the *Record* office yesterday."

"So far," Mr. Cuthbertson replied, with impatience, "my unaided intellect had been equal to understanding what has occurred. What I want to know is how another man got into Thomas's clothes, and—"

"Bevan says that Thomas left the clothes with him. He procured the dead body, which, being a surgeon, and having plenty of money available, he was able to do, and then dressed it up for the part."

Mr. Cuthbertson considered this. He saw difficulties.

"It was a dirty game," he said. "I hadn't guessed that Tom hated me enough to have tried it on. But I don't see how it was done. How could they tell that the body would have been five days in the sea, and be unrecognizable when it came out?"

"Of course it wasn't; and Bevan didn't leave anything to chance. He dropped it into the sea from his yacht, when he was no more than a few miles offshore, with wind and tide coming in. He says he kept it in a salt water tank until then, with a sufficient number of eels."

"But what inducement—?"

"Not money, of course. Bevan had always had too much of that. It was just the malicious pleasure of seeing the mess he could get you in, and perhaps reading that you had been executed at last. At least, that's what Monkhouse thinks.

"He is a clever surgeon, but has always been up to monkey tricks, in which cruelty, and curiosity to see what will happen, have been the most evident impulses.

"The police want him now for offences against the vivisection laws. It appears that he's been warned twice before, and that means more than it sounds, because those laws are administered in a particularly lenient way. I mean lenient to the operators: the animals concerned might give it a different name.

"Anyway, he was warned twice, and, after that, complaints came to the authorities too serious and specific to be ignored. An investigation was ordered to decide whether his vivisection certificate should be withdrawn, and the result was that one of his assistants got frightened, and gave him away.

"Inspector Monkhouse says that the allegations are of an almost incredible character, including that of experiments on the brains of at least one imbecile child that its parents had been glad to part with, which he carried on at his country house. The laboratories at Thames Mansions seem to have been well conducted, and kept on more or less as a blind."

"They haven't caught him?"

"No. But Monkhouse thinks there's not much doubt that they will. He took refuge at first with Sir Isaac Shuster, the brain specialist, who, being a surgeon himself, may have sympathized with him as much as with the police authorities. Perhaps it isn't fair to say that. Anyway, he stole Sir Isaac's private plane during the night; and it's supposed that he flew to Ireland, probably to meet his yacht on some remote part of the coast there."

Alfred Cuthbertson listened to this explanation, perhaps as bizarre as any that his imagination had contrived for the amusement of his fellow men, and the thought that truth is stranger than fiction came to his mind. He might even have uttered this banality, and would certainly have asked a dozen further questions to elucidate points which were still far from clear in his mind, had not the magistrates, at that moment, returned to the court.

"It has been decided," Sir George announced, "by a majority, to dismiss the case without calling for further evidence from the defence.

"Alfred Cuthbertson will therefore be discharged, but I think it is only right to say that he appears to have brought this trouble upon himself by his own folly, and that the prosecution was very properly instituted."

"It is a decision," Miss Lait said, with the flush of angry argument still on her face, "with which I do not agree."

"I said by a majority," Sir George announced in his most pompous turkey cock manner, but his words were little regarded amid the bustle of the rising court, in which reporters dodged and pushed, in their efforts to be first through the door for the telephone booth; and a little group of friends and lawyers pressed with congratulations round the acquitted man and his laughing wife.

* * * * * * *

Sir Isaac Shuster, seated at the desk in his private study, opened a secret drawer, and drew out three bundles of one-pound notes, each secured by a rubber band. There was £100 in each bundle, and the whole sum was the price of dropping the key of the aerodrome at a spot where Dr. Bevan could pick it up. He had been friendly to Bevan, but his regard had not risen to the point of presenting him with a fairly good plane (though it was one that he had already re-solved to sell), nor of getting into trouble with the police for assisting him in his escape. So far, all had gone well. He had aided Bevan, sold his aeroplane, and remained unsuspected of anything more than entertaining one of whose true character he was unaware. But the notes were new. They appeared to have come from a bank in unbroken bulk. Even one-pound notes may be identified under such conditions. Reluctantly, he put them back in the drawer.

* * * * * * *

A week later, an Assistant Commissioner of the Metropolitan Police devoted his morning hours to the consideration of an unusual case.

So far as Alfred Cuthbertson was concerned, he felt that, whatever legal irregularities there might be in his admitted conduct, he had been sufficiently punished, even though his nefarious scheme appeared to have succeeded in its object, and the demand for his books must have risen to a fantastic figure.

But the case of Thomas Birchall was widely different, and of a more serious kind. It had some difficult, even some unprecedented features, but on the whole— "Yes, Monkhouse," he said, "I think it's a case for a jury rather than us. There's the lending of the clothes, and the other articles, to Bevan; and then there's that telegram—that must have been sent because he was afraid that the body might be fetched out of the water the day before he had disappeared; and—yes, I think you can have a warrant and run him in."

ABOUT THE AUTHOR

SYDNEY FOWLER WRIGHT (1874-1965) penned over seventy volumes of science fiction, fantasy, classic mysteries, historical novels, poetry, and non-fiction, many of them being published by the Borgo Press Imprint of Wildside Press.